MIRANDA

AND THE
D-DAY
CAPER

BY SHELLY FROME

BQB

Virginia

Published in the United States by BQB Publishing
(an imprint of Boutique of Quality Books Publishing Company, Inc.)
www.bqbpublishing.com

978-1-945448-57-7 (p)
978-1-945448-58-4 (e)

Library of Congress Control Number 2019956025

Book design by Robin Krauss, www.bookformatters.com
Cover design by Rebecca Lown, www.rebeccalowndesign.com
Editor: Olivia Swenson

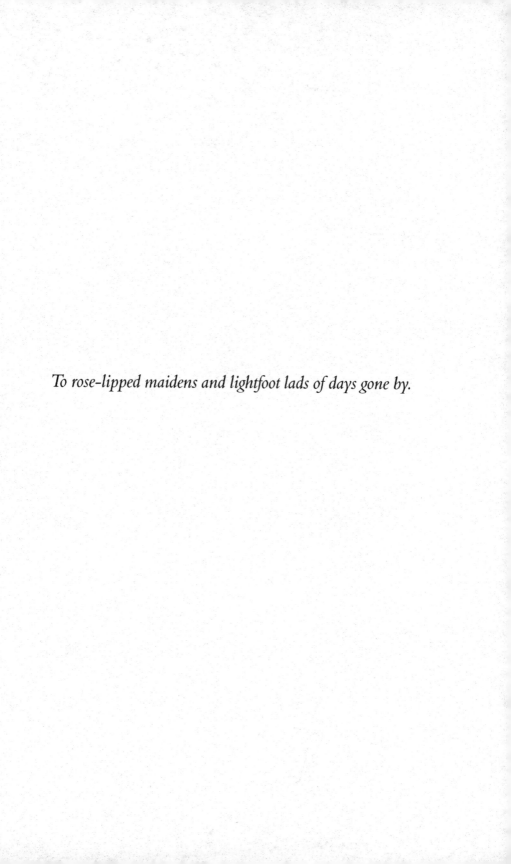

To rose-lipped maidens and lightfoot lads of days gone by.

CHAPTER ONE

Miranda Davis was undaunted as she approached the spring reopening of the tailgate market.

She took in the crisp morning air, shimmering sunlight, and cloudless sky of vibrant Carolina blue. The verdant green of the Seven Sisters mountain range hovered in the near distance along with the crackle of cheery greetings from the popup canopies. Yet again, she reminded herself that whatever cousin Skip had in mind, whatever quandary or trouble he was in, she'd handle it in the same manner she handled her realty clients—upbeat but firm, open-minded but sensible.

Sporting spanking new bib overalls and a bright peasant blouse that echoed her spunky resolve, she passed the pottery display under the Mud Buddies logo and called out, "I see you muddy gals got cleaned up real good." The response was just as chipper. At Trudy's, she ordered a half dozen apple turnovers she'd pick up as soon as she finished her rounds.

Resuming where they'd left off since the closing of the market months ago, Trudy's unblemished Nordic face beamed as she said, "So tell me, how is it going since last time?"

Without missing a beat, Miranda said, "Oh, you know, same old, same old. Thinking about the realty market getting into gear, managing weekends at the Tavern. Nothing new to report."

"Ah. Not to mention that other business I read about that you solved?"

"All water under the bridge," said Miranda, recalling a client's hassle over poison pen letters, a matter Miranda had no intention of hashing over. "Right now it's my long-lost cousin who happened to drop by. See what's on his mind and then the beat goes on."

"Cousin? You never mentioned."

"No big deal. As it happens, I grew up in a little town in Indiana. So did he. As they say, you can take the girl out of the heartland, but not the heartland out of the girl."

"Ah," said Trudy again, obviously confused but wanting to know more. "I can always tell when something's up."

"Nothing's up, Trudy, believe me. Be back in a minute."

Trudy nodded, still beaming as if taking the cue to keep everything on the Q.T. despite her growing curiosity.

Moving on, Miranda saw that the bluegrass trio at the far end was drawing a crowd with a down-home sing-along, segueing from "Let the Circle be Unbroken" to "I'll Fly Away." She hung back a moment, petting the ragtag assortment of dogs, making small talk with the little kids, and holding onto to her let-Cousin-Skip-off-easy objective.

Drifting away from the bluegrass trio, she circled around and cut through the swath between the food vendors and handmade jewelry stalls. At the end of the pathway, all she'd have to do is stop at the picnic area and find out what caused Skip to hightail it all the way down from Manhattan and show up out of the blue.

Though he was a distant cousin, she'd told Trudy he was long-lost because she didn't want to go into it. Point of fact, they had had a special bond when she was a kid. Once, when she was around eight years old and laid up after spraining her ankle, he, age fourteen, popped in and regaled her with stories of Jack Armstrong, the all-American boy. Another time, he happened by on her twelfth birthday, finagled some duds, and took her to the annual costume bash dressed as night stalkers on a raid. But first, he whipped out a bottle of crème de menthe and, straight out of *Casablanca*, said, "Here's looking at you, kid." Which was her cue to raise her glass and spout the WWII regimental toast: "To rose-lipped maidens and lightfoot lads."

Kid stuff back in the heartland. But, truth to tell, as vivid to tomboy Miranda as if it were yesterday.

They'd kept in touch since, mostly exchanging birthday cards. Later on, there was some improv TV show out of Chicago she got wind of. There was also a sketch comedy troupe show that came to Asheville she saw two or three years ago. But nothing had set her up for a call at first light and this clandestine meeting under the spreading oaks.

Unless it had something to do with that e-mail about two weeks ago:

Hey, Cuz. Got a fill-in radio gig in the Big Apple and ran across this clipping from USA Today. It says a small-town rank amateur had a hand last month in breaking a cold case involving her realty client and an unhinged looney. And, lo and behold, that rank amateur was you. Got hold of your Blue Ridge website and wanted to wish you all the best with your new sideline.

Miranda mulled this over at the Dynamite Coffee stand

while downing a hot mocha. Discarding the Styrofoam cup and reciting the old postman's creed, she muttered, "Get a grip, girl. Nothing shall deter you from the completion of your appointed rounds."

She hurried past the remaining vendors, peered here and there, and finally spotted him sitting at a picnic table and holding up a newspaper. Even with his back to her, there was no mistaking that tousled mop of grayish-red hair and coiled beanpole frame.

But he didn't spring up when she tapped him on the shoulder. He only turned slightly, forcing her to sit next to him, both of them positioned cattycorner from an empty field to their right.

"Okay, I get it," said Miranda, assuming it was playtime as always. "We're double agents. You keep reading the paper and light a cigarette. A minute later, you toss the cigarette and leave the book of matches on the table with the coded inscription *Moscow rules*. That's when I take it and slip away to await further instructions."

This was flippant Miranda. The one with the short bob, over thirty, just trying to set the easy tone on this glorious Saturday. But playful Skip seemed to have lost his way. His eyes were bloodshot, underscored by dark circles. And the signature mischievous smirk on that smooth, narrow face had been replaced by a worrisome twitch.

Folding the newspaper with his cornflower blue eyes gazing into the distance, Skip said, "I don't know, kiddo. I tell you, I just don't know."

"Which makes two of us. So tell me again why you couldn't simply e-mail me?"

"Why? Am I holding you up or something?"

"No, you're not holding me up. Look, what do you say we cut to the chase? For my part, as you may recall, I've got a birthday coming up. As my profound wish, I promised myself no more overloading the circuit. However, for old times' sake, I penciled you in between picking up some apple turnovers and taking in this wondrous day. Penciled you in because you wouldn't spell it out over the phone. Insisted on meeting face to face. Okay? Your turn."

Glancing around, taking his sweet time, making sure no one was within earshot, Skip said, "All right."

"From the top."

"Okay. Like I indicated, I was filling in, got a break on a prestige AM station only a few weeks ago. Well then, soon enough, I started doing riffs on that right-wing drivel from Russ Mathews. You know, the stocky pundit."

"Stocky pundit?"

"Far-right commentator. The one who cranks out doomsday pronouncements. Walrus moustache, always leaving the dregs of his cheroots still smoldering in my wastebasket."

"Whatever. Go on."

Getting more anxious by the second, his lanky body beginning to squirm, Skip said, "So, when opportunity knocks, you seize the day. Right?"

"Out with it."

Scrunching forward, he continued, "One night I started to wing it. No more of this 'Yup, it's midnight, folks. Some of these homespun Indiana tales should ease you right off to sleep.' I was antsy. I'd had it with Russ, who'd signed off that night sounding more and more like some fearmonger back in the day."

"And what day was that?"

"World War Two, remember? Shep Anderson on the radio telling us children about those times when Jack Armstrong had to be on the lookout for German U-boats lurking off the New Jersey shore."

"Telling you as a kid."

"Whatever."

More glancing around on Skip's part. More checking the flow of visitors coming and going.

Getting antsy herself, Miranda said, "Will you get on with it? Is there an upshot in our future?"

"I'm coming to it," Skip said, looking right at her this time. "Right after my kazoo rendition of 'I dream about the moonlight on the Wabash,' I lean into the mic and say, 'Guess what? Ole Russ must be on to something. I'm talking the plot against America.'"

"Where do you get this stuff?"

"I told you, I told you. From good ole Shep Anderson and his broadcasts from the heartland."

"So?"

"So I tell the insomniacs all over the Liberty Broadcasting System that at first I thought Duffy was pulling down on the blinds out of longing."

"Duffy?"

"Just your average ginger house cat, left alone, separated from other felines on the prowl. But every night I come home to my sublet, he's perched in the exact same spot, his green eyes staring across the street. So, over the airwaves, I said, 'What if I told you night people something was up in a dilapidated rooming house in Hoboken? Right across the river from the Big Apple?'"

"That does it," Miranda said, getting to her feet. "How am I supposed to follow this? When you're ready to get to the point, let me know."

"Wait a minute. Don't you see?" said Skip, getting to his feet as well. "I stumbled onto something. Just like one of Shep's old timey shows about subversives—a fifth column, enemy agents holing up, in cahoots with alien forces out to shatter our democracy. Before you know it, my ratings climb. But since the weather's getting warmer, those guys across the street aren't scurrying in and out of the cold. They're loitering by the stoop, glancing across the shadows."

"Great. Swell. Very entertaining, Skip. But, as it happens, I've got things to do."

"Are you kidding? I haven't got to the kicker."

Shaking her head, she remained standing by his side.

"Right," Skip said. "Next thing I know, I'm getting negative call-ins. Guys from the heartland telling me to knock it off or else."

"Wait a minute. How do you know they're from the heartland?"

"Because that's my stock in trade. Accents, idiosyncrasies, characterizations. These voices had that same flat tone of strictly business guys from Nebraska, back home in Indiana— you name it. Anyways, undaunted, I tell everyone in radio-land what's going on may have far-reaching consequences. Unless I intercept. The way things are going, let's give it, say, five days—from now till next Wednesday."

"Oh, please," said Miranda, walking away.

Skip scurried after her and held her arm. He towered over her. "Listen to me. Completely different types were out there, hardened New Yorkers. I could hear them talking. Pulling up in a delivery van with a light gray emblem on the side. Crossed cavalry swords like Civil War rebels—totally out of character—plus a small American flag. I tell you, they were carting off concealed stuff."

"I'm not listening anymore."

"You've got to. You have obviously become some kind of tracker. Tracked down a poison pen perpetrator like the paper said."

"Enough. Stop hyping everything up. Look at you. You're coming down with full-blown hysteria."

"Exactly. Because it appears there's no longer any line between entertainment and politics. While messing around, sticking it to Russ Mathews and boosting my ratings, I may have stumbled onto an actual plot utilizing WWII codes."

"Amounting to hype piled upon more and more hype."

"Oh really? You think so? Get a load of this."

Skip reached inside his windbreaker and pulled out a roll of white ribbon attached to a small collar sliced in two. The ID tag hanging from the buckle was embossed with the name Duffy.

"Just cause you're paranoid, missy, don't mean they ain't out to get you."

CHAPTER TWO

Miranda stayed with it a while longer. Perhaps it was the catch in Skip's voice and the pleading look in his bleary eyes, which wasn't at all like the playful older cousin of yore. At any rate, he finally began to zero in on his predicament.

It seems he'd obtained the below-street-level sublet from his old school chum Chris Holden, the one he was temporarily replacing at the radio station. An adjacent alleyway was where he parked his old clunker of a Volvo. The other night, as he descended the steps by the iron railing, things started to percolate. Across the way, that dubious van pulled in, a door opened, and something was dropped off.

While he was watching, a high beam from a tactical flashlight from the direction of the van scanned the iron railing and focused tightly on Skip's face.

"You getting this?" said Skip, gesturing wildly, trying even harder to hold Miranda's attention as her patience wore thin. "As I start to head down the stairs, I spot a manila envelope dangling from the railing by a thread. Inside the envelope, there's a Post-it note telling me to sign the enclosed document from the Liberty Broadcasting System contracting me to abide by the non-disclosure agreement forthwith. I'm given one hour to affix my signature, insert the document in the envelope, and drop it in the rusted mailbox of the abandoned house next door."

"But brave, intrepid Skip crumples it up," said Miranda, hazarding a guess to hurry things up.

"Sleepy Skip, figuring this is totally off the wall and dying to get to bed, tossed it in the nearby trash can. Shortly after, glass shatters via a high-powered pellet gun aimed at my window. Next, a hissing noise from outside turns out to be the leaking tires of my old Volvo. Taken together with the threatening calls at the station, I pack up and split right after the AAA truck comes by and takes care of the flats. I snatch Duffy and, in my panic, cover so many miles that I wind up at a motel in Pennsylvania near the Bucks County Playhouse."

"Where you once appeared in some Story Theater show. I get it. But why not hole up there until you get your wits together?"

"Because when I emerge to get a bite to eat, there's a note on my windshield telling me to keep going and stay strictly on the eastern seaboard."

Miranda shook her head. "However, still scared witless, Skip takes off again, and even more sleepless and fatigued, decides to fake them out and heads due west instead. Then drives south full tilt through the Virginia and Carolina Blue Ridge, miles and miles out of the way."

"How did you know?" said Skip, lowering his waving arms.

"Because, Doctor Watson, you'd been to Asheville during that improv gig I caught a couple of years back. Black Mountain was only a short drive east. You remembered I had just been through an escapade which, in your loopy, burned-out condition made me an operative you could hook up with. All the while checking your rearview mirror and reassuring Duffy the cat."

Dropping his storytelling act, he said, "As you guessed, I was in a panic. I kept remembering the map on Russ Matthews's wall."

"Oh, no. What map?"

"The one in his office. With a check mark for Savannah and Charleston and a red pushpin smack-dab all the way west to Asheville. If I could hide out close by and consult with a crackerjack sleuth and relative . . ."

"Whoa," said Miranda, leading him back to the picnic table, sitting him down, and hovering over him this time. "Let's deep six the crackerjack sleuth bit once and for all. A rattled church lady client asked me to look into poison pen letters slipped under her door. After a bit of poking around, I traced it back to a child she'd abandoned years ago but who, as a lady deacon of the church, didn't want anyone to find out. Ergo, a bit of poking around doth not a crackerjack operative make. Moreover, I had to rely on my ex—a local detective now on the force in Raleigh—to corral said perpetrator and throw away the key. Ta-da! End of story. Are we clear now? Have you got this straight?"

Maybe Skip heard her, maybe not. Closing his eyes, elbows on the table, holding his head in his hands as if all the energy had suddenly gone out of his body, he began murmuring. From what little she could make out, there was something about pulling in at the Black Mountain Motel, tossing and turning, hearing Duffy make a familiar yowl when he was hungry and the deep growl of a motorcycle. Miranda strung it together to surmise that when he crawled out of bed at first light, someone must have slipped in, grabbed Duffy, sliced his collar, tossed aside his white ribbon leash, and split.

His murmuring became harder to decipher yet more insistent. Being Duffy-less without his ginger tabby pal . . . left with five days to carry out his midnight cry of Paul Revere . . . or raise the white flag, get Duffy back, and to hell with saving the country . . . based on a cryptic note discovered at the station on Russ Mathews's desk two days before: *Down to the wire, D-Day minus seven.*

Then the murmuring segued into muffled sobbing.

She tried to console him, patted him lightly on the back, but to no avail.

Miranda slipped away and edged past the Mud Buddies canopy. The air was still crisp, the sky still a vibrant Carolina blue, the Seven Sisters range still a fresh verdant green. But her basic assumptions had been turned around, inside out. Instead of an older cousin she'd always looked up to, who ministered to her and always managed to slough everything off, here was Skip coming apart at the seams.

She crossed over the grassy aisle back to Trudy and the apple turnovers. She wondered what in the world Harry, her confidant and part-time lover, would make of this. Some shadowy plot trickling down and across this great land about to implode in this neck of the woods? *Oh really, Miranda? Give me a break.*

She paid Trudy for the turnovers, taking in the pie lady's

ever-radiant smile emanating from some trouble-free parallel universe. "How did it go? What's up? Something new?"

Miranda merely returned the smile.

Clutching the pastry box, she doubled back and paused at the far end where the bluegrass trio still held forth. The ragtag assortment of little kids and dogs had thinned out, doubtless because the tunes had become quite heart-tugging. At the moment, the lead gal dressed in a hand-me-down cowgirl outfit was wailing, "If you're hurtin', hon, can't you see? If you're hurtin', hon, you can count on me."

There was no way she could piece this all together, let alone fill in the gaps. Skip himself was too discombobulated to lay things out in a straight line. At best, she could only come up with a starting point and, little by little, take it from there.

She turned the corner and hurried back past the vendors. Skip was still at the picnic table, totally slumped now, no longer murmuring a word.

She strode right over, plunked down the pastry box, and, calling on her take-charge self, said, "Okay, kiddo. In my line of work, we speak in tangibles. We put aside overblown concerns. We take soundings. We do preliminary assessments. At the Tavern, before I book an act, I arrange for an audition. As for assessing property, I check out the lay of the land, the condition of the home, the comparable market value. I zero in on the realities."

Slowly raising his weary head, he said, "What are you saying?"

"Given a supposed window of five days left—which

happens to be the allotted time in which I need to book new acts at the Tavern and post new property listings—we'll look into the matter of a purloined cat. If, by some quirk of fate, the scope actually happens to widen and I can draw the salient details out of you . . ."

"Go on," said Skip, sitting up straight, the color returning to his cheeks.

"The purloined cat, Skip. Our sole and only tangible. Steering clear of some gonzo classified maneuvers to save America."

CHAPTER THREE

"You've looked into it, Miranda."

"Hardly," said Miranda, getting more and more exasperated.

"In point of fact," said Harry, "you have contacted every animal rescue site. No one has seen or even heard about a stray, collarless tabby."

"Which means there could be more to my cousin's tale than meets the eye. Like holding the cat for ransom. Who knows?"

"Oh, please, give me a break. Give us both a break."

It was a little past noon on that same Saturday. Miranda was up on Gray Eagle Crest in the cottage she'd gotten Harry as a house-sitting retreat. He was ensconced in the corner of the pine-paneled living room, tapping away at his laptop, dressed in his usual button-down white shirt and khaki slacks. Add his horn-rimmed glasses as an indication the feature he was working on about the community garden demanded his full attention. Indicating, therefore, that he was at work, much older and mature, and she was just fooling around.

Miranda moved closer. "Can you grant me a few more minutes of your precious time?"

"Afraid not."

"Don't pull this, Harry. I'm talking to you."

Harry stopped typing and let out a sigh as if he was about to humor a mate who was highly impressionable. He whipped off his glasses, brushed a shock of graying hair out of his eyes, and rose up from the desk. Snatching his mug of herbal tea, he shuffled over to the armchair by the stone fireplace directly across from the picture window and plunked himself down.

"All right," said Harry, "tell you what. You suggest to this cousin of yours that he quit waiting glassy-eyed by his motel phone. Tell him to go to Precision Graphics down the street and get them to crank out some reward leaflets, which he will then put up in the most likely places."

"Brilliant."

"Afterwards, he can get on that same phone, make amends, beg for a second chance, and promise to severely modify his next broadcast well before . . . When did you say?"

"Revealing all on Wednesday, five days from now, at the stroke of midnight."

"Right. Instead, have him make arrangements to sign the NDA and swear to open his program with something like 'It was all a lark, folks. Actually, I've been searching high and low for Duffy my cat and finally found him lost in, of all places, the wilds of the Blue Ridge.' If by the remotest chance the cat is actually being stowed away, it will defuse everything. Skip will be back on board minus the threat of embarrassing the corporate powers that be, the cat will reappear, and that's an end to it."

Miranda countered, "You're forgetting what drove him out of his digs. You're forgetting he was tailed to Bucks County. He might have been tailed all the way here. And any missing-cat leaflets will amount to zilch, let alone your let's-forget-the-whole-thing scenario and all's well that ends well."

"Look, I am only taking the bits of information you've provided. Moreover, may I remind you that we have a pact. No more craziness. It's over. You got duped into one goofy escapade. You learned your lesson and, as a result, know exactly what you're doing."

"Nobody knows exactly what they're doing."

"Oh, that's clever. That is just perfect. Why do you keep pushing this?"

"Maybe because he looked after me when I was a kid while the girly girls called me names and ostracized me. Maybe because he now needs some looking after."

"Maybe because your tomboy alter ego comes to the fore when you're hung up."

"When I'm motivated, you mean. When a frazzled client gave me a per diem because she was going to pieces."

"Leading to a perpetrator who had long since gone to pieces. Leading to a little detective work despite what was constantly lurking. That's not a realtor making an assessment, lady. That's putting yourself in harm's way."

"Not necessarily."

"Absolutely necessarily if you think about it."

And that's where it stalled. Without uttering another word, they both knew they'd come to an impasse. Harry gazed out the window at the sunlit ridgeline in the distance and sipped his tea.

In turn, Miranda began to wonder why she said that about everyone not really knowing what they were doing.

Perhaps she was reminded of *Middlemarch*, the novel her book club had just discussed. A classic, foisted on them by an English teacher in their midst, about characters who found themselves acting against their better judgment and subsequently messed up their lives.

Breaking out of it, Miranda said, "Okay, I give. I let Skip get to me, all right?" With that, she walked out the door.

Harry caught up to her at her SUV. "Look, let him know we've got a nice thing going here and wouldn't want to compromise it."

"Right."

"That blurb in *USA Today* about the intrepid amateur sleuth was just hyperbole. You have to be sensible and Skip will have to take his situation under advisement."

"Uh-huh."

"Besides, I'm getting to like this little town. The restless transients stop off at the motel on the way to Florida or heading back north. The residents—the Southern folks tied to the mountains along with the new homeowners—let all that fluttering pass them by as they go on with their lives."

"Except for a mad local perpetrator."

"Which was a fluke. By and large, we are nestled in the benign bosom of the mountains."

"What is this?" Miranda said. "A few months doing features at the local paper and you're now a shill for the visitors center?"

"An advocate for preserving precious energy."

Brushing past him, she said, "Well, I need to waste a little more energy, check out the realities, and see for myself. I need to come to terms with one of those pesky transients!"

As a few clouds scudded across the crisp Carolina blue sky, Miranda pulled into the motel on Route 70 across from Blue Ridge Biscuit and Brunch. She figured Skip was sleeping it off by now and Cindy had already checked in for her afternoon managerial shift. There were only a few motorists around—the tourist season wouldn't be in full swing until May—which made Miranda's immediate task simpler. Cindy would be so eager to convince anybody who happened by that she was marking time till she got a showgirl booking in Vegas, she'd carry on and let things slip. Like what may have really happened to Duffy the cat.

The second Miranda entered the cramped office, Cindy began sashaying around, puffing up her amber do, fishing for a compliment.

"Like it?" Cindy asked. "I told Lois at Kim's Cuts to give it more body but keep it natural and loose."

Miranda nodded. It never seemed to matter why you dropped in as long as Cindy could manage to get some attention. She did a little twirl, draped herself over the Formica counter, and blew on her coral-coated nails to make sure Miranda noticed that everything matched, including her wraparound skirt. Only the wrinkles in her lip gloss and eyeshadow were a dead giveaway her showgirl opportunities were severely limited.

"Looking snazzy, girl," Miranda said, easing into what she was after.

"Taking a line-dance class at the Lake Tomahawk Center to keep it going. I tell you, I am primed."

"Yes ma'am, looking good."

More sashaying around the counter, humming a country rock tune, showing off some trendy steps. When she paused to straighten one of the oversized what-happens-in-Vegas-stays-in-Vegas posters, Miranda took the opportunity to jump right in.

"Speaking of the exact opposite of looking good, guess my cousin Skip looked a lot worse for wear when he checked in."

"Your cousin? Didn't know that. Why didn't you put him up?"

"I didn't know he was in town till this morning. That's good ole Skip for you. Everything on the spur of the moment when he's on the run."

"What do you mean?"

Covering up, Miranda said, "I mean, when his plans are up in the air. But I'll bet you made him feel right at home. It was really nice of you to let his cat stay with him."

"His cat? What are you talkin'? You mean the other guy's."

"What other guy?"

Cindy made another face, crinkling her heavy makeup as if she was having a senior moment. Then she sidled up to Miranda. "Later on."

"You mean that's when you first spotted it?"

Lowering her voice, going into her gossipy mode, Cindy said, "Not me. First this guy cruises by—one of those compact rentals from the airport. You can always tell. A plain, white Toyota Corolla. At first I barely noticed, but there was practically nothing else on the road at that hour. He pulls in, gets out, and looks everything over. Like he was casing the joint or something."

Cindy stepped back, leaned over the counter and blew on her fingernails once more, milking the story for all it was worth. "Then he comes in, still casing the joint, and starts coming on to me with this deep, syrupy voice. Looks at the poster, says he can tell I must've put it up. 'Cause he's willing to bet other motels in these parts only have shots of mountains and streams."

"Did he check in?"

"Yeah, sort of. Right when we were changing shifts."

"Okay, go on. What do you mean, the cat belonged to him?"

"'Cause," Cindy said, easing her way back to Miranda, "sometime in the middle of the night, Pete on the late shift says the guy starts up his car. Which was right out front, and he'd backed into the space. Like he had to cut out early or something."

"So is that it? I don't get it."

"No, that's not it." Going over to the plate glass window, tossing in a bit of pantomime, she said, "Not long after, Pete peers out. Says he heard a motorcycle come by but didn't see one. Only a minute or two later, he hears the motorcycle take off. When Pete peers out again, he could swear a cat was staring back at him through the rear windshield of the Corolla."

With her mind racing now, Miranda said, "How secure are the door locks?"

"What do you mean?"

"Could you use a credit card to slip the latch?"

"I suppose. What does that have to do with anything?"

Unable to take the do-si-do any longer, Miranda confronted her. "This guy. The one in the white Corolla. What did he look like?"

"I don't know. Kind of stocky maybe."

"Walrus moustache? Smoked cigars? Smelly cheroots?"

"Yeah, come to think of it."

"Name of Russ Mathews?"

"How did you know? Say, wait a minute. The cops called earlier. What's the story here?"

Miranda had no answer. There was a missing cat. There were wider implications. Without missing a beat, she moved on.

CHAPTER FOUR

Miranda crossed the empty front parking lot and turned the corner just as a mockingbird alighted on the motel roof, ran through bits of its repertoire, and settled on a high, piercing trill. As if taking the cue, Miranda noted an old Volvo out back, past the ice machines and soda dispensers. She assumed it was Skip's and he was still in. But as she zeroed in on the room number Cindy had given her, she saw that the door was ajar. She knocked gently. Then, competing with the mockingbird trill, she called out and received no reply.

The bird desisted. In its place came a low, muffled moan. She called out again, went inside, and found Skip sprawled on the bed as though he'd taken a few steps, staggered, and collapsed.

Still moaning, he struggled onto his elbows, twisted around, and barely managed to slide off the bed and pull himself up.

"My God, Skip. Are you all right?"

"Shh," he said, rubbing the back of his head and wincing. "Wait a minute. Maybe if I can stand without getting vertigo . . . can recall exactly . . . right before I blacked out . . ."

"Look, I think we better—"

"Quiet, please? Now, let's see. Can I think, can I remember . . .? Right. Worried sick about Duffy . . . last night in fact, thought I heard a clicking sound and a yowl . . . maybe a motorcycle tailing off . . ."

"Never mind. What happened to your head?"

"I'm working on it. Yes . . . last night . . . must've rolled over and drifted off."

"Will you forget about last night? Tell me what just happened."

As Skip went blank, Miranda went over and discovered a swollen bump on the back of his head. She rummaged around the room, located a Styrofoam bucket, and headed outside for the ice machine. Hurrying back, she got a towel from the bathroom, dumped the ice onto the towel, and insisted that he sit down on a chair and hold the cold compress on the exact spot.

"Now then," said Miranda, "we have to tend to the swelling and get you to the ER to make sure."

"Wrong. You asked me what happened. I have to at least get my bearings."

"Well get them fast, kiddo, and we're off."

"Hold on, will you? Okay. So . . . after I saw you this morning, guilt seeping in deeper over Duffy, I must've dozed off."

"Whatever," Miranda said, forcing him to keep the compress steady.

"Not 'whatever.' I got up, went to the police station, made a statement about somebody swiping Duffy. The duty sergeant gives me the once-over, doesn't buy my story but jots it down anyways and passes it on to some officer by the name of Ed. I drive back, unlock the door, go in and slip out again."

"Why?"

"Because I could swear I'd been tailed again." He lost the gist of what he was saying and then came out of it. "Oh yeah, I scurried around and pressed my back against a wall like a night stalker on a raid."

Unable to humor him any longer, Miranda carefully removed the compress and dumped the melted ice into the sink before wringing out the towel. "All right, let me guess. After leaving the door ajar, you doubled back, spotted nothing, stepped further inside, got bopped on the head, lurched forward, and wound up out cold, splayed on the bed."

"Bingo."

Miranda added fresh shards of ice, grabbed his overnight bag from beside the bed, and said, "Wait here. I'll pull my car around. Don't move."

"But maybe I'm okay. No memory loss. No nausea, dizziness, or passing out. Just your average clobbered fugitive."

"Knock it off, Skip. We're going to the ER. You never know."

Getting woozy again, Skip said, "We're going to the ER. You just never know."

As the clear skies began to give way to streaks of gray, Miranda was not about to take the fast route onto I-40 to Mission Hospital in Asheville. That would mean competing with the hell-bent eighteen-wheel rigs followed by 240 North with its lanes that suddenly switch to off-ramps in the race to the downtown exits. Instead, she decided to take Swannanoa River Road and then Biltmore Avenue. There would be stop lights, a slower trek, but so would her thoughts slow down and Skip, squirming next to her in the passenger seat, would hopefully cool it down as well.

But on the way to the first four-way light at Buckeye Cove, he began carrying on about pushing forty-five—his fear of winding up like the army of guys who couldn't hack it, retreating to Podunk, selling life insurance, and treading the boards doing community theater. As if taking a page from her partner Harry, he considered waving the white flag and getting Duffy back after asking for a second chance to sign the NDA. After all, he'd only just gotten to the Big Apple, and this was his chance to get somewhere.

"After all," he said, "who needs scruples?"

When Miranda didn't bite, he blurted out, "Ask yourself, what's my currency? It's not my looks, right? It's certainly not my sharp business sense. If you look at my sole cachet, it's nonstop whimsy."

Past Buckeye Cove, he threw in some more second thoughts. "Besides, who knows who might be listening in from the entertainment world if I tone it down?"

She realized he was trying to call on his usual carefree, go-with-the-flow style, but that fearful catch in his voice gave him away.

Another delay before he came out with "Come to think of it, why, out of the past, did fellow thespian Chris Holden keep saying what a nice homespun guy I was as he showed me around? Like he was making sure of what he was counting on when he called me at the last minute."

"Someone harmless," said Miranda to keep him talking while trying to make the drive as smooth as possible. "A fill-in who wouldn't rock the boat. Just an affable throwback to an innocent time."

Skip grew still, obviously taking this all in. At the same time, Miranda's line about a more innocent time turned her thoughts to that incident when she fell out of the tree spying on the neighborhood girly girls' tea party. Her incurably practical mom called her heedlessly reckless. But Skip came by when she was on the mend and told her she had the makings of a great scout. To cheer her up, from out of his bag of tricks he produced his ukulele and sang old timey songs like "You Are My Sunshine" and the good ole "I dream about the moonlight on the Wabash." There was another crème de menthe and toast, and he told her about all the adventures they could go on. And there was that costume party at the big house on the hill, when her mom said her outfit wasn't suitable but Skip insisted it was perfect for a commando raider. And all the birthday cards he sent with sign-offs like *Tally-ho* and *Onward into the fray*.

Driving on, Miranda began to wonder what she was getting herself into. Harry's prodding crossed her mind, as did her mom's. Like that time she was having second thoughts about majoring in business at Chapel Hill, and Mom, who had just broken up with her dad, had said, "What have you got to fall back on? Love and marriage? Or how about a life of foolhardy escapades with your loopy cousin Skip? Wise up, buttercup." And where was her mother today? Running some trailer park south of Orlando with some guy named Fred.

No love or marriage. No foolhardy escapades. No ma'am. No sir-ree. Strictly business.

Breaking into her reverie, Skip said, "Hold on. There's a good point there about good ole Chris. And that stuff Russ Mathews was going on about hidden threats to homeland security. Maybe there was always more to this and all the while I sensed it."

As she came to Swannanoa River Road, despite mulling over Mom's and Harry's cautions, Miranda found herself starting to buy into some subterfuge. Like a character from *Middlemarch* putting aside her better judgement and getting more and more sucked in. "Okay," she said, "as long as we're at it, what exactly did you say when you were on the air?"

"What do you mean?"

"You know, catchphrases you glommed from Russ Mathews that let the cat out of the bag. No pun intended."

Miranda held fast to the right-hand lane, avoiding the cars in line waiting to make a left-hand turn. "Come on. Let's have it."

A good five minutes passed before Skip said, "Unless . . ." Then he began squirming and grimacing and struggling with the slipping icy towel. "Unless it was references to that stuff on Russ's wall. Those Marvel Comics movie posters. You know, Avengers, Captain America and S.H.I.E.L.D. Funny thing, though."

"What?"

"While Chris was showing me around, he seemed nervous. I lingered in Russ's office, and he caught me glancing at a book about Rommel's tactics with his Africa Corp, another about Special Forces, and a calendar with circled dates. Plus a

Stalking Horse logo. It was then he started to freak. Blocked my view of the map with check marks veering west toward Asheville."

"Well now."

"And Russ's scribbling stuff like *down to the wire . . . D-Day fast approaching.* Chris grabbed me by the elbow, yanked hard, and hurried me out of there."

Glancing at him as she drove, she said, "And you capitalized on that?"

"Naturally. One thing you learn about storytelling—you come upon something that lights a fire, you use it. When your listeners egg you on, you up the ante. More fun for one and all than homespun anecdotes and news from Indiana fishing holes."

"Go on," said Miranda, getting even more hooked despite herself.

"Right." He assumed his radio voice. "'Okay, night people. Taking a page from good ole Russ, how many of you know about D-Day or the SAS? There comes a time when you have to strike suddenly. When the stalking horse is in place. When there's only a short window till midnight on this following Wednesday.'"

"Great," Miranda said as she barely missed a car coming up on her right. "D-Day, the SAS, and the stalking horse— whatever that is—probably did it."

"Except for the fact," Skip said, back to wincing continually, "Russ Mathews started it."

"Brilliant. Except for the fact he had no idea what you were up to. Except some higher-ups apparently didn't appreciate your extrapolations."

Skip devolved into muttering to himself, but Miranda listened in. "Wait a second. There was also a red pushpin in the neighborhood of the 9/11 memorial. What is that all about? Do you think there's more than one target? Do you think . . .?"

As she approached the hospital on Biltmore Avenue, Miranda's thoughts veered again. "How did anyone know you had a cat if it was always cooped up?"

Dispensing with the compress which had turned watery, Skip said, "Probably because of those times I felt sorry for him. I took Duffy for rides on those sunny days to check out the territory as he curled up by the rear window. He really liked that, peering out with the warm sun glancing through. That's when somebody must have spotted him."

"Crossing over into Lower Manhattan," said Skip, his manic mood picking up again. "To check out St. Paul's Chapel. The Little Chapel that Stood and survived 9/11. The van, the one coming and going at the ramshackle rooming house. The one with the Confederate logo and a small American flag."

"What about it?"

"The driver was either checking out the old church or following me or both."

She pulled into the visitors' lot for the ER and slipped into a space close to the entrance and shut off the motor. Though it would totally overload the circuit, she couldn't help letting him know.

"Look, I hate to break it to you, but Cindy at the motel let on it was some guy on a motorcycle who snuck into your room at the crack of dawn and sliced the collar. Tossed Duffy into a rental car where he crawled up by the rear window as the rental car took off. The upshot is, Mathews was the driver. Must have flown all the way down from New York to keep you under wraps one way or another."

As Skip sat there in stunned silence, she couldn't help but notice the white compact pulling in a few rows back. It could very well have been a Toyota Corolla. Needless to say, it was another sign the powers that be were on to Skip and their tactics were unlimited, let alone the parameters of the playing field.

Given the strain to eke out what was going on, Mom's and Harry's cliché word to the wise had no cachet.

CHAPTER FIVE

The male doctor with the non-descript face, brush-cut hair style, and green scrubs slipped out of the examining room at the ER and glanced at his clipboard. Then he peered at Miranda as if about to confer with a key witness.

"Can you tell me what really happened?"

"What do you mean?"

Glancing at his notes again, he said, "He could be delirious, but it's hard to tell. It would be helpful to know the exact cause of the swelling at the base of his head."

"Didn't he tell you?"

"That's the problem. Most of what he claims is hardly believable. And the way he flits from one story to the next makes me wonder if there might be complications. Problems with memory, impulsivity, cognitive impairment. There may be neurological phenomena to consider as well as fatigue."

"Fatigue," said Miranda, chiming in. "That's your best bet after being harassed and chased from Hoboken to Bucks County to here with little or no sleep. Plus, there's all the anxiety, having his cat stolen and now the assault. What can you expect?"

The doctor studied Miranda anew, perhaps wondering if her own overactive imagination was a contributing factor. "And what makes you so certain?"

"He told me," Miranda said.

"Yes, but discounting anything he may have said, what did you witness firsthand?"

Miranda had known it was going to come down to this, but all she could offer was "There was a cat collar sliced in half. I did see that."

The quizzical look he continued to give her as he went back to his notes did little to advance Skip's cause. "And the bump? That's the focus of concern. What concrete information can you add about the severity of the blow? The kind of blunt instrument used? The approximate duration he was unconscious on the motel bed?"

Coming up empty again, Miranda said, "Can't you put him under observation, run a couple of tests? Give him some anxiety-free down time? Can't you just do that?"

After examining his clipboard and jotting down a few more notes, he gave her a cool "We'll see."

Miranda nodded, beginning to wonder how much longer her seesaw ride between pulling back from or completely buying in to Skip's sputtering story would go on—or proliferate. How much worse could this conundrum get?

What followed was a rigmarole of red tape, insurance cards, and whatnot, followed by jockeying around as orderlies wheeled Skip hither and yon. Miranda kept pace as Skip continued to grimace, carry on, and complain. She still hadn't found out what medication they plied him with as he went on deflecting, going over stuff he'd already told her, and tossing out a slew of what-ifs. What stood out was the fact that easygoing, carefree Skip had long since been left by the wayside.

After a time, as Miranda kept watch over Skip in his assigned ward while a nurse checked at the main desk about his diagnostics schedule, Skip finally divulged another little bombshell.

"You might be interested to know when you and the brush-cut doctor were going through the motions, I checked for messages on my smartphone while getting into these hospital pajamas and before being confined to this stupid wheelchair. And there it was. And I quote: *What are you stopping for? Unless you want more of the same, keep out of the way. Try Charleston or Savannah on the East Coast corridor like you were told. Or hole up down in St. Augustine on the beach. If you play it smart for a change, in a couple of days when you get the all clear, you'll get your cat back.*"

"Okay, who was the sender? Russ Mathews?"

"Who knows? The cell phone has got to be a burner," Skip said, his tone as wired and jumpy as ever. "Disposable, cheap, a prepaid job. Isn't that obvious?"

"I hate to tell you, but absolutely nothing is obvious."

"Oh really? Druggies and terrorists use them. You destroy the SIM card and get a new one. That's why it's called a burner. It's burned, gone up in smoke. The NSA can't track the positioning coordinates because no one signed up for it or supplied identifying information. Users don't provide any name at all. Cash only. Wham, bam, thank you, ma'am!"

"Where, may I ask, are you getting all this?"

"Life in the big city. Chicago and now the Big Apple. Keeping up on things so I don't get swallowed whole. Hate to break it to you, but for an operative, you're coming up short."

"Look, buster," said Miranda, beginning to lose any semblance of objectivity. "I made it clear that one loopy caper doth not an operative make."

"That's not what that newspaper clipping said. It said 'Small town realtor handles baffling case like a pro.'"

"In point of fact it morphed into something else—a big dollop of madness. My partner Harry put the kibosh on the whole thing by calling the cops, namely, my ex, Detective Dave Wall. That was it. Can we please drop it once and for all?"

Sensing that there was no way she was ever going to convince him she was a one-shot rookie at best, she simmered down and said, "Look, Skip, mixing your assumptions with your bent for playtime doesn't help me get a bead on any of this."

"Uh-huh. Who was it who used to take counter espionage tactics seriously while crossing enemy lines?"

"When my seventy-year-old maiden aunt Zoe prevailed upon her ward Skip, who was a whiz at theater games, to drop in once in a while to humor me. Well, this kid has grown up. Okay? All right? There is no correlation."

"Except that these guys have got a game going. Only they are not playing for kicks."

"Good God, Skip. Will you just give it a rest!"

A nursing assistant came over and asked her to lower her

voice. Caught by surprise, all Miranda could do was nod and apologize.

Skip twisted around expectantly as the RN walked away.

Miranda went over to the water cooler to gain some separation. Taking a few sips she didn't need, she reached for some way to put things on hold. The listings and available property in her bailiwick were fairly limited at present. In fact, in this tight market, she could recite them all by heart. If she could come up with a retreat for Skip like the one she found for Harry . . .

"Tell you what," she said as she spotted Skip's nurse hurrying back toward them down the hall. "Taking a clue from your smartphone messenger, they want you to hole up. Great. But forget hightailing it down the coast. I'll scare you up a short-term hideout."

"That's it?"

"And stash your car. If the medical profession finds nothing drastic and they discharge you, that should buy us a little time."

"And Duffy?"

"Let's assume he's safe for now. He's the carrot on the stick they're dangling. Duffy shouldn't have to consider using up any of his nine lives for the time being."

Skip didn't respond but slowly began to close his eyes.

Miranda took his prolonged silence as a tacit agreement.

Skip's silence was generated by a sedative a nurse had given him that was starting to kick in. It bypassed the throbbing in the back of his head and his abiding agitation and caused him to stop and wonder where it had all gone wrong. At the same time, some part of him knew full well.

Like some fuzzy day of reckoning, the brittle voice of Miranda's maiden aunt Zoe was the first to come to mind: *I didn't take you in to be always daydreaming, boy. There are chores to be done. How are you ever in tarnation going to amount to anything?*

Next, as if he was still a kid, one of Shep Anderson's radio broadcasts came into his memory bank: *Are you ready? Return with me now to the days when sidekicks were loyal. When heroes answered the call. When people took you at your word, sweethearts were true, and duty prevailed. Jack Armstrong, the all-American boy, wasn't just a radio serial. Oh no. Oh-oh-oh no. He was a symbol. He didn't back down and stood his ground. Once again now, open your window wide and answer the call. Are you ready?*

Moving his lips, trying to cut in but not making a sound, he argued that no one taught him to stand his ground. Make-believe was a surefire way out. The curtain closed, the show was over, the program ended. Each time was a new beginning. You can do or say anything and take it all back. How can you lose?

Then it was back to Aunt Zoe. *And so, what have you got to show for yourself? Wife? None. Family? None. Job, position, standing in the community? None. Bona fide prospects leading to self-respect? Not a jot. And those women you've run around with, comediennes making fun of courtship and marriage? Oh, puh-lease.*

The reckoning kept flitting by him in the wake of Miranda's departure, topped by the caption on a bright storybook cover: *The Ballad of the Daydreamer—A Cautionary Tale.*

CHAPTER SIX

At first, Miranda considered her twilight drive back to the countryside of Swannanoa a respite. The rampaging traffic on Biltmore had reminded her of TV shots of New York, Skip at the radio station, 9/11, and a vague, dicey plot. While ensconced in the hospital, she found herself longing to be high above downtown Asheville, perched on the western-facing slope of Sunset Mountain, gazing at the peaceful vista of the far-off Smokies. It happened to be her birthday wish for this next weekend. Hiking, the soft, comforting scent of the pines underfoot, dissolving into the greening of the hardwoods, the burgeoning light shades of the oaks, tulip poplars, ash, beech, and maple. This was nature girl Miranda out on a trek, reminiscent of her childhood days back in Indiana in the woods, free of hassles and girlish demands, wondering when Skip might drop by again to pretend to be Indian scouts.

Breaking out of it, she decided to kill two birds with one stone: furnish Skip with a hideaway while she looked over a piece of property a client received in a divorce settlement. Since the lady in question wasn't scheduled to return from her Mediterranean river cruise for another two weeks, checking the house's sales potential was a return to the realm of the doable.

However, as she cut down Marion onto Alexander and

then a shadowy, tree-lined lane, she saw that this was not some run-of-the-mill, cozy neighborhood. For the entire stretch, the houses were set back with great swatches of woods between them and the road. No cars in sight as Saturday night approached—no lights anywhere, in fact.

She kept going. She couldn't swear to it, but off and on she had the sense she'd been followed. Maybe she had seen a white compact. Maybe it was a flicker of high beams across her rearview mirror every now and then. Maybe it was just her imagination working overtime.

She cut back to Old 70, made a hard right, sped up, and made another hard right until she eased onto the Grovemont section, which no one except residents could navigate with its scattering of unmarked streets. She passed the little lending library nestled on her left and weaved in and out of a half dozen more streets with no names until she turned off at a dead end and eased onto the dirt driveway of a devout feminist she knew who was on her annual retreat in Santa Fe to celebrate the new moon. She switched off the motor and headlights and waited.

After a good ten minutes without any movement whatsoever, she got going again and tried another pass onto Alexander. Soon enough, set off by themselves, she came upon two adjacent Southwestern structures—takeoffs of the Alhambra in Granada, Spain, as far as Miranda knew. It was as if some homesick Angelino had these two buildings hastily put up decades ago, thought better of it, and took off back to LA. The exterior walls were stucco, broken up by horseshoe arches trimmed in thin dark wood. One was a two-story affair with a flat roof, and the other was tiny, framed in weathered teal-blue strips around the front windows. The little house was the one up for grabs and had a one-car wooden garage out back, apparently cobbled together and tossed up as an afterthought.

The larger structure too was unoccupied, but she hadn't run down the owner. Perhaps it also came with a pre-nup arrangement. All told, the entire street seemed like an afterthought that hadn't worked out. And there was still no sign of a single car on the road.

Getting more spooked by the minute as the shadows lengthened and a swath of smoky gray clouds scudded overhead, Miranda reached in her shoulder bag for the keys entrusted to her. "No hurry," the itinerant divorcée had cheerfully instructed. "Whenever you get the chance." Miranda would make sure the smaller place was safe and inhabitable and that there were no marauding creatures, squatters, derelicts, or what have you about. Or someone tracking down Skip.

Hearing rustling sounds, she hunkered down by the trunk of a huge oak. The smaller place was only a few yards away from where she parked by a stand of scraggly shrub, but she held still as a bunch of groundless suppositions began to get the better of her.

As she edged closer to the smaller structure, she couldn't help but be reminded once more of the time she and Skip did their commandos-strike-at-dawn approach to the Halloween bash at the mansion on the hill. Only then she hadn't been alone, knew everyone who would be there, and it was strictly pretend danger. At this moment, she wasn't traipsing around in the gentle Indiana countryside she knew so well. Now, thanks to Skip, more worrisome thoughts flitted through her mind. Did she know for sure she hadn't been tailed from the hospital? Had she been spotted as she entered Skip's motel room and drove off with him?

She snuck around and cast her gaze both ways down the street, looking for even a semblance of a white car lying in wait. Which proved nothing if ultra-right-wing pundit Russ Mathews had noted her whereabouts and passed the information to one of his minions, like the rampant biker who'd clobbered Skip.

Realizing she was again buying into Skip's espionage scenario, she forced herself to trudge to the small house and disregard the two-story faux Spanish building blocking the emerging moon. This was not the Alhambra in Granada, or the Alamo for that matter, and she was not under siege. This was a back street off the beaten path in Swannanoa after twilight. Or, as Harry would put it, it was a matter of logic, awareness, and keeping a close check on her impulsiveness. The way things were going, she was beginning to wonder what part of her would show up.

She unlocked the door and slipped inside. The musky smell that greeted her and the fact that the lights didn't work didn't ease her anxiety. After banging into things, she trudged back to her SUV, grabbed a flashlight out of the glove compartment, and spent the next hour or so locating the breaker panel, getting everything running again, and airing the place out. She located the single bedroom which, from the look of things, must have served as a bachelor pad for her client's ex. She got out a notebook and made a quick inventory of items needed for a few days' stay.

She did this all hurriedly, like the time she entered a ramshackle abandoned house on a dare. Still riding this childish cheap thrill, she scurried back to her car.

After heading back to town and her sensible house on a sensible street with friendly neighbors and the reassuring flood of streetlights, she found a certain comfort in being snug inside. She made herself a snack and some hot chocolate and listened to the familiar low diesel whine of the freight train as it rumbled by at the tail end of Cherry Street past the old depot. She gave herself points for averting her prime shortcoming—getting carried away and in over her head. Like when she'd jumped in the river to rescue a lost little girl stuck in the brambles on the opposite bank. That time she'd misjudged the depth and current of the river and damn near drowned.

Given all she'd been talking herself into and out of, she still couldn't relax as she got ready for bed. Maybe it was because despite her dominant side, she was irrepressibly drawn to diving in and seeing how far she could go. Maybe it was because Skip's dodgy scenario had the greater draw . . .

In the dream, the star-spangled troops were driven back by foreign hordes dashing out from portals in the Alhambra. When the scene switched, Miranda spotted Davey Crocket and Jim Bowie in coonskin caps alongside others in John Deer caps and combat fatigues, raising their fists in defense of the Alamo. Skip blew a whistle and everything went into freeze-frame as he told Miranda they were going to sneak behind enemy lines and report back, like SAS marauders in the Libyan desert.

When she asked what SAS meant, he garbled something about secret commandos dropped in by parachute during WWII. "Don't you remember?"

Just then, a burly figure with a handlebar moustache got behind a microphone, puffed on a stogie, and yelled slogans like "Remember the Alamo" and "America First."

When she protested that the time frames were all mixed up, Skip kept prodding her to move as the battle carried on in the smoke and haze. But she remained stock-still as a tabby cat scurried away before she could stop it. Totally flustered, Skip cried out, "Now look what happened!"

Clutching the back of his head as he fell to his knees, Skip cried out again, "Are you going to get cracking or not? This is not *Let's Pretend*."

Out of nowhere, Harry appeared and said, "Think, Miranda, think. What are the realities? Use your head." Harry returned to his typing in the mountain cabin. Miranda remained frozen.

"No, no," said Skip. "Hang on, don't you remember? How about Field Marshal Rommel's maneuvers during the Africa Corps campaign?" Waving his arms wildly, Skip leaped over a fallen soldier as tanks rolled toward them, scattering desert sand in their wake. "Don't you see, don't you get it— all these maneuvers and tricks? The stalking horse must be exposed before it's too late. Duffy needs you. Your country needs you. It's D-Day minus four!"

At last, she sprinted back through the fog of war, asking

Harry to look out for a white Toyota Corolla. Hovering over his keyboard, Harry announced that the car was a figment of her imagination. So was the commando raid, the smoky battle, and all the rest of it. She was simply losing her grip.

But she kept at him and was warding off the fog and smoke when she woke with a start.

Sitting up straight in bed, she said aloud, "Right, Harry. Just a matter of common sense. Anyone can see that."

CHAPTER SEVEN

Early that Sunday, as Miranda approached Harry's cottage atop Gray Eagle Crest, the irony of it all wasn't lost on her. She'd settled in Black Mountain as a relief from the right-wing politics she'd encountered in Raleigh, which were not unlike the pressure she'd encountered back home in Indiana. No matter where she went in Raleigh, she was bound to get an earful of unwanted advice from other realtors that went something like this:

"You side with those liberals holding rallies in front of the state capitol, word will get out. Your sales prospects will dry up. Get with the program, darlin'."

It wasn't that Miranda ever had any hard and fast political views. She just didn't like putting up with clients trying to feel her out as to which political tribe she belonged. Here, in this little mountain town off the beaten path, it was strictly live and let live. You could count the number of those scrutinizing the ups and downs of the national political scene on one hand.

So what happened? Skip crossed the Buncombe County line and brought the latest ultra-right-wing machinations with him.

But even after she pulled in to Harry's house-sit, mentioned the irony, and broached the subject of the assault, Harry shrugged her off and went back to tapping away on his laptop at his spot in the far corner. She saw it for the obvious ploy it was; he'd posted his latest feature and wouldn't receive his next assignment from the editor till the end of the week.

As usual, the moment Miranda started to move in on him, Harry pocketed his horn-rims, scuffed over to the picture window, and looked out at the cloud-covered ridges. As if he'd been harboring an argument for such a contingency, he said, "Let's chalk if off to pure happenstance. Plus a soft spot for a pixilated old playmate."

"Oh, that's cute," Miranda said, holding her ground. "Look, Harry, Russ Mathews is actually on the scene. And somebody actually bashed Skip on the head. It was lucky I came along and got him to the ER."

Continuing to look out at the rim of the Southern Blue Ridge, Harry said, "Okay, then let's chalk it off to a complete misunderstanding."

"Brilliant."

"As far as you're concerned, maybe, way down deep, with a mother hooking up with yet another assignation in a trailer park and a father you never knew, there's a yearning for an idyllic childhood. Which would account for the way you're being taken in by all this."

Miranda wanted to remain standing until the testy silence got to him. Instead, she countered with "Your psycho-babble aside, under the circumstances, I cannot turn my back on him."

She knew full well the instant she stepped closer, he'd edge over to the kitchen area and either opt for making some tea or yank out a Jamaican ginger beer from the fridge. She took a step, and he proceeded true to course. She followed right on his heels.

"Can we cut to the chase, Harry? It isn't just a stray cat. It obviously goes a lot further."

"How do you know?" said Harry, dropping his calm and sensible ploy. "Did you ever even see the cat? How do you know anything?"

"Well I do know Skip didn't bop himself over the head. I do know he's not being held in a major hospital in Asheville on a whim."

Locating a tumbler, pouring some ginger beer, Harry finally came out with it. "I am not going out there again. Understood? Not going to help you investigate anything that places me in any kind of jeopardy."

Miranda circled the kitchen island, slid the glass away from him and said, "No jeopardy on your part. I promise."

"I'll bet."

"For now, I only need you to hop in my SUV as we go to the motel, then follow me in Skip's old Volvo and park it in a battered garage in the Swannanoa boonies. Afterwards, to occupy your idle mind, I've cranked out a list of slogans, battle cries, and what have you that I've gleaned from the bits and drabs I managed to eke out of Skip. All you have to do is open a browser and see if you can find a pattern—any way to make any kind of sense out of all this sputtering. Any link that could tie in with D-Day and the witching hour at the tail end of this Wednesday."

"You have got to be kidding."

"I wish. Anyway, as I said, simply think of it as a way to while away the time till your next gig."

"I don't believe this," said Harry, peering up as if praying for deliverance.

"Dammit Harry, I have to know how far it goes if it actually is going anywhere. You need to keep from having a frazzled woman on your hands. We're talking less than four days scoping out a maybe, possibly percolating catastrophe."

When he gave her another "I don't believe this," she countered with, "Okay, I'll settle for a what-if."

Practically rolling his eyes, Harry said, "The reason people go round the bend, my dear, is because they're victims of what-ifs. Assumptions that haven't stood the test of cold hard facts. You copy?"

"Absolutely."

"Come again? You actually agree?"

"Taking into account my realtor's sharp eye poking around every nook and cranny, how can we miss? I'm saying let's get off it and start to nail this thing down."

Harry hemmed and hawed some more but to no avail. In no time he was ushered out the door and ensconced in the passenger seat of Miranda's SUV. Completely oblivious to all his misgivings, she tooled down the mountain lane on the first leg of a dubious undertaking he still hadn't agreed to.

CHAPTER EIGHT

U pon returning to the mountain cottage some two hours later, Harry couldn't shake an abiding sense of unease. It had started while traipsing around that shadowy lane off the beaten track in Swannanoa with those two moldy Spanish houses and a crumbling garage that barely housed cousin Skip's rattletrap Volvo. He'd tried to slough it off, telling himself how unreasonable it was to be acting this way over a proposition that was by all indications preposterous.

That loopy escapade Miranda had dragged him into that culminated in gunshots and the apprehension of the unhinged perpetrator would do anyone for a lifetime. He'd assumed she'd fully come to her senses and they were well out of it. But here she was, no matter what he said to her, dragging needless anxiety back into their lives.

If he could convince her that her cousin's problems were not linked to some right-wing conspiracy about to erupt, if he could defuse the whole notion, life could return to an even keel. As for the assault—the tap on the head plus the catnapping—it was a local police matter, surely. The assailant was probably a transient motorcyclist linked to some fly-by-night ransom ploy. By the same token, the sighting of Russ Mathews's rental car also had some rational explanation. Though the cat perched in his back window after he'd hopped a flight down here from New York was hard to fathom.

If there was anything Harry couldn't abide, it was fuzzy circumstances. Which was understandable given his background. He had been shunted off to New England boarding schools while his parents went their separate ways engaging in venture capital schemes abroad, causing Harry to eventually chronicle other people's lives from a remove. To take everything on shaky ground with a grain of salt. To take refuge in sheer objective observation.

Which did little to explain his on-again, off-again relationship with Miranda that, more often than not, tended toward the irrational once a little chaos crept in.

Dismissing these issues, which only exacerbated his anxiety, he made himself another cup of herbal tea, sat back, and gazed out the picture window for the umpteenth time. He then realized there was only one thing for it. Go into gear as Harry the great poohbah of Trivial Pursuit and purveyor of cold, hard facts. He would simply shine a cool light on present day politics and place the elements into separate compartments where they belonged: fantasy, fact, supposition, partisan propaganda, etc. And that went double for cousin Skip and his campfire tales, which he'd summarily file under pure whimsy.

He strode over to his corner workspace, logged onto his computer, got out Miranda's hodgepodge of a list she'd dropped off, and placed a blank notebook at the ready to slot everything in its respective place.

He began with parallels between Skip's alleged findings at the radio station and military history. As he proceeded from one website to another, he found no connection between Russ Mathews's intimations re: Field Marshal Rommel's tank tactics during his Africa Corps campaign in World War II except for a threat and subsequent maneuvers on the part of a foreign force.

Switching to the SAS, he found that it referred to a secret Special Air Service attached to Great Britain during Rommel's campaign, made up of bands of nerveless misfits—not unlike pockets of patriots presently engaged in weekend maneuvers in backwaters of this country's South and Midwest. At any rate, the SAS marauders parachuted onto the Libyan desert to infiltrate and cause havoc. They planted explosives and hightailed it to a rendezvous point. Given their thirst for action, these SAS bands raided suddenly and retreated swiftly, attacking where and when least expected. Such volunteers were allergic to military discipline, which, arguably, made them the forebears of the paramilitary troops running around the backwoods today.

Harry stopped himself. Despite his intentions, he was reaching, speculating. Not only that, he was blending assault and defensive tactics. Who were the perpetrators and who were the defenders?

He segued to Russ Mathews's radio broadcasts. He came upon prerecorded podcast feeds on the syndicated Liberty Broadcasting System with affiliates throughout the South, Midwest, and the Rockies. The voice was deep and resounding, like a tent-pole preacher goading his flock.

The notes Harry jotted down were sporadic but contained certain pivotal words and phrases like "America foremost," "make us safe," "the system is breaking down," "overthrow the establishment, the East Coast elites," and "give us our country back." The words and tone changed from the presidential campaign to the inauguration to the current state of affairs. When Mathews's candidate won the presidency, the rallying cry was "Now we can get our house back in order."

Recently, however, something must have gone amiss with Harper, "our new, pliable commander in chief." Hence Mathews's preoccupation—according to Miranda's notes gleaned from Skip—about the breach in the castle walls.

Admittedly, like Miranda, Harry hadn't been following the shifting news cycle with all its partisan bickering. He hadn't kept up with the primaries and the national election which, on the surface, was all a muddle. The democrats had no clear message and the republicans had broken into factions muddying up global initiatives and America first protectionism.

He pulled back. He may have hit on something but had no upshot to declare. Once again, he dropped it and moved on.

Sticking closely to Miranda's notes, he next searched Mathews's *stalking horse*. Then he melded more of what Skip had glommed off Mathews's desk, plus Skip's tall tales over the airwaves pointing to the supposed deadline in a few days.

Harry learned the different codes for D-Day—the day on which an attack is to be initiated like the invasion in Normandy. If all systems are a go, D-1 is the day before the operation, D+3 is three days after, and so on. As for the stalking horse, according to Wikipedia, it seemed that hunters once used the cutout figure of a horse to hide behind when stalking game. Fowl would flee the moment humans approached but would tolerate the close proximity of what they took for wild creatures. In politics, it referred to the use of a dummy candidate or straw man to determine which way the wind was blowing—a way to test the waters before she or he threw their hat in the ring. A way to take soundings, to assess the lay of the land. Some kind of stalking horse was employed as a tactical maneuver to achieve the endgame.

Harry leaned back, took all this material into consideration, and thought long and hard. Before cousin Skip was allowed to fill in for his friend, Mathews and/or the powers that be must have checked him out. Listened to his homespun tales from the heartland—that so-called "flyover zone." Home of the very folks Mathews referred to who felt they'd been left out, lost their jobs, lost their voice due to the coastal elites and Wall Street financiers. Therefore, pencil in looking Skip over in person to make doubly sure you have the spitting image of the loveable scarecrow from *The Wizard of Oz*. Little did Liberty Broadcasting know that Mr. Homespun saw this as an opportunity to gain notoriety through takeoffs on Mathews and ultra-right-wing politics. Or had no idea what he was doing and was simply having a good time. In either case, discovering Skip's attachment to a stray ginger cat, the powers that be gave the order to swoop in and . . .

Shaking his head, Harry rose. He was buying into this whole thing. Complicit in conjuring up a through line to a clandestine scheme.

He left the cottage and strolled up the rocky slope under the starlit sky. Sensing the chill in the air, he clambered up and around the jutting pines, attempting to clear his mind.

But even after reaching the top of the rise, none of it helped, not even the crisp night air. He'd sectioned off no sharp dividing line between fact and fantasy. Yet, like it or not, something long repressed had been stirred, and he found himself starting to get hooked.

He turned his thoughts again to the recent presidential election and a relative unknown who barely squeaked by. An ex-governor Harper who seemed so pliable at first but apparently hadn't come through for them in the eyes of Mathews and his ilk, leading to imminent circumstances requiring a stalking horse on D-Day.

Harry caught himself again. He didn't want to jump the gun or get ahead of himself. What's more, who knew what Miranda would get herself into if he didn't warn her. But any kind of warning would alert her that something was up and set her off.

He hurried down the steep downward slope, determined to stay objective. Reentering the cottage, he made a beeline for his nook and typed up the scattering of facts, links, and suppositions and saved the file under the heading "A Case for Imminent Right-Wing Maneuvers."

The time was drawing near for Miranda to get the upshot on Skip's condition, and the best Harry could do was give her an update. Sorting through the possibilities, he decided on a three-sentence text:

You could spin it to cause some concern. You could take it as an excuse for right-wingers to let off some steam. You could sit back and simply play it as it lays.

He sent the message.

On second thought, he wished he hadn't typed the words "cause some concern." But in all honesty, he was conflicted and had to include that remote possibility. For the moment, all he could do was wait for her response and gird himself for another round of the cousin Skip follies.

CHAPTER NINE

With Skip's old car tucked away in the dilapidated garage and the little faux hacienda now well-stocked and comfy, Skip was all set to be discharged from the hospital—and Miranda realized that things were still totally up in the air. Skip on the loose again was a real concern. The text message from Harry and Miranda's call back in an attempt to decipher it only knotted things up even more. Especially when she kept pressing and, unwittingly, he let a few things slip.

Keying on Russ Mathews's podcasts, Harry's allusions to antsy backwoods militias echoing SAS marauders, D-Day, a stalking horse, and other items he'd passed on were troubling enough. Not to mention that Skip obviously brought it on himself by hyping this all up over the airwaves and unwittingly giving away the "plan," whatever that was. So it was right back to juggling her worries over Skip and a catnapped Duffy, amplified by some vague alert involving this area in the next couple of days.

Miranda searched her mind for some realty experience she could draw upon. Something she could relate to to still this overloaded circuit. But all she could think of was an unscrupulous developer who surreptitiously bought up parcels of land, then hoodwinked and paid off members of the Planning Commission on the way to site approval for a humongous retirement community. One that sprawled across the once boundless acreage. And nobody saw it coming.

But this analogy got her nowhere.

Again, what the forces that be had been setting in motion might culminate close by (else why were they so insistent he get far away from here?). And also be linked in a chain reaction in the vicinity of the chapel by the World Trade Center that Skip unwittingly cruised by with Duffy in tow (else why were they tailing him?). More to the point, who were the immediate adversaries trying to keep Skip in check? Was Mathews still hanging around to make sure Skip got the message and would clear out forthwith? Or was that the biker's job?

It would really help if she could smack up against some of the players and bring this down to those blessed tangibles. Despite Harry's input, Miranda had to admit she was just racking her brain and still guessing like crazy.

Given a little time before Skip's discharge from the hospital, she headed east out of Swannanoa and decided to clear her mind and while away the next hour or so with some bacon, eggs, and coffee at the Blue Ridge Biscuit and Brunch. Though the place was located across from the motel where Skip had been accosted, a patio was wedged between the rear of the place and the embankment of railroad tracks above. It was a spot that always served as a refuge from whatever it was that was getting to her. It held the promise that the freight train would come by and, in a folksy sense, ease her troubled mind and carry her blues away.

The train didn't just come by. It grinded to a stop and a barrel-chested, red-bearded crewman jumped off a flatbed car and started tossing wooden rail ties here and there to replace the worn ones in the coming days. The crewman, clad in sooty overalls, cursed under his breath every time one of the ties rolled too far down the slope. Each time it happened, a sandy-haired, smooth-faced country boy type seated on a wooden bench to the right of Miranda's wooden table began teasing him.

Draining another from a six-pack of Corona, the country boy seemed to have been lying in wait for the crewman's arrival. It wasn't only the way he held up the bottle in mock salute and hollered "Way to go, Duke!" It was his eyes. Even from this distance, she noticed they were a cool shade of blue that took in every movement, no matter how slight. Like the cardinal that alighted on a fence post a few feet away and suddenly took off again. The leather-fringed jacket and vest and faded Levi shirt and jeans only echoed this mercurial drifter effect. So did the fancy, hand-tooled cowboy boots.

Soon, the exchange with Duke began to get a little heated and drew Miranda in a bit further, succeeding in getting her mind off the fanciful plot against America.

Shielding his eyes from the glinting sun rays playing hide-and-seek behind the cloud cover, Duke peered down from the embankment and said, "So, you gonna tell me what the hell you doing here, peckerwood?"

"Now is that any way to greet kin?"

"That's exactly the way. Seeing it's you and our kinship don't figure in. I mean, what does it goddamn take?"

"Hold on now. You don't want the little lady over there to get the wrong impression."

"Only impression concerns me is one I'm finally making on you." Duke turned his back, straightened up the skewered rail ties and returned to the flatbed to toss a few more farther over.

"As I recall," the country boy said, raising his voice again, "you used to let me tease you some and then maybe come around."

"Well, you recall wrong. If I wasn't busy here, if I wasn't on the job, I'd clamber down there and really make it plain."

"My, my, you sure are touchy today."

The tone of the country boy's voice remained as dry and cool as his eyes, and the expression on his smooth features didn't change, as if making absolutely sure to keep his cards close to his vest.

Before he hopped back onto the flatbed, Duke said, "Can't believe you've been sitting there nursing your beer, waiting, all along fixing to run into me."

"Not so surprising though. Seeing that I had some time on my hands."

"Before what?"

"Seems I got me a gig at the Tavern this Friday."

"I thought it was Travis's gig?"

"It is. But I'm maybe fronting for him and Bud with some new tunes I wrote."

Seemingly taken aback, Duke scuffed around, straightening out ties that didn't need straightening, came right back, peered down again and said, "Oh yeah? Since when? And why drive all the way down from Madison County some six days early?"

"Practice."

"Don't give me that."

Plunking the bottle hard on the table, the country boy said, "Ain't giving you nothing but a last chance. Let bygones be bygones." The eyes and voice still cool along with the blank expression.

"That'll be the day. The name Dupre ain't no password. Get that through your head. Don't entitle you to nothin', leastwise my companionship." Standing tall, Duke signaled for the shortened freight train to move forward.

"Nevertheless, offer's still open!" the country boy hollered over the grinding squeal of the wheels rolling by.

"You got it backwards!" Duke hollered back.

Before the country boy could repack the empty bottles, rise, and exit back into the eatery, Miranda picked up her coffee mug and asked if she could join him. Predictably, the look on his face told her nothing. Only the fact that he stayed seated gave her the clue she could proceed.

"As it happens," Miranda said, "I book the acts as well as manage the Tavern on weekends."

"Well now, how about that? Some coincidence, huh?"

"Like running into Duke?"

"Yup. You never can tell."

Trying to keep her cool as well, Miranda went on. "And, of course, I'm well aware that Travis is the lead singer and

Bud backs him up on the dobro. Plus, there was no mention of a front man with some new songs. Which is all the more curious since this opening gig calls for old favorites."

He smiled the kind of smile that was impossible to read and said, "Depends on how things go. All things come to he who waits."

Playing along despite herself, she said, "Ah yes, haste makes waste."

"What you don't know can't hurt you."

"Never judge a book by its cover."

"Keep your sunny side up."

"And let a smile be your umbrella."

He nodded like a guy who'd successfully sized up a gal at a singles bar. "That's right. As for Duke . . ."

Perhaps teasing again, perhaps deflecting, he went into the storied history of the Dupre clan while keying on Miranda's response.

"Ever hear tell of three Dupre brothers during the Revolutionary War? Who run into a Major Patrick Ferguson, an Englishman who threatened to tar and burn every citizen who refused to pay tribute to the king?"

"Can't say as I have."

"Well now, not only did the brothers three refuse to pay, they and their kin bushwhacked his regiment."

"Why are you telling me this?"

"Didn't want you to get the wrong idea about me and Duke. He's sore that his little sister was sweet on me. But we still got long-ago family ties. Since the victory at King's Mountain in 1780 and our victory with the patriot militia, we don't hold with foreign invasion. Since us and other over-the-mountain boys settled deep in these parts over two hundred years ago, we've kept to what you might call a traditionalist way of life."

The way he underscored the word *traditionalist* gave Miranda the feeling he was really checking her out now. That and the way he then carried on about having to hide the stills and crates from government intervention to preserve a *natural* way of life. Self-sustaining with grist mills and all, and depend on and defend your own kind. He underscored *depend on and defend your own kind* just as deliberately as he'd underscored the words *natural* and *traditionalist*.

By this time, it was more than apparent to Miranda that if she extended this encounter or followed him too closely under some pretext to get a bead on his license plate, it would clinch whatever he was fishing for.

Instead, as he began ambling back inside the restaurant, she said, "By the way, I never got your name."

Hesitating at the doorway, he said, "What for?"

"Because, in case you still don't get it, whoever appears on that stage is my lookout."

With the slightest hint of a smile, he said, "Vin. Just make it Vin."

"Gotcha."

"To save you the trouble, haven't finalized my plans with Travis just yet."

She could have thought more about the backwoods militia notion on her list. But she had more than enough on her plate for the time being.

A short time later, hanging back and playing it safe, she was still seated in her SUV ringing Travis's cellphone, giving it a fourth try. This time he picked up and, as always, minced no words. Including his riffs on his Gibson guitar, everything with Travis was short and sweet with no frills.

"You never know with Vin," said Travis, after thinking it over.

"Okay, how about this? Why would he be tracking Duke down and then lie in wait for him to come by? Is it really something to do with Duke's little sister?"

"Ain't got no little sister."

"Bad blood then?"

"Like I say, you never know with Vin."

"Can you just take a stab at it? Why drive all the way down days early from Madison County? Does he really need to practice? And why wasn't I told about it?"

"Damned if I know."

Easing back a bit, Miranda said, "So, in all likelihood, he may or may not be showing up at the Tavern."

"Or was just pulling your chain." Then, after an interminable pause, Travis said, "As for Duke . . ."

"Go on."

"Maybe Vin is still trying to recruit him."

"For what?"

"Not exactly sure except Vin is bound to be up to no good."

Left with that little zinger, Miranda reminded Travis they'd be setting up this Friday around five-thirty. Then she rang off.

She switched on the ignition, but before she hit the road

and began to wend her way to the hospital, she spotted a shiny white compact pull into the motel parking lot across the way. She waited, but no one got out.

Shortly after, a rusted green Chevy pickup vintage 1940s cruised by, circled around, headed back and idled by the far edge of the motel. As far as Miranda could tell, it had a skewered Madison County license plate and a busted taillight. Then it took off again. This went on a few more times until the pickup drove in and, despite all the empty spaces, backed up right next to the compact until both drivers were within arms' length of each other.

From where her SUV was idling, she could swear the driver of the pickup was wearing a leather-fringed jacket as he extended his hand in greeting.

Needless to say, Mathews was still in town and the local Carolina crew included not only a biker henchman but, in all probability, cool Vin Dupre as well.

CHAPTER TEN

A long with everything else, it dawned on Miranda that she had no backup this time. No ex-boyfriend Detective Dave Wall to step in. Not only was Dave out of the picture now, there wasn't a smidge of verifiable evidence, let alone firsthand encounters on her part.

As she drove to the hospital to pick up Skip and take him back to the faux hacienda, she dickered over what, if anything, she should tell him. The last thing he needed, as if these temporary digs weren't odd enough, were more inklings to set his fevered brain off and running.

And so, during discharge proceedings, she went through the motions and did her best imitation of a doting relative. In turn, she learned that all test results indicated he was fine. As for the blow to his head, coupled with his fatigue, it didn't take more than a tap with a blunt instrument for his assailant to hit and run undetected. In any case, the swelling was minimal, ibuprofen should help alleviate the dull ache, and it was advisable for him to avoid any stress or strenuous exercise for a few days as a precaution.

Miranda didn't mention it, but not only was Skip not the type to frequent a gym, the funk she found him in was so debilitating, there was little sign he was up for any kind of activity. In fact, after she dutifully checked for a white Corolla lying in wait, he hardly uttered a word the whole drive back except for an occasional "Who was I kidding?" and "Why didn't I see it coming?"

Even after she'd gotten him settled in and made him tea with fresh scones she'd picked up next to the Black Mountain Visitors Center, his response was to slump over the kitchen table in the same forlorn way he slumped over the picnic table by the tailgate market under the spreading oak. Only this time he was in full despair.

"Okay," Miranda said, pulling up a chair, "whatever happened to the great conundrum? Caught between getting Duffy back and getting to the bottom of things?"

This time there wasn't even a sigh.

Unable to contain herself any longer, she got to her feet and began trying to get a rise out of him. "You know what I still remember? Being called into the principal's office because I couldn't take *Silas Marner*. Some drivel about an old guy who'd lost his gold and hangs around forever sulking. I got in trouble because I told the teacher if I've got to play pretend, I'd rather listen to stories about Jack Armstrong, the all-American . . ."

"Boy," Skip murmured.

"Right. Jack Armstrong, the all-American boy. I said I'd rather listen to my cousin Skip's adventure stories than sit around in a stuffy English class and be bored to death. When Jack's boon companion says, 'There's a lady stranded who's run out of gas,' Jack says, 'No time for that now, Billy. We've got real trouble to deal with!'"

Slowly propping his head up, Skip said, "You remember that?"

"I remember lots of things." Feeling hemmed in by the

musty stucco walls, Miranda passed through the horseshoe-shaped archway and the compact living room until she reached the front door. Pivoting, she said, "Meanwhile, if you spot a shiny white Corolla or an old, rusty, green Chevy pickup, we may actually be on to something."

"What do you mean?"

"Well, for openers, according to Cindy at the motel, Duffy was last seen crawling up to the back window of Russ Mathews's airport rental."

"Really?"

"Really."

She hung back for a moment, hoping she'd gotten his attention and perked him up a little.

Just as she was about to give up and let herself out, he said, "We? Like Jack Armstrong?'"

"For heaven sake, Skip, I was only making a point. Jack Armstrong may have been stuck inside Shep Anderson's memories, but at least he and his sidekick were actively trying to nail something down. Not running hot and cold. Neither one sticking his head in the sand. Keep an eye out, buster. Who knows how many of his nine lives Duffy has left. The way things are shaking out, unless we actually begin confronting things face-to-face, who really knows anything?"

CHAPTER ELEVEN

An hour or so later, Skip took in the waning rays of twilight filtering onto the slate floor but remained stuck at the kitchen table. Yet again, he thought of his ginger tabby Duffy with those piercing green eyes. And how many of his nine lives he really had left.

In a sense, Skip and Duffy were both strays, a fact underscored by that early evening when he appeared out of the blue when Skip first arrived a few weeks ago, meowing outside the basement flat in Hoboken, asking to come in from the cold. Instead of being aloof at first like most cats, Duffy patrolled the place, rubbing against things to get the layout before he felt safe and established his perch by the front window. It wasn't long before he sprang up on Skip's lap when Skip was home musing over his next flight of fancy, contentedly purring while he was being stroked.

There was little doubt that when Duffy found himself collarless, staring out the back window of the airport rental, he was panicking, searching for a way out, raising his hackles, ready to spring. And what about being fed or ever calming down and feeling secure again—what about all of it? Despite the fact that Skip's own defense mechanism was to lose himself in fantasy, improv, and storytelling, this time there was no line between himself and reality. No way to mess around and take it all back. As long as he could hang onto a silver linings playbook, he could talk himself into or out of anything. But there was no way to dismiss the abiding anxiety running up his spine.

And the thought of throwing in the towel and going along went totally against the grain.

Too rattled to remain in limbo a moment longer, Skip got up and left the room. Wending his way outside, the strangeness of the foliage, the Spanish mission style of the two buildings, and the deserted street only added to his jangled disorientation. Even the vague familiarity of a front porch light was erased by the thick, low-lying clouds racing across the dusky-rose afterglow.

As he warded off the long shadows, the dull ache at the back of his head returned, reminding him yet again that it wasn't another improv or trying something on for size. For the first time ever, there were dire consequences.

As though seconding the motion, he thought he heard the raspy grumble of an old truck engine—perhaps headed this way, perhaps cruising by not far from where he was standing. He wanted to run, but he just stood there, unable to move his feet.

Besides, what did Miranda mean by looking out for an old pickup along with a white rental?

Glancing here and there, he caught sight of the outline of six or seven mountain ridges in the distance. Along with everything else, he was a fish out of water. There was no terrain like this in the heartland and certainly not in the Big Apple. Even during his improv stint in Asheville, he stuck close to Haywood and Park. Under the reassuring glare of the downtown streetlights and the toothless lady who set up shop by the Flatiron Building, slapping her knees with clacking spoons while keeping time with a foot drum.

But he wasn't in Asheville. He was dangling, hiding out in the middle of nowhere.

He heard the grumbling engine coming from another direction. But he was so far out of his element he couldn't say whether it was traveling west, east, north, or south.

Something else caught his attention. It may have been the same galloping paranoia, but he could swear there was a light flickering by the other side of the larger building. The one with the cascading tile roof, arched corridors, windows, and doorways. In his mind's eye, he could picture someone slipping into place to spy on him and signaling some guy in an old truck.

He hunkered down and made his way through the thick underbrush. He had to know what was going on. Couldn't keep going on this way till his nerves got so frayed he'd become unable to function. No use to Duffy. No use in this world at all.

Just then, at the far edge, he spotted her waddling up the exterior terracotta staircase, shifting between the oversized stairs and the stucco wall leading up to an arched landing. She was heavyset, wearing a shapeless, sack-like muumuu of mismatched tiers of orange and coral. Tugging a sack as she went, she flashed a flashlight here and there to light her way. What really caught his eye was the wary way she halted every other step and looked around. Her round, childish face and wide eyes reminded him of his days as a drama counselor in a woodland camp for slow learners. He used that same wide-eyed look when he told the kids they were going to act out fairy tales and invite their parents and friends to see how special and talented they were.

If he could earn her confidence, maybe she would intercept whoever was tooling around before the guy noticed the porch light and came barging in. Or, just as bad, yanked up the garage door and came upon his old Volvo to seal the deal. If he could buy a little time, he might start thinking straight again.

He waited while she tried the door. It was a faded Mediterranean blue, flimsy and warped. Sure enough, after she yanked and pushed a number of times, it creaked and gave way. She mounted the tile stairs beyond, reached the landing and peered inside. Skip followed suit, easing up higher, trying to get a peek himself. As she flashed her light around the mustard yellow walls and a ceiling accented with wooden beams, he could tell that the place was bare like an empty ballroom, and the dusty terrazzo floor made her slip when she shuffled forward.

Impulsively, he framed himself in the doorway and said, "Oh, hi there. How's it going?"

She wheeled around, reached inside her burlap bag, and whipped out a willow stick as if it were a magic wand to ward off evil spirits. With her mag light in hand, she reached into the bag and pulled out a sparkling five-pointed star. She waved both objects and said, "I call upon the five elements of air, water . . . earth . . . fire and . . . and . . ."

"Spirit," Skip said, raising his hands in mock surrender. In his rush to humor her, he blurted out, "Do you have a crystal? If you add it to the tip of the wand, that'll increase the power ten times over."

Her eyes widened as she lowered the mag light and star. "Crystal? You mean the pretty kind that breaks real easy? The van that gets them little figurines and unicorns and such from rich ladies donations has to drive real slow so's they don't break. Wouldn't never put no such thing on the tip of this wand."

She reached down and shone the bright light directly on his face. "Are you the owner? The village witch promised it was un . . . un . . ."

"Unoccupied? No, I'm not. But I'm set up next door, thanks to the broker who is acting on behalf of those rich ladies who are off somewheres."

Stepping away, she said, "Uh-oh. Am I in trouble? Don't want that. Preacher Bob won't let me into the food pantry. I'll have to give this dress back to the village witch and she and the others won't help me anymore with stuff and—"

Raising his hand like a crossing guard this time, he said, "It's okay, stop. We can work this out if you'll do me a little favor. What's your name?"

"Uh-uh, you'll tell on me."

"Friends don't tattle."

"You mean it? You'll be my friend?"

"Cross my heart."

She looked all about as if making sure there was no one within earshot and then whispered, "Annie."

"Great, Annie, listen."

Shaking her head like a rag doll, she came right back with "No, no, it's too late." She dropped her wand and started pacing. "Can't make the witch happy and clear the place for her and make Preacher Bob happy. Not and play with you. No, no, no. Oh, golly, I am so confused."

As if caught on stage in an improv that was sinking fast, he darted over and rummaged around in her bag until he came up with a broom made up of willow bindings and birch twigs and began whisking the threshold. "Watch, Annie, see? I'm sweeping away all the negative energy, all the static. Nothing can harm you."

"Really?"

"You bet," Skip said, his imagination clicking away. "And now you're going to keep both places free from harm. For the village witch and her gang to hang out in, to make Preacher Bob happy, plus doing a kind deed to cover for me."

Annie trained her light on the threshold where he'd swept and said, "How can I do all that?"

He put the broom and star back in her sack and ushered her outside to the landing. "If, in the next few minutes, some bad person appears, drives up and has no business being here, not like you and me . . ."

"Oh? Drives up? Really?"

"Yes, 'cause we're hooked up with the real estate lady. Miranda. You must have seen her out and about. Hanging out at the tailgate market and such. She's in charge."

"The cute spunky one in overalls?"

"The very one."

"You know her? Know her real good?"

"Absolutely. She's my cousin."

"For sure? Cross your heart and hope to die?"

Skip went through the motions, leaving his right hand plunked across his chest.

"I like her," said Annie, beaming.

"Good. So this is what you're going to do. You're going to shoo the bad guy away. Tell him you're the caretaker in charge of trespassers. This is private property and it's to stay that way."

"I'm what?"

"Guarding against intruders. Keeper of the keys." He reached inside his trousers, plucked out a latch key Miranda had given him attached to a braided loop. He dangled it like a magic charm and handed it to her.

Annie gazed at it, unclasped the loop, affixed it like a necklace, pulled back, and thought it over. "Guarding what?"

"What do you think? What do you imagine rich ladies stored away while on a faraway boat trip?"

"Precious crystals of course."

"Bingo. You got it. Did you see that old, crummy garage?"

"No."

"It's there at the end of the drive. That's where precious things are stored for safekeeping."

The whole time he was hyping this up, he was hoping against hope Annie didn't want to see for herself and expose his old Volvo.

Squinting, Annie leaned out the door and looked up into the sky, like a school kid priming for a tough exam. She moved her lips, possibly silently repeating some of the instructions he'd given her, just as the squeal of old, rusty brakes cut through the stillness.

CHAPTER TWELVE

A s a vehicle door creaked open and slammed shut with a thud, Skip whispered to Annie that they were going to only take a looksee. Maybe the driver would keep on going.

But he had to see for himself. So far it had been irate callers' voices over the intercom at the radio station, furtive figures across the way from the sublet in Hoboken, a nondisclosure form dangling from the iron railing, a shot shattering his front window followed by slashed tires. All this followed by a note on his windshield in Bucks County, Pennsylvania, Duffy's sliced collar, and a blow to his head here in the Blue Ridge. But no actual perpetrator he could lay his eyes on.

He reached for Annie's hand as he set off down the terracotta stairs, but she shook him off and brandished her willow wand. Catching up, she tiptoed behind him into the brush. He bent over as if showing a wary child how to play hide-and-seek.

Making his way at a steady clip into the shadows as she continued to lag behind, he crouched so low behind a thick scrub pine, he could barely make out the green pickup. Perhaps it was the exact vehicle Miranda told him to keep an eye out for; perhaps he was just seeing things. But no, there it was, complete with a lean figure standing by the grassy verge.

A few yards away, Annie was having such a hard time

crouching in her tight muumuu. Motioning her to keep down, having no idea how to play this if the guy lingered, Skip remained hidden behind the pine as fleeting thoughts crossed his mind. Notions like, What if Duffy is stowed away in the trunk and not holed up with Russ Mathews? What if it's part of an exchange, if Skip will only show himself and swear not to call the police? Or, while the guy is preoccupied with Annie covering for him, Skip could sneak around, search for the trunk latch, yank it open, and see for himself.

As he dismissed this last notion out of hand, something must have emboldened Annie. Naïve as can be despite Skip's effort to wave her down, she stepped right out onto the verge and flinched when the shadowy figure let out a "Well there then now" in a lazy Southern drawl.

Holding up her wand like she was shooing away demon spirits, she said, "Be gone! You don't belong here and will have to leave."

"You don't say?" the guy said in that same amused tone. "What gives you that idea?"

"It's my job."

"Oh, is it now?"

"That's right. Owe it to the village witch. And Preacher Bob. And the real estate lady who divvies up the keys for rich ladies who don't want nobody trespassing."

Surprised that Annie could speak up like that, Skip dropped down on one knee. Which did nothing for the headache that had returned full force and a sudden gnawing concern over what Annie might be in for. Like everything else, things had ramifications you couldn't dismiss in the name of pretense.

The guy brushed right past her and headed for the front door of the little house, doubtless hell-bent on coming across the bedroom, maybe riffling through Skip's suitcase, bureau drawers, and what all he could find.

Skip forced himself to creep forward until he spied Annie, highlighted by the porch light on the top front step, blocking the guy's way.

"And what do you think you're doin', missy?"

"Be gone, I said," Annie called, waving her wand in all directions.

The guy reached up from the bottom step, grabbed the stick out of her hands, snapped it in two, and tossed it into the brush not more than a few yards from where Skip was hiding.

Annie yanked off the latch-key necklace, spun around and locked the front door, spun back and said, "See? I don't need no wand or nothing. I will tell Preacher Bob and report you."

"Oh, will you now?"

"'Cause I see you real clear and remember stuff. Officer Ed knows I remember everything about the blanket factory burning down. And what souvenirs I took and have stashed in my bag, which I can go get and show you."

Standing to the side now, the guy could have been mulling over if this was worth the trouble, how far he should push it. Skip was frozen to the spot, prodding himself to do something.

The silence was broken when Annie said, "So shoo, like I said. Go home, go back where you belong."

"Tell you what," the guy said, his tone laidback again.

"I'm gonna ask you a few questions. You come up with good answers and I'll call it quits. You come up with bad answers, I'll tell Preacher Bob and you'll never hear the end of it."

"Then you got to swear you know Preacher Bob, and promise to do right, so help you, cross your heart and hope to die."

A barely audible chuckle as the guy said, "I'm gonna do right, missy. But not right now." Another beat and the guy said, "So, you got the rules down?"

Annie did another of her stargazing routines and said, "Yes, sir. Pretty much, I guess."

The guy drifted past the front windows, as though expecting Annie was too dumb to realize he was after a glimpse of some telltale confirmation.

"Now then," he said, continuing to shuffle here and there, "you sack out at this itty-bitty house whilst keeping your eye on the big one. Which, given this stretch of woods between, don't seem hardly likely."

She gazed at the latch key, looked up at the sky again, and came out with some hocus-pocus. "Don't never question the power of those who bide the Wiccan Law. What evil ye send forth comes right back to thee."

Cursing, the guy cut over to his left and headed down the weedy drive straight for the rickety one-car garage masked only by the sprung, warped door.

Tripping over the front steps, waddling as fast as she could, Annie screamed, "You can't do this, can't trespass, not after the broom swept things clean!"

Skip tried to break out of his feebleness and failed as Annie reached the garage just as the guy hollered, "Who you think you're messing with? You see the tire tracks through the weeds here? You see this crummy garage no rich lady would cotton to? Out of my way!"

He raised his hand to smack her, and her fleshy arms raised to shield her face. Skip darted out of his hiding place, fearful to step in but feeling responsible for the mess he'd gotten her into. But the best he could muster was to flatten himself against the corner of the house by the rutted drive where Annie was carrying on.

When the guy said, "What you hiding there you don't want me to see?" she came up with, "Not hiding. Protecting. Making sure."

"I'm warning you, dummy. Step aside."

"Ain't no dummy. A church wagon goes everywhere, I seen it! Picking up and bringing things fine folks don't need once they're all prettied up. Money goes to the pantry so's I can eat. You touch me, you mess up the fine things and you're in even more big big trouble!"

There was more muttering that Skip couldn't make out. Something about "What fine things?" and Annie going on about "Crystals you can see through that break real easy."

Forcing himself to peek out while avoiding any eye contact, he caught a glimpse of the guy's hand-tooled cowboy boots. The moment the guy hit Annie and shoved her to one side, Skip sprang back. Annie screamed, "Assault, assault!" and Skip quivered as the garage overhead door shook with the pounding of the guy's fists.

Remembering Miranda told him it was off its track, Skip flattened himself harder against the edge of the house and held his breath. Presently, the screaming and pounding stopped. The crunch of scuffing boots over gravel drew closer and closer up the rutted drive. Spinning around, Skip made a beeline in the opposite direction, tripped and scurried into the brush.

"Assault, assault!" Annie cried out, even more insistent this time, her voice getting louder and louder, echoing at the grassy verge by the road. "I'm gonna report you to Officer Ed!"

Her cries were eclipsed by her shriller scream close by the truck's throbbing motor, the strain of the worn engine picking up speed and trailing away. In its wake it left Annie's moaning "Not fair, it's not fair" and Skip's shaking body riven with guilt.

CHAPTER THIRTEEN

Miranda's notion of a brief hiatus that Sunday evening was short lived. It started with a call from Skip's cellphone around eight, which gradually became incoherent. Something about taking crazy Annie to a Waffle House because it was the least he could do and dropping her off at a witches meeting to report back about a ceremonial location. All this mixed up with an encounter with a "hell-bent, laidback Southerner" while Skip hid in the bushes. Now it seems Skip was rattled over the return of this same guy in "that old Chevy pickup."

Trying to simmer it down a notch only seemed to make things worse as Skip threw in so many contingencies, Miranda could hardly get a word in edgewise. Soon there was no solution except to drive back there and see if she could settle him down. After all he'd been through and having just been discharged from the hospital, she had to at least assess the situation and make a determination. In a sense, she felt like a crisis management case worker on call.

When she finally got there, it was pitch dark. And there was no mistaking the state he was in as he struggled with the overhead door at the end of the rutted drive as if priming himself for a quick getaway. It was even more off its track than the last time she'd seen it, and it was all she could do to get him to back off while she barely managed to raise the door up again. Then, as handyman Miranda forever dealing with property in the throes of deferred maintenance, she retrieved her toolkit, got the rollers back in position, leveled the tracks, tightened the bolts and screws, and sprayed some lubricant while Skip held the flashlight and commented things like "What if he'd managed to crank the damn thing open? What then?"

With the overhead door problem solved, she stepped back and lowered it to the ground as he said, "Great. In the meantime, it'll be easy to open and he'll see my car right away."

She managed to escort him back inside the house by saying "I know, I know" and "Let's talk about it." She got him seated at the kitchen table and made him some instant cocoa with milk, harboring the hope it might help calm him down so that she could get to the bottom of this.

However, after taking only a few sips of cocoa, he jumped up and went over to the front window. "Poor, addled Annie had to cover for me. Pretty pathetic, wouldn't you say? All of it started because I couldn't see any of this coming. Thought it could be my last chance. Latch onto this late-night gig and winging it, using whatever I could latch onto to gain some notoriety. What if? What if? Always what if. What if I hadn't gone along with Chris Holden's offer in the first place? Damn that he was granted a leave of absence. Why from the get-go couldn't I sense there was something iffy about it?"

"Look, I know how you feel, but it's all water under the proverbial bridge, kiddo."

What little Miranda knew about handling people who were stressed-out was to refrain from being argumentative.

See things from their perspective and take it from there. Granted, she didn't do so well with ex-lovers and, nowadays, Harry. But, at the moment, this was the best she could do.

Skip stopped talking altogether as he kept staring into the darkness, ostensibly out of fear the Southern guy could barge in any second. At that point, she dropped being understanding and segued to that old standby, logic.

"What do you say we drop all the what-ifs? Let's assume it was the same beat-up Chevy pickup. The guy I met may have lost it here for a second, but he couldn't discount what he ran into."

"Like what?" Skip asked, fixing his gaze directly at her this time.

"Think about it. Thanks to you, Annie had a key to lock the front door. For all intents and purposes, she truly was a sleep-in caretaker. He—whose name is Vin Dupre by the way—was trespassing and didn't dare poke his head inside, which would be bordering on breaking and entering. Not to mention shoving Annie around as she screamed and told him she's going to notify Officer Ed, which is tantamount to accusing him of assault."

"Vin Dupre? Another henchman? How many are out there?" Acting like a little kid, he snuck out the door, skirted by the brush at the side of the yard, waited a while, and proceeded to scour the deserted lane in all directions. He glanced at the trees, examined the road again, and scurried back to Miranda's side. Out of breath, he studied Miranda for the longest time, nodded, and went off on another tangent.

"You know something? Between diagnostic tests, I dozed off on the gurney. Pictured Duffy at his wits end trying to contact me, rattling the blinds in some mountain cabin nearby."

"Right. Then started looking for a PI in the yellow pages."

"Looking for help, you mean. One eye open because Pinkertons never sleep. Did you know that? Thus the term *private eye* so that clients can get some shut-eye. Good grief, Miranda, why can't we do something?"

Throwing up her hands, disregarding the fact that he trailed right behind her, she opted to boil some water, make herself a bracing cup of instant coffee so she could call for a timeout and stay alert on her drive back home.

Avoiding his bloodshot eyes as long as she could as he remained framed within the horseshoe arch separating the two rooms, she made the coffee, sat at the table, and gulped it down. At the point when his eyes began to get to her, she said, "Look, I explained it to you. My foray into the world of detection was all a fluke. And besides, there still isn't a helluva lot to go on. Who wants what and how far are they willing to go? That to me is basically the kicker."

Still no word from Skip. Still the same, imploring bloodshot eyes until he scuffed over to her and leaned on the table. "You're right. That's it. That is the question. What did I stumble into? Who wants what? We can damn well at least start with the *who*."

"Oh, really?"

"Yes, really. Think about it. The Liberty Broadcasting doesn't just have affiliates. They must have henchmen. Guys who can get on the phone and tell you to knock it off. Trail you over to the World Trade Center. Pin a cease-and-desist agreement on your railing. Shoot out your window and puncture your tires. Trail you over to Bucks County and pick up the trail again to this little mountain town. Text you to beat it back over to the shoreline and down out of the way. They must have a whole team of trackers."

"Including Mathews? Some tracker."

"Granted he's just a mouthpiece. But Mathews knew I broke the code, was responsible, and had to make amends. I'm saying the powers that be have me pegged as a whistleblower, on the run, hovering dangerously close now to whatever in the world is going down. So, they got Mathews to hop a flight, enlist their local backwoods squad, flush me out, put me under wraps, maybe stash me away somewhere—who knows? That is the long and short of it up against some relentless patriot game."

Miranda mulled it over while finishing her coffee but still had no answer for him.

"Look," said Skip, "there's still a window of at least seventy-four hours. I've got money stashed away in an account at the Bank of America. I know there's an ATM machine in downtown Asheville. In the movies the PI always says, 'I get a per diem plus expenses.' You must have received a per diem for your last case. You as much as told me so."

Miranda gazed up at him and caught the catch in his voice when he said, "Don't you see? I ain't much, but until I get the hang of it . . . I'm saying we can't let Duffy down. Can't turn a blind eye on this whole crazy business."

"Listen, Skip. It's not that simple. It's light years beyond simple."

"Understood," said Skip. "Exactly. I'll take that as a yes." Eyelids drooping now, he let out a sigh of relief and scuffed off into the tiny bedroom.

Miranda got up and started to go after him. But by the time she got to the bedroom door, he was flaked out on the bed. "Skip?"

There might have been a murmur, it was hard to tell. The only thing apparent was that, at this point, he had totally had it and was nodding off.

Miranda said, "Hey, we'll be in touch, okay?"

Still no answer.

"Take stock. Come up with a more comprehensive game plan. Who's running Mathews, what's the big deal? Words like that."

She lingered for a moment, left the room, and called out that she was locking the door behind her and making sure everything was safe and snug.

In the silence, thoughts of a per diem aside, she decided the Pinkertons were right. A timeout, day or night, was totally out of the question.

CHAPTER FOURTEEN

While driving back in the dark, it wasn't lost on Miranda that she'd turned the corner and was in the throes of unfinished business—Vin Dupre checking her out and selling her short, the way they'd been knocking Skip around and prodding him to bail out, Harry's text intimating current political implications riding on this whole gambit.

As for Skip's offer, at best she'd send him a bill in case her services amounted to anything in recovering Duffy the cat, getting a bead on whoever had accosted Skip, looking into Vin Dupre's troublesome incident with Annie, and so forth. Depending on how any of it played out.

Turning her thoughts back to Vin while continuing to encounter little traffic at this hour, she didn't appreciate his ruse of using her Friday night country-folk fest as an excuse for driving all the way down from Madison County six days early. Especially when it turned out to be a lie that he was fronting for Bud and Travis. Anyone using her in any way really ticked her off.

And then there was his pride in the history of the rebel patriot militia clan. Plus, something he said about *depend on and defend your own kind*. And there was his lying in wait by the tracks for his kinfolk Duke to join him. Join him for what? Recruit him for what? Why here, why now, and so what?

What's more, soon after their little exchange, there he was circling around in his old pickup, landing in front of the motel to rendezvous with Russ Mathews. Was he one of the broadcasting system's henchmen? Did Mathews actually rent a room, have a biker come by before first light, sneak into Skip's room, slice off Duffy's collar, and hand the cat over so Mathews could drive off? Then have the biker put Skip out of commission for good measure? Then have Vin comb the back roads of Swannanoa at dusk to flush out Skip?

Was this all part of a reconnaissance crew covering territory from New York south? And, though she'd never laid eyes on the creature, was it in turn linked to some political subterfuge with Duffy the cat's nine lives hanging in the balance?

As she pulled into her driveway, she nailed at least one thing down. As any floundering PI knew, once the game was afoot, things snowballed in all directions. Closer to home, at least one key suspect was on the prowl.

CHAPTER FIFTEEN

A few hours earlier, Vin Dupre left the shed in the hidden grove off the old Mill Road east of Black Mountain. Shaking his head, he walked back and entered the junk trailer. Still edgy, he switched on the light. To accommodate him, somebody linked to Mathews's crew must've siphoned off electricity by welding a transformer wire.

Which was all well and good. But just to make sure there were no telltale signs left from this latest incident, he went over to the cracked mirror above the sink.

No, there was nothing that heavy, slow-brained gal could report to this Officer Ed she'd been carrying on about. No lingering scratches under his pale blue eyes that would set him apart from any other thirty-something country boy with sandy hair. What could she possibly say except that he was slim in a rambler kind of way and drove an old green pickup? Besides, it was hard to believe anyone could take seriously any of that mumbo jumbo, mixed-up crap coming out of her mouth. And a bruise maybe showing up on her arm where he'd shoved her out of the way wouldn't prove a thing. She could've gotten it any which way.

Still and all, he wished he hadn't lost it back there and banged and jerked on that goddamn stuck overhead door. Not at all like a chill dude who saw things from afar and hardly ever let himself get riled. But what can you expect after the long ride down so's he could intercept Duke at the exact spot and time when he was due to unload those railroad ties? And still get turned down again flat. Not to mention meeting up with Russ Mathews who let on this Skip character hightailed it out of the motel. That happening despite Mathews arranging for him to get knocked cold to finally convince him to cut out and lay low or else.

Afterwards, if that ain't enough, Vin finds himself on a wild goose chase looking for a beat-up gray Volvo clunker, winding up after a bunch of dead-end leads in Swannanoa somewheres off the railroad tracks. Tooling in and out and up and down unmarked back roads 'cause some gas station attendant swore he saw a person with glasses lagging behind an SUV, "drivin' one of them old foreign Swedish jobs but never come back out again in the Grovemont section." All this at dusk, followed by that loony fatty in the woods, peeking out like some nosy brat. Giving him, a perfect stranger, a hard time though he came on friendly like. Well, who wouldn't get testy, coming up empty after going to that much trouble? All for a fool assignment well beneath his calling.

The topper was having to navigate clear down this jagged drive to where he was now as it was growing pitch dark, blind switchbacks looping the whole descent through underpasses while the Norfolk Southern freight was straining, looping and climbing up above on the opposite side. As if Duke was giving him the finger heading back to the same spot in Black Mountain where he'd brushed him off for good this time.

Getting testy all over again, Vin reached into the back pocket of his jeans for the half-pint of Jack Daniels and took a deep swig. Checking his watch, he saw there was still time till he was to check back in with Mathews. That is, to tell him off and just plain let him have it.

He opened the squat little ice box and yanked out a can of Coors wedged next to a carton of milk. Shaking his head over the sight of the milk carton, he opened the beer, reached into the wall cabinet above the dinette window for a large plastic glass, poured the beer, and added enough Jack Daniels to do some good. He kicked back on the sprung vinyl couch, propped his feet on a wooden crate, and took stock.

The way he operated was to never let on. Never do or show anything that would give himself away. But the way things were going, sent out on these fool errands, he damn well had to reinforce his creed.

He drained the glass, poured himself a second spiked cold one and pretty soon began to feel more like his old self. Even started to half sing that old tune. "You're loaded again. Ain't you handsome when you're high?"

He got out his old Gibson guitar by the side of the couch and changed the lyric to *Ain't you foxy when you're high?* He segued to a riff on a new number he was working on, the part where he was laying waste a number of Yankee Bluecoats at Shiloh. When that stalled on him, he shifted to one where he took care of some joker messing with his woman. Took that dude down in short order.

He laid the Gibson aside and realized the whole problem was he'd been lying fallow. Wasn't having any fun. Like the good times back when his kin hid the bottles of corn liquor they'd distilled under mounds of hay for pickup. So when no one was looking, he snuck up, set the haystacks on fire, hid high above in the hops field, and watched the explosions as all hell broke loose. Each time any of his kin asked if he'd seen anything, he gave them that choirboy look and shook his head. Shame about that cute little gal that got burned some. But that's the way it goes. Nowadays, they called it collateral damage. Which means to look at it from afar, which was his custom anyways. Or had been till getting stalled and sent out on lame, dead-end pursuits.

Feeling edgy yet again, he got up, riffled through a stack of pamphlets and what all the outfit left for him on a rack, and grabbed a map. Near as he could tell, this Skip character's escape route made no sense. If they'd let him be, he could have cooled his heels somewheres around eastern Pennsylvania. But no, he swings west and straight down 81 South, veers off onto 40 West, and veers off again at Black Mountain, less than thirty miles from where the action was gonna be. The last place on earth Mathews and his crew would've wanted him to run aground.

He went through the rack once more till he came across a copy of last week's *Black Mountain News*. As he scanned it, what did it for him was an article with photos of some weird poet-type with long, white scraggly hair. The long and short of it was that this dude settled here because it was small, friendly, and a live-and-let-live kind of place. Nobody talked about politics. They accepted you no matter what you did or didn't do, what kind of car you drove, or where you lived. A big house or a single-wide sitting on a concrete block or a tent in the woods didn't make no never mind. You take everything with a grain of salt.

Which led Vin to think about the gal sitting in back of

the Biscuit place. The cute, feisty one in the bib overalls and short hair taking her sweet time with her lunch. After a little do-si-do, she still didn't pick up on anything. Not talk of patriot militias, or depending on and defending your own kind, none of that. Seems all she cared about was the opening lineup for her Friday night do at the Tavern, the only place in these parts Vin knew about. And she was a hoot matching him old sayings. They could've kept it going with "Never a borrower or lender be," "The early bird catches the worm," "You catch no fish if your line don't get wet," and so on. Feisty, no sweat, and let it all hang out. Typical Black Mountain outlook if the paper was right.

Which told him what about how things got stuck here? Not a helluva lot.

Realizing it was just about time, he snatched his cell, hit the unlisted number and, soon as Mathews picked up, started right in.

"Hey now, Russ. You simmered down some?" Giving him no chance to respond, Vin kept at it. "You see, truth be told, you must've brought this all on yourself. What kinda posse hounds a quarry some eight-hundred miles till the quarry winds up in the exact neck of the woods where the posse don't want him to be?"

"Did you find him?" The deep radio voice came right back at him.

"Listen to me now. I'd say you been wasting my time and my special knack with demolition and such over some fool who only put his foot in it or something."

Vin could hear a wooden match scraping against the side of the box and that unmistakable sucking sound as Mathews began drawing on a fresh cheroot.

"You getting my drift here, Mathews, or am I talking to myself?"

More inhaling, sucking and puffing until, "I don't hear anything."

"Then hear this. You say he's a storyteller. We've got lots of them up in Madison County, some I know who've even done gigs at this Tavern here. They take stuff and blow it up so pretty soon you can't tell gospel from bald face lies."

"Tell that to the callers."

"What? At your radio station? Late night insomniacs? Is that what you're all fired up about?"

"Fellow travelers. Diehard members of our base. Need I remind you the broadcast reaches all over this land? Need I remind you of the stakes and the timeline?"

"Over some clown holing up till whatever you got in mind blows over and he gets his cat back?"

"Holed up where, Dupre? Parked his old Volvo where?"

"Who cares, dammit?"

"Talk to me. I need to pinpoint the exact locale and eradicate this glitch."

Vin shot right back with "Maybe somewheres in Swannanoa after a tip from a gas attendant. That do it for you?"

"Where exactly in Swannanoa, wherever that is?"

Vin plucked out his half-pint and took a deep swig. "Get this in your head, Mathews. I have had it with you. The dude went to the Black Mountain police station 'cause it was the Black Mountain Motel where you got Zeb to grab his damn cat. Which to my mind was all he cared about anyways, no matter what crap he run off at the mouth about. So you can cross me and Zeb off any more dumb ass assignments. You read me?"

More inhaling and puffing until Mathews said, "Once more. Where exactly in Swannanoa and what's the word on your cousin Duke?"

Vin took a deeper swig and came back even harder. "Jesus, Mathews, what does it take? I did you a favor 'cause you didn't know diddly about these parts and I had a little time to kill before the van gets here with the goods. You want to get to this character so bad, dangle some bait 'stead of running him aground. And that, fella, goddamn ties it."

Giving Mathews no chance to get in another word, Vin hung up.

He reached into the wall cabinet, got out the carton of milk from the squat little fridge, and poured some in a bowl. He went outside, cut through the weeds, unlatched the shed door, hunkered down and placed the bowl on the dusty floor. But the orangey cat cowered in the corner behind the rusty gas can, arched its back, hissed and swiped its paw, its green eyes fixed on him all the while.

"Now don't you go giving me that. Ain't my fault they dropped you off here. I am bringing you some milk only so's you don't up and die. Which is no skin off my nose anyways."

The hissing eased just a tad, but its back was still arched, paw extended, green eyes still piercing.

"Hey now, I've got a good mind to set you loose on the highway and time it till you get flattened. I give the odds of your survival at best as one in three."

He shoved the bowl of milk further in, stepped out, and secured the latch. He eyed the scudding clouds for any sign of stars. Not that he was superstitious, but he eyed the sky anyway in case this recent tomfoolery in any way set things off course.

Coming up empty, he went back to his old truck, cranked open the squeaky passenger door, and grabbed the rest of the kitty litter Zeb foisted on him. As he traipsed back to the shed, he ripped open the green bag, spilling some on his way before reopening the shed door and dumping half the bag in a prepared bin. After securing the door once again, he reached once more for the pint of Jack Daniels in his back pocket.

A few more swigs and he began to see that nominating Duke, and even enlisting Zeb for that matter, had its drawbacks. Be that as it may, if he could get ahold of himself, he was still in the catbird seat. Unlike the heel-dragging politicos, unlike everyone in play that he could see, he was the footloose shadow man, the one no one ever saw coming. If he could just damn well cool it down.

Which led him to the score so far. Testing out firebombs from Ocala, Florida; up to Macon, Georgia; Florence, South Carolina; and back to Madison County for a little layover. Each time he struck, he upped the ante, expanded the chlorate mixture. He liked leaving a trail of fire after each explosion. He liked the fact they were all everybody-welcome churches and meeting halls no matter your skin color or sexual orientation. He liked help gutting that notion, watching it all going up in smoke and flames in the dead of night, bigger and better than ever.

But he didn't like each church being empty of people. Nobody racing and screaming left and right. Where was the fun in that? Where was the surprise? Everybody pushing and shoving, folks getting trampled and throwing blankets over the ones writhing on the ground. Where was the big to-do, TV cameras, interruption of scheduled broadcasts, the special hullabaloo?

This next one better be worth the candle. Uncle Lucian better have a doozy of a payoff up his sleeve. What was this march from Florida to Georgia to South Carolina and now here all about, unless it shook everything to pieces? And the footloose, shadow man finally getting his due with nobody ever being the wiser.

CHAPTER SIXTEEN

T hat Monday, Miranda left the house first thing, looking for a telling lead, a notion of what Vin Dupre
might actually be up to, something to build on. She
had it in mind to catch Trish Wheeler as she got ready to
make her rounds while plying herself with coffee and pastry
in the coffee shack right off old US 70.

It was true that Trish no longer had the knack and was
relegated nowadays to cleaning houses. But in her heyday,
when she first started appearing at the Tavern with her folk
tales and songs from Madison County, she was as quick and
sharp as they come. Lately, you had to wait her out until she
got rolling. But she must know about the Dupres and could
give Miranda an inkling how Vin possibly fit into the overall
picture.

Luckily, the little frame structure had just opened shop
and the truck and delivery van drivers hadn't stormed in yet,
exchanging stories about exasperating customers. And, sure
enough, there was Trish in the far corner by the window,
gazing out at the cloud-rimmed reaches of the southern
Blue Ridge range, moving her lips as if trying to remember
something she had to do.

Miranda ordered a hot mocha. While she waited, she tried
to conjure up a surefire approach. Nothing came to mind.
And so, mug in hand, she crossed the plank flooring and

seated herself directly across Trish's miniature table, figuring she might as well play it by ear.

"Hey, Trish."

"Mmm" was Trish's reply. She didn't even bother to look to see who it was.

"How about that? I recognized you right off the bat. Remember the first time we met? Swapping quips at the Tavern? Just had to come over and say hey."

This opening gambit was greeted by another "Mmm."

Undaunted, Miranda said, "I booked you then and there. You must remember. Because you outdid me three quips to one and tossed in some down-home lyrics to old timey tunes for good measure. I mean, how could I ever forget?"

Trish kept gazing out. Not even a "hmm" this time. Miranda began to notice that she seemed even more scrawny scrunched up in the glancing light of early morning. Perhaps she hadn't been eating right. Her high cheekbones were more prominent, and she'd added flecks of pink onto her coarsely chopped gray hair. But her hazel eyes had a glint as she suddenly glanced up, took in Miranda's presence, and nodded.

It only took a bite of her Danish pastry and a few sips of black coffee before Trish said, "Know why Southern spinsters have sworn off sex? Too many thank-you notes."

Giving her a thumbs-up, taking the cue and assuming she could cut to the chase, Miranda followed that one with "Yes, ma'am, that was one of the zingers. Bless Madison County. Great source of folkways among those that time has forgot. Now then, while I think of it and while we're at it, I was wondering if you could tell me . . ."

But, as if catching on that Miranda was after something, Trish cast her gaze back into the oblivion of the mountain range and began moving her lips again.

Setting aside her mug of coffee, leaning in, Miranda carried on anyway. "Just for interest's sake. About the Dupre clan. The patriot militia, the traditionalists and all. Is any of what I've been hearing lately still true, hearsay, or old history? It's just come to my attention and as soon as I spotted you, I figured you'd be the very one to ask."

At first, it seemed hopeless trying to get a rise out of her. There was hardly any reaction. Tossing it out there anyways, Miranda said, "At any rate, getting right down to it, lots of bikers still around up there. Am I right?"

Keeping her gaze past Miranda steady, Trish said, "Some got Confederate flags everywhere. Except when they're on the prowl. Removed from the back of the truck cabs in that case. Except for the tiny ones where the black leather saddle bags go on the Harley."

"Right. Gotcha. Is that a Dupre trademark?"

"Which one you got in mind?"

"Oh, I don't know. Take your pick. Duke maybe?"

Mulling this over for a few seconds, Trish started to brush Miranda off and then changed her mind. "Ain't Duke's style. But one of them characters pulls the visor down from his black helmet. Black knight of the ridges, I used to call him. Next thing you know, your whole pumpkin patch is all tore up. You hear the roar in the middle of the night, but soon as you jump outta bed and poke your head out, he's gone."

"Taking a wild guess, who do you suppose it could it be?"

"Why you want to know?"

"As I said, it's all come to my attention."

Trish's beady eyes darted around before she said, "As for the black knight, can't hardly tell. Does his mischief mostly at night. But what does that have to do with the price of eggs or you and me at the Tavern or any such thing? What's really on your mind, girl?"

All of a sudden, Trish sat up straight, excused herself as if she was about to use the ladies room, took a few steps, then turned to stand directly behind Miranda's chair.

"Okay," Miranda said, twisting around, "forget it. Just tell me about Vin Dupre. I recently ran into him. Don't know him from Adam, but he starts pulling my chain. Tells me he's got an arrangement with Bud and Travis to front at my spring opening this Friday. But Bud tells me no such thing, and I sure know nothing about it."

Trish drifted around, sat back down. Her hazel eyes hardened and her cheekbones started to twitch. "Now look here. I haven't completely lost it, remember most everything. Haven't you had enough man troubles to do you for a while? I hear tell you got an older fella stashed away, on the string so to speak. Up on Gray Eagle Crest they say, writes for the paper."

"That is beside the point. Not what I'm getting at," said Miranda, pressing a bit harder.

"Well, whatever, you best leave it be. Yes, ma'am, Vin seems as cool as all get-out. But pretty soon things start to happening. Like he's in three places at once. Pretty soon some fella who's taken a shine to some gal Vin's got his eye on ain't around anymore. Other weird things start happening."

"Such as?"

"Heard tell about a little barn burning, if you must know. Explosions and such."

"Involving Vin you mean. Or others? Or a whole bunch of them?"

"Who knows? Who cares? What are you going on about? First it's old times sake, then it's militias, then bikers, then it's some upcoming gig, now it's . . ." Trish gazed out into space even harder this time, as if it finally occurred to her what she'd been silently moving her lips about.

Just then a flatbed truck pulled in front with a humongous piece of farm equipment shackled on the wooden bed. The second Trish spotted it, she sprang up out of her seat and said, "You think I got time for this? You got any idea what my cleaning schedule is today over by that assisted living complex? You want me to be late? Get all behind, and then what? A body has got to eat. Pay the rent."

"Okay, I get it. But if you could fill me in a little more, I'll make it up to you. I swear."

Trish peered at the entrance as the door opened and two ruddy-faced, burly figures in overalls stomped in, arguing in thick Southern accents. The only discernable difference between the pair was the red beard on the taller one and the stubble on the other.

Covering up for their benefit, Trish said, "Dang, look at the time. You can leave the tip, sister. Steer clear, if you take my meaning. That's the long and the short of it."

Before Miranda could say another word, Trish was barging past the burly pair who reluctantly stepped aside. In no time, she was gone.

Ignoring the continuing argument over whether it was

worth the grief over hauling equipment down all this way, Miranda remained seated, nursing her lukewarm mug of coffee as the bickering duo carried on at the service counter.

In marked contrast to the way things were going, she was reminded of a British crime show she watched off and on. There was always a masked figure traipsing around in the dark, whacking people over the head, like what happened to Skip but a whole lot worse. The inspector and his sidekick, who had the authority to grill people, sifted through the limited list of suspects until some telltale clue appeared just in time to end the show.

In this case, the only factor that applied was the springboard. In the matter she handled for that church lady realty client, it was poison pen correspondence. In the Brit mystery, it was the first incident. In this conundrum, it came about the moment Skip unwittingly blew the whistle on whatever was being set in motion.

At the moment, there were also glimmerings of the playing field. A ramshackle house on a cul-de-sac in Hoboken where guys were loading stuff in a van in the middle of the night. There was a chapel by the World Trade Center. Something somewhere in this vicinity was also in play.

Taking her cue from Skip, she shifted her thoughts to ringleaders and flunkies. The guys in Hoboken were involved. Russ Mathews was in cahoots with a phantom biker who might be a member of the Dupre clan, conceivably the black knight Trish alluded to. But Vin Dupre was the only one so far who was actually caught in the act, accosting poor crazy Annie while using a fake opening gig at the Tavern for cover.

At any rate, it was too early to wake Skip who truly needed his sleep. So who could she pester at this hour and make some more headway?

All she could think of was Arlo. He'd been around, was well acquainted with the music scene, and might be able to draw her a clearer picture of Vin than the fuzzy one she'd glommed from Trish.

Arlo was her jack-of-all-trades at the Tavern. Because he was a Native American, the drawback was that he was often on Indian time. Which meant he gave himself enough space in case the weather was perfect for hunting, fishing, or hiking so as to be fully enveloped in nature. As a result, stuff was often in disarray, which was bound to be the case at 8:15 a.m. with the sun glinting through the cloud cover, adding to the balmy temperature and light breeze. At times like this, it was hard for him to keep his mind on any conversation, but it was worth a try as long as she could keep from beating around the bush like she had with Trish and focus solely on adding to her profile of Vin. Namely, what was his mindset and what was he capable of?

It was no surprise to pull into the Tavern parking lot and notice his birch-bark canoe, with its flaring topside and spruce-root stitching, perched atop his van, secured and all set to go. The only question was, which young lady had he talked into being his companion and when was she due on the scene? Plus, how talkative would he be given this short notice? As soon as Miranda entered the high-ceilinged former warehouse, she gave herself a window of about twenty minutes before the mystery girl of the moment showed up and Arlo slipped away.

It was no surprise to come upon Arlo's muscular form, floppy coal-black hair, and easy smile doing a little preliminary work till the missy of the moment arrived. At the moment he was eyeing the file of spotlights and Fresnel flood lights at the back of the house. The lighting instruments in question hung neatly in a row from a long steel pipe slightly above his shoulders.

"Well now," said Arlo. "Just in time to cut the gels and make yourself useful." As always, he never asked such things as "What brings you here so bright and early?" The purpose of a visit would doubtless be revealed in short order with no effort on his part.

To ease into it, she checked the number of spotlights and Fresnels as he tightened the C-clamps with his crescent wrench. She assumed the gels he wanted cut were a combination of amber, special lavender, and no-color straw— something to do with spotlights aimed from opposite sides, one cool shade and the other warm, with a pale straw wash from the Fresnels to fill in the gaps. The intended effect was a warm ambiance bathing over the performers in keeping with the advent of spring and this weekend's cozy theme as the audience settled back as though in their easy chairs.

A few minutes later, she sat on the wooden flooring with a scissors, assorted gel sheets, and metal frames and casually began tossing things out. "Now that I'm here, just wanted to run something by you. No big deal."

"Ah, no big deal suits me just fine."

"Anyways, met a guy by the name of Vin the other day.

Vin Dupre. He tells me he's slated to front for Bud and Travis."

"Oh," Arlo said, pulling out the shutters on the spotlights.

"Fringed leather jacket. Fancy, hand-stitched cowboy boots. Casual approach, cool twinkle in his eyes. At first, that is."

"Uh-huh."

She let this sink in before she added, "Funny. First I've heard about his fronting here. And Bud doesn't know anything about it either. I called him."

Out of the corner of her eye she could see him slowing down as he attached the safety cables, clipping them on as a precaution once he pushed the button on the motorized hoist sending this main pipe skyward. But at the moment, he seemed more intent on running Vin by his recollections than making sure a fixture didn't come crashing down on the patrons.

Finally he said, "Drifted back this way, huh?"

"At least five days early. And since you've been rigging lights and whatnot since I don't know when and are well acquainted with Bud and Travis . . ."

"Yup. Rigging and well acquainted, that's me." Looping one of the cables around his wrist, he said, "Hey, you never know," then shook his head.

"So, what was that all about?" Miranda asked, still being as offhanded as possible.

"Well, if you start handing me those gels neatly tucked in those frames, maybe I'll tell you."

"That's good. But how soon do you reckon? How old will I be?"

Sometimes he picked up on her banter. This time he didn't. She handed him the frames and proceeded to cut and insert the remainders while he attached the gelled frames in front of the lenses. She continued to hold back as she reached into a box and handed him some new high-wattage bulbs and offered to discard the others.

"Burned out," Miranda said. Knowing she was starting to push it a bit but fully aware of the time, she added, "Maybe we've got us a theme."

Arlo also let that quip go before he said, "Fishing for something, are we?"

"Why, whatever do you mean?"

"The Miranda I know never comes around this early. The Miranda I know can't be too careful who she allows up on that stage."

"Okay, you found me out."

Giving her one of his slow, mischievous smiles, Arlo said, "Well, now that you mention it, lady, seems the fella you got in mind came by the other day. And did mention Bud and Travis. Must have taken me for some kind of honcho around here."

"No doubt," Miranda said, discarding the used bulbs and remaining by the trash bin.

Teasing, really making her wait for it, a few more minutes went by until Arlo said, "So, next thing you know, he gets out his guitar and wants to know what I think of his latest."

"And what did you think of his latest?"

"All's I remember is something about smoke in the mountains. And clearing out strange critters. But I was too busy looking through the catalogue for a new followspot."

"Nothing in the song about setting fires? Explosions? Barn burning?"

Arlo gave her one of those quizzical looks and spent the next few minutes adjusting the cables that held up the lighting pipe to make sure there was no give or tilt. He gave her another mischievous look and said, "Does this have anything to do with building inspectors and making sure everything's up to code? 'Cause that fellow might come by again and you'd best have the alarms up to snuff."

"Why is that?"

"Well, could be the way things turned out, he had it in for me."

"What for?"

Arlo walked down to the stage, hopped up, looked back, making sure that the lighting instruments were positioned in line with the center of the performance area.

"Come on, Arlo, tell me."

"Too nice a day, Miranda," said Arlo, teasing her as usual. "Rather ponder over cool running streams and rocky rapids."

"A clue. Just give me a clue."

"Well, when a fellow packs up his guitar, pokes you in ribs and says 'Why ain't you back in Cherokee where you belong?' . . ."

"Like he was sizing you up, seeing how you were taking it. Maybe dead serious."

"May-be," said Arlo, stringing the word out as he was fond of doing.

"And that's it? Didn't take it any further? No threats? No more racial slurs?"

Spreading his arms wide, throwing his head back, Arlo

spun around in a slow circle. "Against me? A pure and true Native American? No mixed blood? One who walks in beauty?"

One glance told her that Arlo was now on Indian time, basking in the balmy morning breeze slipping in and the presence of a shy, ponytailed girl, no more than eighteen. She was patiently framed inside the steel door opening, holding a wicker picnic basket.

In that same moment, Miranda couldn't help recalling a time when she too was that bright eyed and innocent. When there were no possible repercussions and a birch bark canoe trip on a sunny day with a handsome, carefree Indian guide had the promise of pure delight.

Miranda nodded to the girl, knowing full well her parley with Arlo was over. She was about to slip by her when Arlo hopped off the stage and called out, "Hey now, let it ride. Just put up some more smoke detectors. 'Cause this Vin Dupre might very well have brush fires on his mind. Clear out all us non-whites. Bring back the good old days."

As usual, Miranda never knew if Arlo was kidding or issuing a warning. Based on what she'd gleaned so far, she took it as a warning.

CHAPTER SEVENTEEN

Miranda parked by the town green and took stock. From all indications, Russ Mathews had two Madison County henchmen on call, one of whom was Vin Dupre: songwriter with a mercurial temperament, part-time tracker with a mountain militia lineage that harkened all the way back. And there were intimations of bigotry and barn burning. The other henchman was a biker, perhaps the black knight Trish alluded to, perhaps someone else.

But she still had no idea of the rest of the cast of characters or an overall agenda. And, at the rate she was going, with the clock ticking away, how could she ever hope to step in?

She hoped Skip would come out of it and really lend a hand.

In the meantime, perhaps if she touched base again with Harry, if he could do some more research and provide her with an overall framework, she could tell if she'd run into a smoke screen or missing link and/or was getting closer to crunch time.

Figuring Harry was always up and cracking by now, making sure to avert another of their harangues, she sent him one of her patented clipped messages:

Really need to know how far this thing goes. Cut through the

*conspiracy and right-wing BS and get to the kicker. Really appreciate
anything you can dig up.*

On purpose, she left out any allusion to Skip's latest
altercation, along with her efforts vis-à-vis Vin Dupre et
al. She wasn't at all certain what else she'd kept from him.
But that was par for the course given their pact to keep in
touch but afford each other lots of personal space. Relying on
one another yet making sure they weren't getting into each
other's hair.

Which called for terseness and a touch of flippancy. She
wondered how Jack Armstrong would handle this developing
situation. Then again, as far as she knew, Jack Armstrong was
never one for flippancy.

By the same token, Harry didn't know exactly what to make
of Miranda's message. How seriously was she taking Skip's
quandary? How much effort should he put into deciphering
the muddle of today's right-wing politics with its deflections,
guessing games, and talking points?

He had gone along so far, kept the ball rolling out of
curiosity. Not to mention the fact that he had nothing better
to do until his next assignment.

Still thinking it over, he padded over to the picture
window and took in the way the soft sunlight dappled the
tree line at the crest of the ridge. But it didn't ease this little
dilemma. He knew full well if he sloughed off whatever
sleuthing Miranda had in mind or made light of it, she'd be
off and running. And if he verified any of the contingencies

he'd noted as a matter of fact, she'd take it as a green light as she'd done once before.

It was the old Catch-22. Only this time she was personally involved. Call the state she was in nostalgia, call it kinship and comradery, call it what you will.

He retreated to his laptop in the far corner, booted it up, and just sat there, immobile, staring at the seaside image on the screen saver. Gradually, the silhouette of a girl runner dashing away began to intrigue him. Was she forsaking her beach companions in favor of something beyond the horizon—something more enticing, something she'd forgotten, or something more pressing?

By extension, what if some political faction was sick and tired of all the posturing and heel-dragging inaction ascribed to the current administration? What if cousin Skip had inadvertently stumbled onto a credible scheme?

Which prompted the notion that Russ Mathews, like the beach runner on the screen saver, was driven by something he had to do. Why else would he have stopped broadcasting live, shoehorned old podcasts in their stead with no forewarning, and hightailed it down here, if Skip hadn't let on that something was imminent? And Mathews didn't want to tip off his nemesis, the mainstream media, about impending surreptitious plans. Had to cover up his blunder of leaving plans in plain sight. And he certainly couldn't afford to have Skip out there on the loose, about to spill it all to, say, the *Asheville Citizen Times* or any media outlet that was equally as liberal.

With his curiosity fired up again, Harry logged onto

his recent document filed under "Inklings." He keyed on Mathews's catchy rallying cries like "the system is breaking down" and "there's a breach in the castle wall." Dicey tips without giving the actual game plan away.

He began pecking on the keyboard and made a separate list of the clues Skip had glommed and broadcasted, like D-Day and the stalking horse.

Scrolling down to the notes he took from Mathews's podcast archives, soon the dates began to stand out. In point of fact, neither he nor Miranda had paid any attention to the final days of the national election because the two of them were in the throes of that Halloween debacle brought on by local family secrets that finally came to light. All the while, Harper—a moderate, former governor from a Rocky mountain state—slipped in and won by a relatively small margin of electoral college votes. His success was evidently due to his campaign manager's focus on the opposition's sins of omission, thus leaving the "regular folks" from the South, Midwest, etc. out in the cold, as the "East Coast elites and Washington insiders continued to kick the can down the road." At least, that was all Harry got out of it.

The more Harry thought about it though, nothing jibed with *the breach* and *the system breaking down*. Nor did issues Harry was only vaguely familiar with, like Russian hacking and fake exposés on social media to sow discord and chaos. There was also the crime rate, urban blight, companies pulling up stakes and laying off workers in the Midwest, and so much more that Harry couldn't begin to get his mind around it all.

Getting nowhere pursuing this tack, Harry got to his

feet, left the cottage, walked across the lane and proceeded up the rise. Reaching the top, he aimlessly scuffed through the flotsam of discarded pots and pans, tent stakes, canteens, and whatnot until he came upon the broken-down hikers' shelter. At that point, he stood stock still.

He couldn't help recalling that time in the darkening wind and rain soon after taking advantage of this house-sitting stint. Checking out the lay of the land, he'd panicked over the sight of a burly figure lumbering out of the shadows. Scrambling for cover, he'd twisted his ankle, made a beeline for his car, peeled out and drove down the switchbacks for dear life. But he hadn't actually encountered anything. Only tapped into his longstanding fear of the unknown and getting directly involved. Keeping at a safe remove was clearly the better course of action.

So, why couldn't he continue to play at it and see how it shook out? If he came up empty—after vicariously taking part without actually venturing forth and sticking his neck out—if playing the armchair detective didn't pay off, he could always pull out and be no worse for wear. Miranda would give him points for trying and be beholden to him for bringing her up to speed given the impossible timeline, thereby saving her a great deal of wasted effort and no blame from any quarter.

Nodding to himself, he ambled back down the rise, returned to his post, got on the Internet, and perused the headlines. He could only find stories about outbreaks of severe weather throughout middle America and drought in California, plus volatile financial markets overseas. Closer to home, he came across reporters' consternation over the new White House press secretary's deflections over policy initiatives.

Harry made a mental note re: the new president's lack of initiative.

In the news from *The New York Times*, he found a reference to a crucial vote by the senate that was tied to bringing certain hot-button issues onto the floor for debate. No other details were given. Harry put this development on the back burner, sensing he had touched on something significant but unable to put his finger on it.

Moving on, he came upon a link to the alt-right *Sentinel*. In this week's edition, there was an editorial advocating "swift and powerful diversionary maneuvers." There was also a piece about the thrill of chaos when things are about to come undone. Emotions running high when you're living in historical times. The moment of danger as your finest hour as long as whatever you've set in motion is highly visual. Pre-apocalyptic and captivating.

This potentially incendiary proposition was attributed to Lucian Clay, a native of Carolina's Blue Ridge and Harper's (the current foot-dragging new president) chief strategist.

But what did it all mean? What was a chief strategist? And where—unless Harry was letting his imagination get away from him—did Russ Mathews fit in, except as a mouthpiece for the syndicated Liberty Broadcasting System?

Harry found links to the tabloids that filled the racks of drugstores and supermarkets everywhere, with their provocative conspiracy claims and celebrity scandals that had no basis in fact.

Taken together, it was far too much to take in, but he

couldn't dismiss any of it out of hand. It took some thought and a great deal of tinkering until he settled on sending Miranda an equally cursory reply he hoped would satisfy her for the time being and keep her in a holding pattern:

I'm on it. If any of this stew of innuendo and breaking news applies to your cousin Skip's predicament, I'll let you know. In the meantime, make do, sit tight, and keep your eye out for that cat.

CHAPTER EIGHTEEN

It didn't take much to get Miranda off and running again. By plying her with his older, wiser, "sit tight" directive, Harry only succeeded in ticking her off.

She opted for continuing to play it as it lay and relegating Harry's rummaging around to the backstory. If she managed to throw a monkey wrench in the works and keep Skip in one piece, that would be fine. If, in the bargain, she got Duffy the cat back, so much the better. As she was fond of telling herself, in this world you are what you do.

As for her current Plan A, what she had in mind called for making sure crazy Annie filed a complaint after being jostled by Vin Dupre. This would lead to Miranda's liaison with the police. That done, she'd hook up again with Skip. But this time, to humor him and keep him from going off the rails, she'd put things on a professional basis.

Picking up from where she left off, Arlo's pointers reinforced the notion that there certainly was more to Vin than meets the eye. There was no way Russ Mathews would return to the motel in his rented white Corolla just to meet up with some Appalachian errand boy.

Moreover, the fact that Mathews and Vin could carry on with Vin's truck backed into a handicapped spot so that both driver's sides were adjacent, was further indication they regarded Black Mountain as a sleepy little mountain town with an easygoing attitude. Add Skip's complaints to the dispatcher that fell on deaf ears and you got more of the same. More often than not, you had to come up with something startling to get anyone's attention—a fact that more often than not stuck in Miranda's craw.

Giving Skip additional time to sleep it off and continuing her aim to shake something loose until Harry came up with the big picture, she decided to get hold of Annie right away and press the issue. Time to damn well intervene instead of continuing to skirt around the periphery.

She checked her watch and realized she could catch the tail end of the Monday soup kitchen breakfast at the Methodist Church. Though she had no idea of Annie's haphazard schedule apart from reporting in at the homeless shelter on the outskirts of town, she frequently spotted her sauntering by the church, taking advantage of the free meal.

But when she got there, the only ones left were a raggedy-looking older couple holding hands, and Mae in the far corner of the small dining room fixated on the last vestiges of her breakfast. Mae was a tiny, birdlike creature with a shock of wispy gray hair and an impish face that seemed permanently fixated on items of wonder. At this moment, it was the lineup of crispy bacon, a scoop of scrambled eggs, two slices of wheat toast, a pat of marmalade, a pat of butter, and a small glass of orange juice at the outer edge of her plate. Some said she had autism. Others said she'd always been this way since her parents abandoned her long ago, slipping in and out of the here-and-now whenever the mood struck her.

Keeping it light and easygoing as always, Miranda pulled up a folding metal chair and said, "Hi, Mae."

"Hi," said Mae, keeping her focus tight on the business at hand, namely, finishing her breakfast in an orderly fashion.

"Have you seen Annie?"

"Yup. You just missed her."

"Oh, where was she off to?"

This question seemed to throw Mae off. She carefully began to rearrange the items on her plate. Crisp bacon pieces were slid between two slices of toast and a helping of scrambled eggs. One slice of toast got buttered, the other slathered with marmalade and put back in position. She took a swig of orange juice, sighed, and then said, "Much better. All the ducks in a row."

"Good job," Miranda said. "So, how was she? In a hurry? Same as always? Or nervous and upset?"

"Yes."

"All of those things, you mean?"

"Didn't know what to do."

"About what?"

Again, Mae was thrown off. Unable to find the answer on her plate, she looked up at the ceiling tiles. Finding the answer there, she said, "About telling."

"Going to the police station? Maybe telling Officer Ed?"

With her eyes fixated back on the plate, Mae said, "Too many things. 'What would Preacher Bob say? What will the village witch say? What will happen if I do? What will happen if I don't? Will I get another bruise?'"

"I see. Annie was in a muddle."

The hazy sunshine glinting through the blinds seemed to bother Mae. As if on cue, the raggedy couple got up with a scraping of their chairs and left. Miranda went over, tinkered with the blinds, shutting off the glare altogether, and sat back down.

"Most of the time," Mae said, "I like the soft sunshine best. It doesn't get in my eyes at my spot at this table. But the scrambled eggs were kinda runny today and threw me off. Made me dawdle till I got things right."

All set now, Mae took a bite of butter and marmalade toast, crunched on a bit of bacon, slid the scrambled eggs aside, and chewed it all up. Fully satisfied, her impish face beaming, she said, "Like the eggs, Annie was not herself this morning."

"Right, I get it. So, where was she off to?"

"Didn't I say?"

"Not really."

"Hmm?" Another beat passed before she said, "I told her to go back in the kitchen, ask for some crunchy French bread, get her ducks in a row."

Miranda caught on. Impressionable Annie was headed for Lake Tomahawk where the waterfowl gathered around the tiny island by the wooden bridge. After tossing crusty crumbs into the water, Annie could watch the ducks lining up and hope her priorities followed suit and straightened out.

Things, of course, didn't work that way. However, by shooing off Vin, Annie became Miranda's only lead, front and center. Miranda would have to catch her in time, do a quick patch job and sleight of hand to resolve Annie's quandary. And then use her to link up with the police and keep this show on the road.

By mid-morning the scene at the lake took on an almost eerie tone. The Seven Sisters mountain range in the far distance changed colors as skimming dark clouds and intermittent flickers of sunlight made them appear gunmetal gray, iridescent blue, and back to gray again. In concert with the pulsing breeze, the hues of the lake itself followed along. In addition, the swing sets, monkey bars, and sand box next to the parking lot were devoid of nannies and children; likewise, the strollers and joggers circling the footpath were missing. Even the mallards and yellow-billed ducks that cavorted around the island by the wooden bridge seemed oddly still and wary, as though they were waiting for Annie to come out of her funk. She sat on the bank facing them, discarding pieces of bread to no avail before shoving her trusty burlap sack aside and slumping back on the bench at the water's edge.

The rumpled, orangey muumuu she had on apparently didn't help the funk she was in either. It was only when Miranda went over and reached her side that she noticed the blue-black bruise on Annie's fleshy upper left arm.

Turning her moon-like face in Miranda's direction, Annie said, "I am so confused. Preacher Bob says I've got to do right. The village witch says the bruise on my arm tells her everything is out of . . . out of . . ."

"Whack?"

"Yes. Got to read the signs and cast the right spell. But the signs are all a jumble. Mae says you can go ahead with things once you get your ducks in a row. But they won't even come over to me." Pointing every which way, Annie said, "See what I mean?"

Miranda nodded as the clouds continued to echo the notion that everything was in flux.

Taking this all in, recalling her few encounters with Annie and what she had to go through to get anywhere, Miranda decided to take charge and make it really simple: Get Annie to file a complaint about her bruise. Add it to the one Skip already filed vis-à-vis his stolen cat, plus the assault he'd suffered and his recent stint in the hospital. Thereby getting Officer Ed Wheeler on board or standby or whatever she could muster. If nothing else, she'd learned by now through her ex, Detective Dave Wall, you don't act strictly on your own. Things are going to remain more or less static if you have no link with law enforcement.

"Gotcha," said Miranda, patting Annie on the back. "Only one solution. Get out your book of spells."

"The one the witch gave me? That I once told you about? That very one?"

"Absolutely."

"But . . . I mean, what for? Most of them are for a bunch of people in a circle."

"No problem. I'll find a two-hander." Miranda said this not knowing for sure she could find one that fit the bill but groping for anything to get cracking.

"But why would you?" said Annie, squinting and scrunching up her face.

"Because I need you to do right for me and Skip."

"Who?"

"The guy you helped and came to the rescue for when the mean guy in the truck came by and hurt your arm. Because that's what you're good at."

"Doing right you mean? Really?"

"You said you needed to make Preacher Bob proud. And stay on good terms with the village witch. Here's your chance."

"But only if you mean it. If you truly think so."

"Bingo. Girl scouts honor."

Shrugging, Annie got on her knees and scoured around her sack until she came up with a dog-eared pamphlet. As soon as she handed it over, Miranda riffled through the soiled pages. She had forgotten there were almost two hundred spells and rituals listed. Among them were hand-fasting, the mystical pentagram, opening the circle, solitary moon rites, weaving webs, and all the rest of it.

Doing her best to hide how bound and determined she was, Miranda skimmed past the ones she couldn't fathom until she came upon a quick two-hander exorcism.

"Okay, we've got to pass you through three gates to three worlds—land, sea, and sky."

"But I don't know that one," said Annie, struggling to get to her feet. "Don't know anything about it."

"Doesn't matter. It'll get you right back on the do-gooder path. Ready? I'll be the gatekeeper."

For a moment, Miranda felt like she was a kid again, out in the woods in small town Indiana. A time when she read comics and played marauding raiders with Skip to save the day and restore the kingdom. Cousins who later fell out of touch as adults and only infrequently saw one another.

"On your toes now, Annie. Get yourself a handful of grass."

Dutifully, Annie reached down, scraped up some grass and held it up.

Positioning herself, holding her arms straight out like a turnstile, Miranda said, "What do you want?"

"What should I say?"

"To get on the windward path."

"To get on the windward path," Annie repeated.

"Right," Miranda said, scattering the blades of grass as well. "You may pass."

Miranda had her repeat the ritual, scooping up lake water and letting it run through her fingers until Miranda let her pass, and then had her throw her head back and reach up, straining to touch the sky until Miranda said, "Yes, yes, land, sea, and sky. Your quest is true" and let her go by.

Coincidently, the skimming dark clouds gave way to lighter, fluffier ones; sunlight glinted on the lake water; and the ducks and mallards slowly began flitting around. The ducks weren't in a row, but the lead duck began quacking as if recalling what he was meant to do.

"There you go," Miranda said, shoving the pamphlet back into the sack. "All you needed was a little shove."

"But what about my bruise?"

"It's evidence."

"And the thing he threw at me?"

"What do you mean?"

"When he was about to drive off? When I leaned in the truck window and said I was gonna tell? When he grabbed it from the passenger seat and threw it in my face?"

"Threw what? What do you mean?"

Annie dug into her sack, sifting and sorting until she came up with a shiny new green bag of cat litter.

Like everything else, it didn't work out quite the way Miranda expected. Because the incident took place in Swannanoa, Miranda had to take Annie to the Swannanoa sheriff's office and deal with a sullen deputy by the name of Roy. The problem wasn't that Annie had to run her complaint through the dispatcher's computer. It was the fact that Miranda had nothing to do with this. She couldn't ask for a BOLO (be on the lookout) on Vin's old truck or request any criminal history or any of that. At best, she'd have to go back to Black Mountain, catch up with Officer Ed with whom she'd had her share of set-tos, and con him into collaborating with Deputy Roy.

Coming to terms with this snag, after dropping Annie off at the food pantry under the auspices of Preacher Bob and assuring her that she'd done her duty—the police would handle it, and she was free and clear—Miranda pulled over by the old Black Mountain train station, now defunct, and called Skip to pass on the kitty litter lead.

But after allowing for four rings on her smartphone, she ended the call. She certainly knew what it was like to be so wasted you needed to sleep till noon.

Given the realization that nothing was holding still, she couldn't help wondering about the latest turn, possibly closing in on Vin during this phantom footrace.

CHAPTER NINETEEN

E arlier that Monday morning, Skip received another message. It wasn't an anonymous notification on a burner cellphone prodding him to get back on the East Coast and keep driving south. This time it came directly from Chris Holden, his old drama school chum from Chicago—the very person who'd prompted him to sub on his late-night radio show that set the ball rolling. For some reason, Chris had taken a plane to the airport in Hendersonville and would be on his way to the Biltmore Estate in Asheville to meet up in two hours at the courtyard. And Skip had better be there, looking presentable, "or else."

At first, Skip was so taken aback he didn't know what to do. He was barely able to crawl out of bed and pick up his cell at the sixth ring, assuming it must be Miranda. There was no chance to make a coherent reply. Apparently, the fact that he'd picked up the phone was all the confirmation Chris needed.

It took Skip another half hour to get himself together, wash up, shave, and fling together a buttoned-down white shirt, beige slacks, and a rumpled khaki blazer snatched from his travel bag. The neutral, Harold Everyman outfit wouldn't do zip to fade him into the background or alter the haggard image in the mirror. A few days ago, his smooth face and tousled grayish-red hair might have passed muster as harmless Skip. But the face staring back at him now was hard-pressed. And the knot in his stomach and the chill up his spine had become wired in.

He took the call from Chris as a summons to crawl out of his hole and face up to the realities as far as Chris could relate exactly how things stood.

After the incident with the volatile guy in the pickup, whom Miranda identified as Vin Dupre, exposing Skip's old Volvo out on the road was out of the question. So he called for a cab from east Asheville and arranged to meet in front of an oversized Shell station Miranda had passed when she carted him to the hospital. He gave himself a half hour to walk there in a roundabout way and, if the coast was clear, cross over to US 70 where the multiple gas pumps sat by the access ramp to I-40 West.

As for breakfast, there wasn't time. He vaguely recalled the improv troupe carpooling during the gig in Asheville and frequenting a French Renaissance mansion that a Vanderbilt tycoon built for his bride. For some reason, his lady had to have a separate monstrous bedroom in addition to a banquet hall, great dining room, humongous library, thirty-five guest rooms, and all the rest of it to accommodate the escapees from Gotham in the Gay Nineties. The prospect was so remote from anything Skip had come across, he saw it as a fantasy backdrop to a dicey encounter.

His hope was that the courtyard Chris alluded to was adjacent to a food court where he could get some coffee and cinnamon rolls to gird him and keep him on high alert. There was also the notion he might need to keep from being boxed in in case things went badly, which by now was a distinct possibility.

His trek to the Shell station on this balmy sunlit day went without incident. As luck would have it, the cabbie was on time, but once on the highway, he was unhappy with the eighteen-wheel rigs that kept crowding him, tailgating and roaring past right and left. In his deep, Southern drawl he muttered things like "If the good Lord wanted us to rush about like this, He would've given us a heavenly sign long before construction through His mountains and streams."

Skip had no answer for him and other scripture-like revelations as they got closer and closer to the Biltmore exit. The last thing he needed were ominous pronouncements about the sins of omission and commission.

Forcing himself to come to terms, he noted that he hadn't had anything to do with Chris Holden, hadn't even been in touch for the past six years until this recent fill-in proposition. For all Skip knew, Chris must have gotten a big break. Parlayed his smooth, slick voice on the late show at the Chicago affiliate to the stint in the Big Apple. Chris also must have moved on from his classy TV ads modeling a line of clothing from a Windy City chain to an upscale Madison Avenue account featuring him lounging in some East Side penthouse or displaying a pricey watch. Or sipping cognac, dressed in a Brooks Brothers suit, ensconced in a first-class cabin on a luxury cruise. Which would account for his taking a leave of absence. Any comparable gig must have been the motive when Skip jumped at the chance to sublet Chris's

Hoboken apartment at no charge and take advantage of this golden opportunity.

This pampered image of Chris lingered in Skip's mind—perfect features, perfect figure, mellow voice, studied gestures—as the cab veered off the highway. But it didn't jibe with the present nervy prospect and only added to Skip's anxiety.

His musing faded when the traffic on Sweeten Creek heading to Lodge Street became congested, as if every visitor to western Carolina had chosen this particular morning to converge upon the largest private residence in America.

When they passed the gate, maneuvering became impossible. Skip paid the driver, promised he'd look into the lessons from the scriptures soon as he got the chance, and went on foot the remaining half mile or so.

The first thing that caught his eye was a field of blooming yellow canola fields as far as the eye could see, filling the air with a sweet heady fragrance. A buxom tourist was frolicking in the blossoms waist high, in a mood Skip couldn't possibly fathom as his anxiety level ticked up yet another notch.

Soon after, he was among the throngs traipsing past the formal gardens laden with a sea of bright tulips, pink and flaming orange azalea bushes, and all manner of roses fully cordoned off, fully under control. In fact, counting the fields of canola, everything was orchestrated: all the pleasure gardens, reflecting pools, marble statuary, a lily pond, and the landscaping along the carefully swept carriage roads leading off to who knew what. Nothing left to chance, not a shrub, not a blade of grass.

And therefore, nothing remotely resembled what Skip had been through or was possibly in for. In fact, it all seemed to be mocking him and his fairytale notion of reinvention in the Big Apple in pursuit of some happily ever after and his preposterous current aim to put things right.

Jostling his way forward, asking for directions from out-of-towners perusing their guide maps, he located the open courtyard between the Atrium, souvenir shops, and the Old Stable Café.

Though Skip was only a few minutes off schedule, it seemed Chris had already corralled a small table in the corner and garnered a tray replete with a carafe of coffee, cups and saucers, Danish, rolls and butter as dozens of patrons stood in line a few yards away hoping for somewhat the same. In that same instance, Skip noticed that the crisp, self-possessed look on Chris's perfect features, which had served him well during his leading man roles, had given way. Neither his designer sunglasses nor his powder blue leisure suit seemed to help. And when he spoke, there was hardly a trace of his affected, mellow tones. Bypassing any hello, he got right down to business.

"All right," Chris said the second Skip reached the table. "Let's have it, buddy. What got into you?" Apparently too wound up to contain himself, Chris kept at it. "I told you they had you vetted. The homespun tales on WKSC Chicago—gliding down the Wabash on a homemade raft and all that nostalgia crap on YouTube. Appealing to the very constituents the Liberty Broadcasting System covets."

"Whoa. Give me a break, will you?"

Wiping his sunglasses with a cloth napkin and slipping them back on, Chris said, "No small talk, Skip. There isn't time."

"Okay then," said Skip, seating himself with a clear exit in mind, "what constituents?"

"Who do you think? The core. The folks in the flyover zone where you hail from. The heartland, glued to the affiliates' broadcasts—the damn target audience. I mean, what the hell were you trying to pull?"

"You didn't mention anything about constituents."

"Isn't it obvious? Use your brain. You look just like the scarecrow from Oz . . . I was damn well counting on the same hapless Skip!"

Positioning his metal chair away from the wall and toward the footpaths and gardens, Skip poured himself some coffee out of the steaming carafe, added a dash of cream and brown sugar, gulped some of it down, and said, "What do you mean, counting on?"

"Oh, come on, cut the tap dance."

"Tell me," Skip said, trying to get his bearings. "Counting on what?"

"First item, we clear the air," Chris said, emphasizing his words as if dealing with a wayward child. "Then a short drive and some hanging contractual obligations. Then a quick meeting to make absolutely sure. That's the deal, pal. So tell me, what were you trying to pull?"

"I don't know," Skip said as he took more sips of coffee. "Maybe I wanted to make the most of the opportunity. Maybe it was the callers egging me on."

"Terrific. Tell me another one."

As Skip nibbled on a Danish trying to get a bead on this so-called agenda, Chris took out a pack of cigarettes, lit one with a silver lighter, and took a deep drag. Which in itself was unsettling because, as far as Skip knew, Chris Holden never smoked.

"Hold it," said Skip, plunking down his cup, switching to the offense. "Enough of this cloak-and-dagger stuff. For openers, I'll have you know, they swiped Duffy."

"Who?"

"My cat."

"What cat? Since when?"

"Since I noticed him shivering around the iron railing and took him in when I first landed in the Big Apple. Last Wednesday, after my second riff on Mathews, they hung a non-disclosure form on the very same railing in front of the very same sublet you so kindly offered me. On a deserted cul-de-sac, where something dodgy was going on in that ramshackle, abandoned rooming house across the way. I hightailed it out of fear and wound up east of here last Friday night. Then and there is exactly when they nabbed Duffy. Do I have to go on? I mean, good grief, Chris!"

Chris waited a few moments before coming back with "Okay, maybe I should have mentioned something. But there wasn't time to go into any of that and get you situated."

"'No time,' he says. Why all this pressure? Firing shots through the window, messing with my tires. Warning me to keep going. When that didn't work, snatching Duffy, then hitting me over the head so I'd land in the hospital. Then

sending some character named Vin in a beat-up green truck
to track me down. That's right. Playing hardball. Just another
contingency you failed to mention."

Chris seemed completely at a loss. He coughed, then gave
up on trying to appear cool as if practicing for a cigarette ad
from yesteryear and stubbed it out on his saucer. "Look, you
started this."

"Wrong-o, *you* did. How come you offered me this gig
out of the blue? What's the matter? Did they get to you? Did
you have to skip town?"

Taking out another cigarette from the pack, sticking it in
his mouth and leaving it unlit, Chris said, "Enough. Quit
deflecting. Quit trying to spin this. Are you going to tell me
what actually got into you in the precious minutes we've got
left?"

"Precious minutes?"

"You heard me."

Still stalling, Skip sketched it in for him. He alluded to
the time he listened to Indiana's own Shep Anderson telling
his homespun tales of the days of Jack Armstrong when he
himself played war games like Commandos Strike at Dawn.

"Don't tell me. You're going to pin this whole thing on
Shep Anderson?"

"I'm going to tell it to you from the moment I took a peek
at the stuff on Russ Mathews's wall and strewn across his
desk when you hustled me out of there. Figuring it was all
hype anyways, I slipped some of it in with little cliffhangers
like good ol' Shep used to do. 'Always a lull before the storm,
gang. But take it from me, they're busy as bees. What do you
suppose they're up to?'"

"Except you were supposed to play sleepy-time music and toss in bits of nostalgia."

"But I was on a roll. How many chances does a guy like me have left?"

"Who cares?"

"Oh, that's easy for you to say. What really made you bow out and throw me a bone?"

"I mentioned auditions as you may recall."

"No, you didn't. Anyways, you could've still done the radio show. Auditions aren't the same as being hired and on call."

Chris shoved the unlit cigarette back in the pack and yanked off the designer sunglasses, fully revealing the strain in his red-rimmed eyes. He glanced at his gold watch for the umpteenth time.

"Level with me, Chris. Why are we both in this bind?"

Chris grabbed the carafe and refreshed his cup of coffee but didn't drink any. In the meantime, the lines to the Old Stable Café continued to grow, the tourists as agitated as Chris.

Ignoring the harried couple looking in their direction, Skip said, "Tell me, damn it. You really expect me to believe that you hopped on a plane so we could hash this out? You expect me not to think there's an axe over your head and you're in cahoots with a bunch of subversives?"

Another delay before Chris came out with "It doesn't go any farther than this. Understood?"

"Great, swell. My lips are sealed."

Leaning forward until they were almost head to head, Chris affected a conspiratorial tone. "Okay. A couple of weeks ago, after I got home—back to the flat I sublet to you—I couldn't find my smartphone. It dawned on me that I had left it in a matching blazer at the station. I went in early the next morning . . . I mean, how was I supposed to know there was a high-level meeting between Russ and Lucian Clay?"

"Who?"

"Lucian Clay! Unlike Mathews, who's virtually a foot soldier, this is Clay's bailiwick! And, good God, no wonder. You're playing Shep Anderson, go on the air, and la-di-da, blow it."

"Okay, okay. Go on. What's with you, Russ Mathews, and some character named Lucian Clay?"

"Call it a fluke. Hearing voices at that ungodly hour early in the day, I approached, wondering what in the world was going on. When the conversation became clear, I froze—right in the hallway by Mathews's open door. I couldn't help monitoring Clay feeding Mathews variations on some D-Day code: spin cycles from WWII, déjà vu from the days of foreign cells and a fifth column in our midst, militant nationalism and taking our country back—all that kind of stuff. Next thing I know, they spotted me. I'm about to get fired or who knows what, so off the top of my head, I made a deal. My lips are sealed. Your folksy drivel till the smoke clears and there's absolutely no fallout. 'Vet him, harmless as mom's apple pie,' I said. No one would be the wiser. No attention would've been drawn if only you'd stuck to our bargain instead of spewing Clay's imminent D-Day code all over the land.

"Oh, damn." Checking his watch again, Chris suddenly rose up, left a tip, and ushered Skip out of the courtyard.

Despite Skip's protests, Chris herded him to a special access parking lot where a limo was waiting, along with, Chris told him, an airtight contract that, this time, he was damn well going to sign. A final settlement with the powers that be would be made when they reached the center of town.

"For all intents and purposes," Chris said, in a tone that was getting more jangled by the minute, "this was the best bet for both of us. In the meantime, we'll be no worse off and you can be ensconced in a beachfront bungalow in St. Augustine with your damn, stupid cat in tow until the whole thing blows over. What could be better?"

"But—"

"You want to save your hide? You want to save your dwindling prospects? You cross the Liberty Broadcasting System and that is all she wrote, believe me. You'll be dead in the water in more ways than one."

With his mind racing, Skip demanded, "What exactly do you mean by 'a final settlement'?"

Chris glared at him. "Whatever I overheard never happened and whatever you came across on Mathews's desk never existed. Eradicated from both our memories. An ironclad understanding between all four parties, signed, sealed, and delivered. End of story."

Skip reluctantly got in the back seat of the sleek black Lincoln, Chris close by to his left, a ruddy-faced driver behind the wheel.

Skip found this quickie exchange had all been set up: an ample arm rest and writing pad between the two of them, duplicate copies, notary stamp, and a Montblanc pen in a leather sleeve at the ready. A few minutes after the limo took off, Chris prodded him to make a cursory scan of the contract and sign the documents.

Skip hemmed and hawed, asking for the meaning of the legalese, stipulations, and disclaimers that he'd never come across in his life.

Checking his watch yet again, Chris snapped. "Never mind, never mind. Recess is over, just get on with it. It's T-minus seven minutes and counting."

Fumbling for his smartphone, Chris hit a speed-dial number and began rattling things off as fast as he could. "Hey, no worries, all set, we're coming in. Turns out it's all a big misunderstanding. He was just messing around. Picking up on stuff, concocting an old-time radio show like the second coming of Shep Anderson from your very own Indiana affiliate. Wouldn't know déjà vu or real WWII paranoia if it hit him in the face. But he'll do anything to make amends, keep his mouth shut, is dutifully spooked, and will stick his head into the sand for now and forever."

Then and there, it struck Skip that the more you cross the line, the more you ramp up the jeopardy till they're hell-bent to put you permanently under wraps. With perspiration beading on his forehead, Skip pressed a button and slid his window down to get some air. He peered out at the driver's side-view mirror on the passenger side to see where they were on the northern end of heavily congested Biltmore Avenue. Soon enough, he caught sight of someone on a big motorcycle—his visor masking his face, all in black leather—weaving in and out, appearing and disappearing, about a dozen cars behind.

It could very well be the same guy Miranda spoke of who

snatched Duffy and came back to finish the job and really send Skip to the hospital. It was the deep *rum-rum-rum* of the Harley engine that truly brought it all back. At the motel, he'd heard that identical growl at the crack of dawn, turned over, barely pulled himself out of his fitful slumber, and discovered Duffy was gone. At the motel again, hours after meeting up with Miranda, he'd heard it once more, played a little hide-and-seek, then caught the sound trailing off, meshing with the blow to his head.

Chris prodded him hard as can be as they approached Eagle Street and the heart of the city. By this point, the biker and his big Harley were only a half dozen cars behind.

Turning back sharply, sweat trickling down his forehead, Skip said, "I don't like this, Chris."

"Well, you better grow to like it before we get to Number One Pack Square."

"Before we get where?"

"You heard me. Sign, initial, and date the papers. Close the books and relieve them of any more goddamn reconnaissance!"

Just then, as the driver hit the brakes to avoid slamming into a delivery truck, Skip could hear the *rum-rum-rum* revving closer still.

No sooner had the limo driver gotten back in gear then Skip jerked the handle, shoved the door open, and threw himself out onto the pavement. Close enough to the pale-brick walkway, he crawled on scraped hands and knees, narrowly avoiding the screeching tires of an oncoming semi-trailer. Ignoring the blaring horns and the motorcycle coming on full bore, he scrabbled forward and made a dash for it.

In the blur, all the buildings seemed pristine and freshly polished. Coming across a French Broad Chocolate Lounge, he knocked over the flimsy wrought iron patio chairs and ducked inside.

Ignoring the searing ache in his hands and knees as he flitted around the squared-off wooden posts, all he knew was he had to get to the rendezvous point to have some inkling of what in the world he and Miranda were up against. What it was all about. He'd settle for a glimpse. He couldn't take any more talk, any more hints of a lurking, shadowy menace.

He accosted a pixie-like waitress in a Tyrolean smock, who backed away pointing and jabbering that Pack Square was close by.

Dashing back out onto the tree-lined walkway, he followed the pale-brick pavers as they began to curve and widen out into the spacious entranceway of a humongous glass building, stretching and bending as its endless panels of glass reflected the rays of sunlight and cottony clouds. The sign above the glass doors said "Biltmore." A slab of marble at the edge of the grass declared the building's address as 1 N Pack Square. Not a soul or a car was in sight.

The second he heard an approaching vehicle, he scurried behind a trimmed hedge.

At the same time, two figures emerged from the glass building. One, Skip could identify, was burly Russ Mathews. The other figure was slight and trim, sported a dark suit, and peered over his bifocals. Both men stood there, stock still as the vehicle's engine grew louder.

The limo swung into the circular entranceway and came to a screeching stop. The driver burst out, circled the hood, and yanked Chris out, pulling him a good distance from Mathews and the dark-suited figure. Within seconds, the limo pulled away, leaving Chris standing there, swaying on his feet. The revving Harley hurtled into the circle as if out of nowhere. There was a roar and a thud as the bike impacted Chris, throwing him headlong. The Harley wobbled and righted itself before picking up speed, its engine back to full throttle as it trailed away.

While Skip remained frozen to the spot, another limo pulled in and all traces of Chris were whisked away.

Within moments, well-dressed couples began spilling out of the building, doubtless on their lunch break. Many disappeared into sleek, late-model cars that appeared in the circle. The mirror images of cottony clouds continued their swaying dance across the glass-paneled building as a breeze kicked up.

Presently, the only one left in the vicinity was Skip, still gazing in disbelief behind the hedge. The back of his head renewed its throbbing, much more intensely this time, but it was no match for the chill running up his spine that showed no sign of ever relinquishing its hold.

CHAPTER TWENTY

Back in the Swannanoa hideaway, Miranda leaned forward across the kitchen table and tried once more to get through to Skip.

"Are you getting this? Preliminary diagnosis: multiple fractures, multiple contusions, internal bleeding, and damage to his spine. In short, this buddy of yours, who dropped in out of nowhere, will be out of commission for a while."

Skip continued to look off into space as he mumbled yet again, "Couldn't sell out, Miranda. Cast a blind eye."

It was now mid-afternoon on that same Monday. After getting nowhere trying to make any sense out of what he was doing in Pack Square, it took her well over an hour to go to the ER and get the skinny from staff members about Chris Holden's condition. All had been aghast as a battered figure was dumped at the emergency entrance by a surly limo driver who sped away before anyone knew what was happening.

And here she was, pressing even harder, waving her hands. "Hello? He's going to live, okay? It's official. Can you fill me in now, dot a few i's and cross a few t's?"

But all Skip could do was recount one of storyteller Shep Anderson's radio tales about a spooky old house, the neighborhood gang goading the smallest boy into crawling up to the front door. The gang then ran off the instant an old man and his guard dog appeared out of the darkness, but the smallest boy stood his ground.

Gazing directly at Miranda this time, Skip muttered, "And then Shep said, 'There comes a time when you don't turn your back. When you lay something on the line.'"

The next thing Miranda knew, he was pleading with her. "Don't you see? It's the old Catch-22. Damned if you do, damned if you don't."

In that same moment, Miranda found herself patting his hand. "Look, you didn't just run off. You came back and checked things out. You get points for that."

"I don't know, Miranda. I just don't know."

"Stop saying that. You went back out there, on your own initiative."

But all Skip would counter with was "We've switched roles, haven't we? Now you're the grownup and I'm the one who needs coddling."

"Will you get off the guilt trip and quit muddying the waters? You mentioned this new character, this Lucian Clay. The first to drop in was Mathews, then your buddy Chris, now Clay. Taking a wild guess, has he returned to his old stamping grounds all of a sudden? Is that it?"

It took another interminable beat until Skip finally started to come out of it. "All I know is he caught Chris eavesdropping at the station back in the Big Apple. Blamed him for bringing me on board, and apparently was hanging an axe over both our heads. Maybe as a front man for the parent company, Liberty Broadcasting."

At this point, having had more than enough with all this sputtering, Miranda took charge.

"Maybe, maybe, maybe. Enough of this. You hire me, I call the shots. And you never go off again on your own, half-cocked. Get it?"

"Got it."

"Good. If anything," Miranda went on, warming to this definitive tack, "you're relegated to scout and legman under my watchful eye. As it happens, my significant other and crackerjack reporter Harry is already on tap researching how far this thing goes, thus accounting for needed information and the like. Information is key to any progress. Not sputtering or getting into a funk over Shep Anderson's code of the hero. You copy?"

"Maybe . . . I guess."

"Keeping in mind my time living with a detective ex-lover," she said as she walked into the mini living room, "plus my run-ins with the local cops, from now on we operate strictly by the book. Which also means I'll keep track of expenses and bill you later if anything comes of this. Which, under the rules of engagement, is up for grabs but at least we'll try to be professional."

Nodding, sitting up now, Skip said, "All right, speaking of things coming to something, what about Duffy? Where are we on that score? And how about some restitution for Chris? Maybe he was playing both ends against the middle, but he didn't deserve to be cut down like that and trashed."

"Fine, but let's not jump the gun here."

Conscious of how far she'd gotten ahead of herself, Miranda called for a recess. She was also well aware that neither of them had had a bite to eat. She opted for a nearby barbecue joint where, given the fact that it was well before rush hour, they'd be virtually alone. He would fill her in about the details leading up to the assault on Chris. Once that was established, she'd earmark the remaining missing pieces of information for Harry to look into. Next up, she'd deal with the lead she got from Annie regarding Duffy as a result of Annie's worrisome encounter with Vin.

Waving Skip off, who was now on his feet champing at the bit, she resorted to the old standby: "First things first, pal." Ushering him out of the house to her SUV despite his protests, she said, "Come on, Skip, this is a new regime. Get with the program."

As she started the engine and Skip reluctantly quieted down, she pondered over the vague connection between his cat and Vin in his beat-up green pickup. She added it to the other vague connections, which included this mysterious Lucian Clay. Sometime soon, she told herself, it would all have to jibe.

She took the backroads until she crossed over US 70 and managed to evade the hell-bent traffic trying to beat each other onto I-40 and south to the airport. The very spot where the main perpetrators were apparently shuttling back and forth.

But even after arriving at the rustic picnic tables at the barbeque place and scanning the Carolina's Best Ribs and Fixins menu, she wasn't able to sit back for a minute. In the background, the agitated hum of the traffic from the nearby on-ramp kept reminding her once more of the opposing players on their never-ending rounds.

At the same time, a recent *Middlemarch* discussion about leading characters going off on a tangent came to mind.

Like Mary Anne Evans, the author herself, had done. Like Miranda and Skip were doing now, attempting to take the initiative on an impossibly foggy chase.

CHAPTER TWENTY-ONE

A short while earlier, drawn by the sputtering roar of the Harley Road King touring bike, Vin stepped out of the junk trailer onto the ragged weeds and gravel. Zeb braked hard a few yards in front of him and killed the motor. He flicked up his dark visor revealing the scowl on his chiseled features, cursed, and dismounted as he kicked out the jiffy stand with the heel of his boot.

The way Vin saw it, it was bad enough having to deal with kin like Zeb when Zeb was raising hell. Like when he was put behind bars for malicious mischief, trespassing, breaking and entering and all. But it was all part of his identity as rogue biker, nodding every time folks up in Madison County said "Here comes trouble." He was out to make everyone sit up and take notice and give him his due. But Russ Mathews ordering cat swiping, clobbering, and now this, whatever in hell it was, meant things had gotten totally out of hand.

"What the hell?" Zeb yelled out, pointing to the deep dent in his front fender, splayed signal lights, twisted throttle cable, and torn saddlebag. "Six hundred dollars for a new fender. Got to remove the retaining bar, loosen the calipers, mess with the spacer and axle forks. Hoist it and use ratchet straps so the whole damn machine don't fall over me."

"Okay," Vin said as Zeb circled around the hefty black bike. "What happened?"

Throwing his hands in the air, Zeb said, "You getting this?"

"Not yet, Zeb," said Vin, waiting him out.

"Hell, just look at it. And you just heard the freakin' engine and shot-to-hell idle. Which means prying under the housing covers, pulling away the hand grip, plus replacing the signal lights and stitching up the saddlebag."

"Are you gonna talk to me or what?"

"Yeah, I'm gonna talk to you. For kin and glory, you said. Take our country back."

"That's what they say."

"Oh yeah? But what about Duke having no truck with it? What about some outfit called the Liberty Broadcasting System I seen neither hide nor hair of? What about piss-ant flunky errands I'm sent on that ain't fittin' for a hell-bent dude like me?"

Vin saw there was nothing for it but to slip the pint of Jack Daniels out of his back pocket, offer him the rest of it, and hope he didn't bust into the shed and take it out on the cat. Not that Vin gave a damn about that ornery thing. But things were whacked out enough without adding Vin's lame assignments to the mix.

At first, Zeb kept pushing him away. It took a while until he simmered down, to get him off the C-clamps, socket wrenches, and slotted brackets that fixing the Harley was going to take, and only then did he start to fill Vin in and halfway make some sense.

Zeb leaned against the flaky bark of an old sycamore, drained the dregs of the pint, and tossed it far off into the shrub. "So, there I was, tailing this limo. Mathews said I had to get used to Asheville anyways. You know how I hate all them half-men half-women crawlin' around everywhere you look. But right after I was supposed to be shed of all that and long gone."

"Right after what?"

"Right after they'd lay the wood to the two peckerwoods in the limo—that same clown fella and some buddy of his from back east. Right after I was to buzz and spook both of 'em for good measure."

"The clown by the name of Skip, you mean."

"You got it." Then Zeb was off again, smacking his fists, eyeing his bike. Making Vin trail after him.

Wheeling around and pointing his finger as if it was all Vin's fault, Zeb said, "What is all this pussyfooting around? Mathews having me slice a damn cat's collar, get clawed and bit while I'm at it. Then sneak around some more and tap this clown fella who's so shaky he's about to faint anyways. But can't bring the cops into it, Mathews says. Just enough so's he's out of it for the time being. But then this Skip, this clown fella, takes off again and Mathews swears he's gotta be flushed out for good."

Despite the fact that Zeb outweighed him by at least thirty pounds, Vin grabbed him by the lapels of his leather jacket and yanked. "Are you gonna tell me what happened or not?

Zeb shoved Vin back on his heels. "Another screw-up is what happened. Leaving the other dude flat, this Skip busts out of the limo. So I cut around, smack into a one-way, double back and spot what's got to be the other one by his lonesome. Mathews signals me to take him out. Put a big hurt on him."

"Not Mathews. Mathews doesn't have the clout. Must have been relaying, must have been you know who."

"Yeah, well, anyways I gun it, must've been hitting over sixty, and clip this other one good. Clipped him so hard and kept goin' so fast I'm gonna have to spend hours at the Old Fort garage to get this baby up to speed."

With that, Zeb mounted his bike, fired it up and, with the motor flaring and choking, hollered, "I tell you, Vin, what the hell? This Mathews is flying by the seat of his pants. Where's the honcho in all this, and there's only two days left!"

With that, Zeb took off, as PO'ed as when he came busting in, if not more so.

As the sputtering Harley trailed off, Vin scuffed back into the junk trailer, plunked himself down on the sprung couch, and started in on another round of Jack Daniels from the carton on the side of the little fridge. He'd put this off and put it off, but now he saw that Zeb, besides being a loose cannon as always, was right. Things were on the verge. For the past six weeks, Vin's contract called for him to waste three churches from north Florida, to Savannah, to Charleston. It was fun as always. But he still never knew why. What was the plan?

Then this Mathews busts in, treats Vin and Zeb like field hands, some other eastern character gets taken care of while Vin is left to guess, lying in wait in the shadows 'cause the pattern has gone plum off-kilter.

Getting antsier just thinking about it all, Vin stalked out

of the trailer. As the late afternoon sky clouded up, he peeked into the shed. The cat slunk back in a dusty corner and eyed him warily, hunching its back.

Grinning despite himself, Vin said, "That's right, tabby. You get yourself primed, 'cause the way things are goin', you just never know."

The cat stayed still, like it wanted to hear more.

Knowing it was the whiskey talking but obliging the cat anyways, Vin went on. "In my case, damn well wasting my great potential. Harkening back from when they hid all them moonshine bottles 'neath the piles of hay, and little Vin comes by with the lighter he's swiped. Sparked them haystacks, hightailed it up the hill, and watched folks running and hollering every which way. And when Momma said, 'You see anything, Vinnie?' 'Golly no, Momma, what happened?' Now that's what it's all about. You set things off and no one's the wiser. Like the good Lord himself. It don't get no better than that."

But all Vin got for his troubles was another hiss, the green eyes fixed on him clear as can be.

"Well," said Vin, "that's what you get confiding in an ornery stray cat."

Vin stepped back outside, secured the latch, and let his smile slide away as he thought about this storyteller everybody was so bent out of shape to nail down, who'd, it seems, slipped away again.

He reentered the junk trailer, got out his old Gibson guitar and started working on his Civil War song to get his mind off things:

Yankee blue, time is a-comin'
Yankee blue, it's on its way
No more whisperin', no more wonderin'
Gonna be a brand-new day . . .

But again, he reminded himself, he hadn't been let in on the plan. And had no idea how this beanpole storyteller bungled his way down here and gummed up the works.

Nevertheless, all it took was a few more swigs of Jack Daniels and he told himself the smart money was on Uncle Lucian finally tapping Vin's potential. Reaping what Vin had already sowed, with that day of reckoning right around the corner.

CHAPTER TWENTY-TWO

The afternoon stretched on at the BBQ veranda as Miranda took in every detail of Skip's escapade. She did so while picking at her mixed greens salad and Skip hemmed and hawed while barely tucking into a serving of ribs, grits, and fried okra.

When he reached the point in the story where he'd been hiding behind the hedge at Number One Pack Square, the guilt got to him again.

"Don't you see? I let a friend down."

"Oh no, are we back to that again?" Miranda slid her salad to the side. "All right, how about this? You go along, sign the nondisclosure agreement, sell out, and wind up holing out in a bungalow on St. Augustine Beach as the malevolent forces do their worst. There's all this collateral damage, and you may or may not get your cat back. But, then again, members of the phantom reconnaissance crew come for you in the middle of the night because the powers that be don't want any leads left alive. Not after whatever god-awful thing they've got in the works comes to pass."

Taking this in, ever so slowly putting down his fork, Skip said, "You think?"

"What are the odds? How many are there? Who besides Russ Mathews, Vin Dupre, and now this Lucian Clay has either of us actually laid eyes on? Prove me wrong."

While Skip thought it over, Miranda broke in with another tack. "Now, while you're at it, consider this. You have no idea this wasn't a setup. That your alleged buddy wasn't in on it, putting you out of commission for good this time to save his skin and be back in their good graces. On the other hand, you've got leads. You didn't take off but scooted back to check out who's actually calling the shots. You even got a bead on this ringleader, this Lucian Clay. So here you are, back in the harness, pooling your resources with me. You have a chance to put a stop to this and get Duffy back to boot. Be pro-active instead of licking your wounds and waiting for the next shoe to fall. Maybe even get a commendation from the Jack Armstrong all-American foundation."

Skip fiddled with his napkin. "Well, if you put it that way."

"Go on."

"I guess I could give myself a reprieve. Until the smoke clears."

"Ah, thank the Lord. As long as you quit running hot and cold and deal."

Tearing into a braised rib, Skip said, "You know something? You have turned into one tough momma."

"I have turned into a fish out of water trying to make a dent."

Working on her salad again, it wasn't lost on her that even the poison pen fiasco was subject to close inspection. Here, she reminded herself for the umpteenth time, she was taking on some amorphous broadcasting system and ultra-right-wing power play with an equally amorphous imminent game plan.

And so, in her mind's eye, she returned to some idea of the

scope of this caper. Taken into account Skip's latest escapade, it had wide-ranging implications. Meaning that she had to weave a thread between Mathews's broadcasts, the purloined cat, Vin and the hit-and-run biker, this alleged ringmaster, and beyond.

With this firmly in mind, noting glimpses of that old purposeful glint in Skip's eyes while tackling his food more earnestly, she broke into the lull and said, "Right. Okay. Better check back with Harry and get an update and some inkling of a timeline."

Skip gazed at her and said, "It's amazing how much selling out is involved if you want to stay in the good graces of the parent company. If you're willing to do anything to stay on board. If, like Russ Mathews, you'll sell your soul, make amends any way you can to keep things under wraps. But if you go on the air and even try out what it's like to rally the troops, you're in for it."

Eyeing his glass of iced tea, he said, "Well that's just too bad. No vintage crème de menthe but this will have to do. To rose-lipped maidens and lightfoot lads."

Noting the newfound glint in his eyes, she recalled this was his favorite toast, borrowed from a crack unit of the Brit commandos during WWII. It had been employed during their pretend raids when Miranda was a kid: getting set to crash the Halloween party at the mansion on the hill, on surveillance going after trespassing hunters crossing Indiana farmland. And, of course, just to celebrate her birthday and past and future escapades.

And so, to keep his spirits up, she said, "I'll drink to that." She raised her own glass of sweet tea, took a quick sip and said, "Be right back. Need a stronger signal on my cell and a smidge of quiet away from the traffic."

"To check with Harry, you say?"

"At mission command post atop Eagle Crest."

Noting the quizzical look on Skip's face, she added, "Like I said, I need to know how far this goes. To help us keep things cracking."

"What have you told him so far?"

"Enough to keep him on board, leaving out anything that would cause him to start mothering me and cramp my style."

Skip nodded as though he understood.

She left the veranda and walked around to the rear of the building, past a set of dumpsters, the distant ridges serving as a backdrop under a lingering overcast sky. She hit the speed-dial number, half hoping for a juicy promising lead, half assuming she'd run into another evasive directive to play it safe.

The second he picked up, she said, "What have you got for me?"

"Meaning?"

"Come off it. You're supposed to provide me with the lay of the land and current developments."

"Uh-huh . . . okay, just a second."

Even with the swoosh and hum of late afternoon traffic on US 70 behind her and I-40 ahead in the near distance, she could make out the rattle of cups and saucers in his kitchen, the squeak of the faucet, the thump of water hitting the bottom of the tea kettle, and even the click of the knob as he turned a burner on.

When he got back on the line, she said, "Tell me you've

been checking into it like I asked, Harry. Tell me after all this time you've come up with something."

The clink of the teaspoon against the ceramic cup only prolonged matters, but she waited him out.

Before the inevitable high-pitched whistle of the kettle, Harry came out with what he'd gathered from the *Sentinel,* the far-right website, coupled with Russ Mathews's podcasts and other various and sundry notes he'd taken. The key, he said, to get the base all fired up appeared to be the thrill of chaos: diversionary tactics that are highly visual and pre-apocalyptic.

When the kettle whistle died down in the aftermath of what Miranda took to be more claptrap, she said, "Terrific. But apart from all that, what does it tell me about what Mathews is doing here instead of running off at the mouth during his live broadcasts? To the point where they had to snatch Skip's cat and opt for sending him to the hospital? And, to top it all off, what do you know about a hit-and-run at Pack Square today around noon?"

The clunk of the kettle was followed by a switch in Harry's tone. "Hold it, hold on a second. What are you talking about?"

"Events. Not right-wing hot air. What is actually going on hereabouts leading inevitably to what?"

Taking his time fixing and stirring his tea, Harry modulated his tone and said, "Okay, you tell me. What does a hit-and-run on Pack Square have to do with anything?"

"I don't know exactly, and I don't have time to go into it. Speaking of which, apparently Mathews can't hack it and there's an addition of some guy named Lucian Clay calling the shots. It would help to know if it's limited to a regional plot—say, backwoods militias or clans joining forces, like the Dupres and the Clays, if that's the link to this Lucian guy. Or, the way things are shaking out, a springboard to a national ploy involving this selfsame Lucian?"

This time there was no sound at all on the other end.

"Harry, are you still there? Not to put too fine a point on it, but with the countdown ticking away, it's vital to know the parameters. I've discounted your local vandals notion out of hand and I really need to know if it comes down to some Carolina deal or is much, much bigger. I mean, all the static aside, what is the actual story here?"

With the silence continuing on the other end, it came to Miranda that Harry had no idea of Chris Holden's existence or any part of the latest happenings. And to keep this from getting more convoluted with explanations and arguments, she had to keep it that way.

Still no reply until Harry came back with, "Miranda, what did I tell you? What did I distinctly advise you about coming down to earth and not going off half-cocked.?"

"You're deflecting, Harry." It was starting. To tone it down, she said, "Tell you what. Just do the research on those two possible clans. Plus keep checking on the news cycle. Soon as you come across anything that intersects with anything remotely like an impending D-Day, let me know. I'll take it under advisement. In the meantime, enjoy your tea. Catch you later."

Miranda ended the call before Harry had a chance for another word to the wise. Though it was hard to admit, some part of her missed the old Harry when there were no squabbles. The ease they'd established, the intimacy, the plans they'd made for leisurely hikes and trips to the Smokies and folk festivals. At the same time, she knew she was well past the point of no return and would have to reserve all comforting thoughts for later.

With the narrowing timeline, she came up with a fallback source. Not an expert per se, but a person who sometimes was involved in area protests and social issues who might be able to give her a leg up on a Clay clan leader. In return, she could offer him an opening for Bud and Travis this Friday in lieu of Vin Dupre's fake ruse. Chase Austin couldn't command an audience as a feature attraction, but he was a well-known blues-harp virtuoso, was between gigs, and certainly had nothing better to do on an early Monday evening. And he might give her some quick insights if she could get him to open up.

It was odd how seeking information and actually getting anywhere required different tacks with different people. Some might out and out lie because they had something incriminating to hide. Some were reluctant or teasing and played games with you just for the fun of it. Some were inarticulate and didn't know how to be forthcoming even if they wanted to. Chase leaned toward the feeling you out and playing games.

He didn't answer at the primary number. But after three more tries at three different locations, she got hold of him at his ex-girlfriend's place. Out of the promise of some extra coin and fondness for Bud and Travis, he agreed to meet her at El Arroyo, the Mexican restaurant a mile east of town just off US 70, in an hour or so. But that still didn't mean she wouldn't have to speed up the teasing at her expense.

Warding off questions about how things were going vis-à-vis what Harry had to offer, she convinced Skip that if they were going to work together given only a window of little more than two days, the best bet was to move him to her den with its spare cot and bathroom next to the garage. Not only for expediency's sake, but there was no percentage in his remaining in his hideaway, in fear that Vin Dupre or the motorcycle maniac or both might be cruising by gunning for his hide.

"Okay, fine," Skip said. "But I've been thinking. That stuff in Mathews's office that set me off."

"Tell me later," Miranda said, ushering him back to her SUV.

"No, wait a minute," Skip said, standing his ground. "Like the SAS, the Special Air Service. If, like those days of old, if these guys are so desperate to keep things under wraps, there must be a covert operation in the works. But where is it going to come from? What impending sneak attack is so hush-hush they would send Chris, Russ Mathews, and this honcho Lucian Clay Chris ran afoul of scurrying after me?"

"Ran afoul of where?" said Miranda, moving in on him.

"Didn't I say?"

"No."

"Back at the radio station. In New York."

"What was Lucian Clay doing up there?"

"Who knows? Checking up on things probably."

"Okay. But for now, Harry is researching, looking into

Clay's political influence and such. Maybe that will give us an inkling."

She drove him back to Swannanoa, helped him pack, and had him follow her in his old Volvo while keeping an eye out in his rearview mirror. Once at her place, with the Volvo out of sight in the garage, there was unpacking to do and getting him acclimated.

But then he jumped in again and segued to "And what about Duffy?"

"Later. I may have a lead, but at the moment I'm trying to set the edges of the puzzle, so we don't keep running off in all directions."

But Skip kept it up until she promised to keep Duffy in mind. Before Skip had a chance to cut in again, she told him that Chase Austin was a longtime activist folk singer who might be able to divulge something about the reactionary scene in these parts.

That said, she retreated upstairs to her study and penciled in some pointed questions. All the while, she reminded herself that Chase would rather blow on a blues harp (his gritty Hohner harmonica) and rally the troops with his protest songs. But if she could play it just right, she might glom something useful and carry on.

To set it up, she called El Arroyo which, given the recent spring rains, would feature a gently gurgling creek to live up to its namesake. She reserved a table for two down the far side of the patio and ordered a bottle of Don Julio to be kept in reserve until she got there. Pressing the issue with the receptionist, who was having trouble with her English, she made sure it was the high-quality, straw-colored reposado tequila produced in the state of Jalisco, home to the city of Tequila. The last thing she needed were a few remarks from Chase about blue agave harvesting and how the cheap kind required salt licking and lemon to get past the taste, among other Chase-like deflections.

After setting things up at El Arroyo and feeling as primed as she was going to be, she was confronted with a knock at her bedroom door. And there was Skip, lovingly eyeing a Daisy Red Ryder air rifle BB gun with its lever-cocking action, burnished wooden forearm and steel barrel.

"Found it in a closet in the garage," said Skip, "plus an ample supply of BBs.

"You were supposed to make the bed and unwind."

"I know," Skip said, checking out the front and rear sight on the 1938 classic. "But I wanted to get some idea of where I was. And I haven't come across one of these since good ole Aunt Zoe finally relented as long as I promised not to shoot my eye out."

"So?"

"So, how come this pops up if it isn't a sign? Something that's going to come in handy?"

Snatching the air rifle out of his hand before brushing past him and padding down the stairs with him close behind, she said, "It didn't pop up. You rummaged around. The previous owner left it. He had this fixation of protecting the nests of baby wrens and mockingbirds out back who were menaced by pesky squirrels. And I happen to take a few potshots now and then to do likewise. Okay?"

Replacing the BB gun in the cabinet above the work

bench she added, "Now will you please get in your pajamas, cool down that on-again, off-again brain of yours, and watch some DVDs while I'm gone? Give it a rest and allow me some breathing room so I can make some progress here."

Scuffing away, Skip returned to the den and stood there facing the oversized dry-erase board. Miranda eyed him for a moment as he erased last weeks' realty items and began to make a rough sketch of what appeared to be an outline of the eastern seaboard. Then he stopped. With his hands clasped behind his back, he seemed to be doing a take on a wartime Brit squad leader about to apprise his charges of enemy strongholds.

She couldn't help giving him a thumbs-up and was soon on her way.

CHAPTER TWENTY-THREE

The twilight afterglow filtered through the El Arroyo outdoor patio, and the nearby brook rippled quietly. The tables were empty save for the one occupied by Chase and Miranda seated face to face in a private area.

The setup was exactly the way she'd pictured it. Chase was dressed in his usual faded denim shirt rolled up at the sleeves, leather belt with turquoise-and-silver buckle, and stone-washed Levi's. It all dovetailed with her abiding image of his flowing white hair, General Custer–like handlebar moustache, and pointed beard.

But his deep, gravelly tone was muted as he took sips of the mellow tequila from the double shot glass. In short, he just didn't buy it. How come she was so obliging all of a sudden, offering him an opening gig this Friday after previously telling him his rendition of sixties protest songs didn't cut it anymore? More to the point, what happened to flip Miranda who put down the Moral Monday rally in Charlotte, quipping "When it gets to be an immoral rally, let me know."

All of this caused Miranda to pull back and take stock. When she was pursuing her broker's license, her mentor, otherwise known as the broker in charge, kept telling her to reassess her tactics when the deal was in danger of falling through. He likened it to efficient problem solving when you were under the gun. Both parties want something, but something stands in their way. Both parties are asking, *What's in it for me?* In this case, time was of the essence solely for Miranda, and Chase already knew what was in it for him.

In other words, this transaction between Miranda and Chase was a gig in exchange for some information—a bead on who or what she and Skip were up against.

"Okay," said Miranda, realizing she had to disarm him from the get-go, "maybe a battered relative of mine has gotten to me and brought the protest scene closer to home. Maybe I got involved."

"Uh-huh. I see."

But obviously he didn't see. Luckily, there was no chance of Chase pursuing her motives any further. It wasn't his style. He just wanted to make sure Miranda wasn't jerking him around.

Chase eased off and seemed to warm to the idea of humoring her now that he had the prospect of a little work and temporary relief from his lady friend's harping over his casual ways.

"Okay, boss lady, break it to me easy-like," said Chase. "Maybe I can accommodate you some, long as it requires very little effort."

Spotting the harried waitress rushing out of the main dining room toward them, Miranda got up, retrieved the fancy bottle of Don Julio before the girl could painstakingly try to fill his shot glass without spilling it again, and gently told her that Chase would pour his own. Plus, to forget the nacho platter. He could order something afterwards. For emphasis, Miranda told her she had already paid for the fifth of tequila and was running on a tight schedule.

The waitress gladly relinquished this chore and scurried back to the main dining area.

Returning to their table, Miranda slid the squat bottle over to Chase and said, "Now then, we are back live. What can you tell me about Carolina backwoods clans, gatherings, and secret militias? Specifically, the Dupres and the Clays."

Chase poured himself another double shot and thought about it.

In the withering silence, Miranda took a few swigs from her iced coffee, hoping against hope to salvage something. As if oblivious to her plight, the creek gurgled quietly and the twilight afterglow held steady. Chase's mottled hand reached for the shot glass and he poured himself another drink.

A few more minutes went by until he managed a wry smile and said, "So, where were we?"

Miranda pushed it now. "Look, Chase, you said you might be able to give me a tip. Well, here I am, no ulterior motive, still waiting."

"Well now, missy, not exactly a tip. Still don't exactly know what you're after. Secret roving militias? Gathering of the clans?"

"Any such thing, any such gatherings. That's all I ask."

Chase dug out the Hohner 532 harmonica from his top pocket and made it quietly wail. It wasn't long before she recognized the old country tune whose lyrics went something like "What have they done to the old home place? Why'd they have to flood it? Why tear it down?"

Picking up on this little clue, Miranda gave him a little prod. "Environmental preservation. Some kind of protest. Am I right? Am I close?"

"Tit for tat, you say?" said Chase, obviously nailing her down after her previous put-downs of his sixties protest songs. "I get to open for Bud and Travis. Get to do my old tried and true. Like this one. Like—"

"Cut the tap dance, Chase. Yes, yes, and yes. 'Tearing down the old home place.' Where were you? What was going on that pertains fairly recently to what I'm fishing for?"

"Well, now that you mention it, I do seem to recollect some such thing."

He drew it out as if he had all the time in the world and it tickled him no end to get her riled up. Or maybe because the shoe was on the other foot for a change. At any rate, the upshot was that in Madison County last summer, some logging company from back east wanted to do extensive cross-cutting of a mountain range, erect a sawmill, widen the road for huge trucks to transport the milled lumber, and so forth. The combination picnic and protest Chase attended was organized to serve notice of the dire consequences this would have—flooding the bottomland with the run-off from neighboring ponds and creeks, not to mention the effect on the government protected trout hatcheries, mountain streams, plus clogging access to and from the main road.

"Whoa," Miranda cut in. "Let me guess. You were blowing on this selfsame blues harp, doing your 'why'd they have to tear it down' tunes. But who was there? How about storytelling Trish doing her thing? But, more importantly, a bunch of Dupres including Vin wearing his signature leather-fringe jacket and vest and hand-tooled cowboy boots. Plus a menacing Dupre on a big fat Harley."

"Hey now, I don't have no photographic memory about a shindig I attended some eight or nine months ago."

"But that's the gist, isn't it, give or take one or two characters? Protecting the status quo from way back when, which is right up the Dupres' alley. And now let's add the Clays."

"Clays?"

"Yes."

"Boy, you sure are getting pushy. You mean plural?"

"Of course I mean plural. Because they don't cotton to some Yankee firm bulldozing the mountains and streams of their dear home place."

It was back to the agonizing pouring, sipping, and blowing a few riffs on the blues harp. At the point when Miranda thought she was close to screaming, Chase slipped the Hohner back into his top pocket and said, "Anyways, only one Clay I can recall."

"Are you sure?"

"Only reason I remember is 'cause he was way off to the side leaning against an old Sycamore. Thin as a rail, dark suit when everybody else was in shorts, T-shirts and such. Plus dark glasses. But most of all, giving me a high sign like he was tipping his hat when I broke into Barry McGuire's 'Eve of Destruction.' And every number afterwards about things going to hell and gone."

"You remember all that?"

"Now that it comes back to me, yes. I asked Trish who the mystery dude was way over there, apart from everybody."

"And she said?"

"Lucian Clay. Said the name over and over like part of a rhyme she was working on. 'Lucian Clay, Lucian Clay, some day'll pass your way.' You know how she does lately. Comes up with some catchy rhyme scheme. Figuring on one of us, maybe Bud or Travis, biting and offering to add chords and a melody line. Trying some way to get it back together now that her memory's slipping."

"Right. But what else did she say about him? Where is he stationed? She must have said something."

"Hey, that's it, lady. It was a Trish thing. So let's let it go at that. Except . . ."

"Except what?"

"Just a rumor, mind." Dragging it out for all it was worth. Taking a long sip from his double shot and letting out a satisfying sigh, Chase leaned back and said, "Guess who's got the new president's ear. Whispering behind them closed White House doors, cooking up strategies."

"Lucian Clay."

"The very one."

When Miranda returned home, she padded down to the den to check on Skip. She found him dozing on the cot, still in his street clothes, his unopened suitcase nudged against the nightstand.

The dry-erase board soon caught her eye. He'd embellished his rendering of the eastern seaboard replete with dashes leading from Hoboken across to lower Manhattan; back to Hoboken; down and across to Bucks County, Pennsylvania;

heading west, then all the way south to the Blue Ridge and Black Mountain and over to Asheville.

Still fixated on what she'd gleaned from Chase, she pivoted and went straight back to the cot the moment she heard him sigh and roll over.

"Skip."

"Hmm?"

"The person your old college buddy mentioned. The one who's in charge, who caught him eavesdropping back at the radio station."

"Who?" Skip said, yawning, stretching his arms.

"The main honcho Chris spoke to over his cellphone in the limo, reporting in that he had you in tow. The one you spotted when you peered over the hedge. Was he slightly built, wearing a suit and dark glasses?"

"Yeah, I guess."

"Could our ringleader also be our current president's chief strategist?"

Skip's bleary eyes widened as he sat up straight. "You think? Lucian Clay? Holy cow. Does it really go that far?"

CHAPTER TWENTY-FOUR

After a fitful night of tossing and turning, Miranda rose early Tuesday morning to once again intercept Trish at the coffeehouse. Predictably, Skip was fast asleep given his first worry-free rest in days. Miranda's plan, if you could call it that, was to prod Trish and somehow nail down a Lucian Clay–Dupre connection and establish the scope of the playing field once and for all. To present Harry with a lead that would set him digging into the archives of the web and news cycle until a nefarious D-day plot began to emerge. One earmarked for late the following evening with Clay hovering in the background, whispering into the recently elected president's ear. Then she'd pass the ball to the authorities. There were now too many juicy pointers to slough this off as sheer coincidence or right-wing paranoia.

At first glance, the layout was perfect. The place was empty at 7 a.m. save for the sleepy tousle-haired girl behind the coffee bar and Trish in the usual far corner window fixated on the early morning light glinting off the far ridges.

Miranda wasted no time plunking her cup of coffee down on the little table across from her, figuring on a leeway of at least fifteen minutes to cut to the nitty-gritty and get on with her agenda.

"Hey, Trish," said Miranda as unobtrusively as possible. "Just a few follow-up questions and I'll be out of your hair. Needless to say, I'll return the favor. Maybe feature that ballad you've been working on. That is, when it's ready, of course. Run it by good ole Chase again and see if it flies."

Still fixated out the window, possibly biding her time till her coffee and pastry came her way, Trish murmured, "So you heard about the changes, huh? Can't say I'm surprised. That's your stock in trade, ain't it? Working the grapevine, lookin' for talent and new material."

"That's right."

But before Miranda could get on with it, Trish began humming to herself, never once gazing in Miranda's direction, even when she broke into the refrain:

"Passed by here, passed by here,

Like a shadow I'd've known him anywhere."

"Great, Trish, perfect," said Miranda, flipping out a notepad, pen at the ready. "Don't tell me, let me guess. The guy in the shadows was Lucian Clay. Had to be. At the gathering last summer up in Madison County. You spotted him in the shadows, apart from everyone. 'Lucian Clay, someday'll pass your way.' Chase told me all about it. Said you were still at it, polishing the lyrics. So, what's the connection with the Dupres? Lucian some kind of backwoods commander, is that it? Moving up in the world to DC?"

There was a long delay as Trish turned her head and took Miranda into account as if noticing her for the first time. Another pause before Trish said, "What are you talking, girl? Runnin' off at the mouth like that? It's a song. You don't make it into some blabbering news item."

The waitress scuffed over with Trish's order, trying not to spill the coffee that was filled to the brim. Trish looked up at the girl. "Ain't that right, missy? It could be a tale from the Revolutionary War, Civil War, whatever. Could be anything or plum made up out of my head. Make it what you will. That's what keeps it goin', not some hot news flash. Now ain't that dang right?"

Yawning on her way back to the counter, the girl said, "Beats me. Half the time I don't get it. Boyfriend starts in with stuff like 'Ripple in still waters.' I mean, what's up with that?"

"You see," said Trish, taking a big bite out of a Danish pastry. "It's transportable. Transports you here and there and anywhere like dang poetry."

Fed by the energy from this lead, Miranda flipped through her notes. "Except, while burning the midnight oil, I sifted through it, saving the good stuff. And here you go, straight from the horse's mouth. 'Black knight of the ridges. Visor and black helmet, riding roughshod on his big Harley.' 'Vin Dupre . . . barn burning, explosions, blasts from here to kingdom come.'"

Trish dropped the pastry onto the plate. With her high cheekbones twitching, she called, "I never, I never! Now you take that back."

"But you did. Just the other morning, sitting in this exact same spot."

Trish's eyes locked as she appeared to be searching for some way out of this memory lapse. Coming up empty, she jerked straight up, knocking her chair over, spilling her coffee all over the table. "You quit that, you hear? You ain't foolin' anybody. I know you, girl. Passing stuff around when you MC. Trying to get a rise out of folks, all in good fun. 'Cept pretty soon word gets around. Kin gets wind of it. Before you know, it ain't tall tales or dreamin' stuff up. It's Trish tellin' tales out of school and my song swap prospects are done. Left to housecleaning for folks I don't know, much less can stand, and an endless life of misery."

While Trish was carrying on, Miranda caught sight of that same flatbed truck pulling in front and the same burly pair up to another round of "I told you so." The red-bearded one in the lead; the stubble-face one grunting and chiming in. In no time, their remarks were broken off as they made a beeline to Trish's side wanting to know what Miranda had done and why in hell she was pestering Trish again.

Thrown off guard, Miranda tried to tell them it was only a misunderstanding, but they didn't buy it. Redbeard told her to shove her notepad where the sun don't shine, clear out, and mind her own damn business.

"That's right, girl," Trish said as Miranda raised her hands in mock surrender and turned to go. "The reason you got no friends is 'cause you're always trying to start something. Get somethin' going."

Miranda still had no idea what she was talking about. Maybe Alzheimer's was creeping up on her fast. All the same, Miranda felt sorry for her and certainly hadn't set out to do any harm. "Look, Trish," she said, getting on her feet.

But Redbeard cut her off and prodded Miranda out the door. "Come on, move them feet. I recollect Trish telling you to steer clear just the other morning."

"That's right," Scruffy chimed in, only a few steps behind.

Miranda glanced back and saw that Trish wasn't responding, reverting back to that blank look as the waitress straightened Miranda's abandoned chair before mopping up the coffee with paper towels.

Miranda started to drift left to the sloping gravel parking space. But the two guys cut in front, blocking her way. Pressing harder, Redhead said, "You'd best get it through your head, putting your nose where it don't belong'll get you to a bitter end. Known fact: woman's got to know her place before it all goes haywire."

"Ain't that the truth," said Scruffy. "No good comes of it every time."

"Once you turn a blind eye to it," said Redbeard. "seems it keeps getting worse. I'm talkin' giving gals free rein nowadays."

Pretty soon, Miranda found herself hemmed in against the narrow wooden porch banister. Unable to take their barnyard odor and their proximity, she countered with "'She never mentions the bad times or the bad things he's done. 'Cause she's a good-hearted woman with a two-timin' man.'"

Redhead stepped right into her face this time. "Don't you mess with that Willie Nelson song. It's *good*-timin' man not two-timin'. You just crawl back into your hole and stay there, you take my meanin'?"

"'Cause nobody likes a smart-ass woman," said Scruffy, crowding her as well.

Miranda pivoted, spotting the Madison County plates at the tail gate of the looming flatbed truck as she smacked into a hanging drainpipe. She spun around again, tripped over the edge of the porch, fell onto a rut in the gravel drive, and skinned her knee. She could hear Scruffy mocking her, calling out, "Serves you right!" as she got up, scuffed over and slipped behind the wheel of her SUV. She just sat there for a time, unable to erase this dodgy encounter nor the image of Trish flinching at the sight of the burly pair.

"Now what?" Miranda muttered aloud. It was still quite early—not even twenty minutes had gone by. In the swirl of her mind, she thought of going home to attend to her knee. She told herself she wasn't simply engaged in fact-finding conversations. She was engaged like the DCI inspector on that endless British series and his young sergeant interviewing likely suspects, weighing alibis, confronting witnesses, sifting through physical evidence and clues. Even though they had a whole team at their beck and call.

She had had her ex as backup, and that whole fiasco Skip had read about had left her unscathed.

As her resolve slipped away, visions of Skip's plight filtered through her mind along with what had befallen Chris Holden, the bruise on Annie's arm, and all the rest of it. She found herself peering at the fluffy scudding clouds under the bright Carolina blue, reminding her of her saunters last spring along the ancient Cherokee trading path and the Rutherford Trace, traversing the clumps of dogwood, groves of cherry blossoms, meadows, and the like.

All of it was eclipsed by the throbbing in her knee and her pathetic retreat at the hands of Madison County's very own Redhead and Scruffy.

She sprung out of her car and burst back into the coffee house, shoved one of her calling cards into Trish's lumpy purse, and told her to give her a call when her ballad was set and ready.

Redhead tried to rise from his chair, but Miranda shoved him back down. "Forget trying to be mannerly, pal. Totally out of your league."

Looking up, his jaw hanging open, Scruffy said, "What are you, tetched?"

"No, that's just the way it goes nowadays. Guess us smart-ass gals will never learn."

Miranda noted that the blank look on Trish's face remained fixated out the window. She was doing a great job with her cover-up act, joining forces with the parting clouds and all she could corroborate if she wanted to but didn't dare.

Outside by the flatbed truck, the words of the broker in charge came back to her:

There you go again, in a rush, tipping your hand. So you're up against it. You don't have to act like an apprentice. Everybody's after the same thing: closing. Always striving for closure. Quit barging around, one minute doing good, the next losing your grip. Keep your eye on the ball and close the deal.

CHAPTER TWENTY-FIVE

M iranda had just finished dabbing antiseptic on her scraped knee and applying a bandage when Skip appeared at her bedroom door clad in pajamas.

"Okay, you managed to slip out at the crack of dawn while I was still conked out. How come? And what's happened to Duffy? Is he still alive, starving, caged up somewhere? Or did they toss him out the car window and he's lost in the brambles, traipsing around some godless mountain pass?"

"Hold on, Skip."

"No, you hold on. I've tried to cool it because you said you might have a lead. But so far you keep deflecting, keep telling me you have to know how far this thing goes. Well, I drew the rest of the dots for you on the dry-erase board and want to get cracking. Which was your sole order of business when you said you were in it for the cat."

"For starters."

"Whatever. Well? How about treating him as a link to what in the world is going on and how far it goes? Or, at the very least, unfinished business?"

Miranda took in the fact that for the first time his eyes were clear and focused and he was totally wide awake. "What do you mean, you drew the rest of the dots?"

"If you'd get off your duff, I'll show you."

With that, he turned and left. Miranda drifted after him

down the stairs into the den, noting once again the vertical line on his drawing dividing his escape routes with a crude drawing of the US and the peppering of dots across much of the South and Midwest, including Indiana and their old stamping grounds. Without giving her a chance to respond, Skip jumped in and told her the dots were an approximation of the affiliates of the Liberty Broadcasting System: the outfit championing Russ Mathews's conspiracy claptrap and the proud sponsor of Shep Anderson's old homespun tales during the days before today's polarized political climate.

Breaking in, Miranda said, "How do you know all this?"

"The map in Russ Mathews's office next to the old timey one. Part of his war room. It just struck me last night while you were out. There was a big LBS logo in the right-hand corner. Plus, a circle around Washington, DC. At the time and for some reason, I never made the connection. Just thought of it as wishful thinking—me as a cut-rate Shep Anderson."

It took a bit of staring on Miranda's part before she caught on. Then she began to incorporate these factors into her list, erasing and editing as she went, underscoring the leads she'd garnered so far along with the loose ends.

"Okay," Skip said, "I'll bite. What are you doing?"

But Miranda didn't answer, concentrating and checking it twice. Then she stepped back and let her own highlights stand.

1. *Recent set of explosions south of here, maybe heading this way and beyond.*

2. The career of Lucian Clay, leading to greater political influence up to the present day.

3. Breaking political news signaling something imminent, possibly by the stroke of twelve tomorrow night.

4. Any of this requiring a stalking horse—"diversionary measures and the thrill of chaos." Just plain shaking things up.

"Talk to me," said Skip. "And who, for Pete sake, are these highlights intended for?"

"Harry. Who else? Mister archives, research, and purveyor of leading evidence."

She reached into the nightstand, plucked out a calling card, and handed it to him. "All you have to do is call his cell, remind him who you are, and read the list to him. Call it unfinished business. Remind him he was supposedly sifting through hype and innuendo and was up on your predicament while I more or less was sitting tight."

"Not so fast. What do you mean, more or less?"

"Leave out the latest mayhem, which would cause no end of his playing mother hen, which would stall this whole operation."

"But you still haven't said a word about the lead on Duffy. You leave me hanging and now you toss this at me."

"Just think of our little trio as partners in crime."

"Oh, terrific. Except that two of the partners have never met and this one is being given the brush-off."

"Which will be rectified forthwith if you will quit wasting time."

Before Miranda could slip out and hit the overhead garage

door button, Skip grabbed her arm. "And what, pray tell, do I tell him as to why you didn't call him and tell him yourself? Plus, what you're up to, let alone what you've been up to? Plus, what's happened to Duffy?"

With her expedient trajectory firmly in mind, she came right back with "All right, all right. Just say I'm going out to see a man about a cat, giving this aspect due diligence, but leave out our overall game plan. As soon as I return, we'll compare notes, connect some more dots, whip up an early brunch and take it from there."

She cut him short before he had a chance to voice any further objections and in no time was on her way to intercept Officer Ed.

She had every reason to believe her hunch would pay off if she played it right. Unlike her hit-or-miss poking around, there was a lot of water under the bridge between her and Ed Wheeler. The deep funk he'd been in since her ex had left for the big time in Raleigh, and Ed's partner Tyler, over ten years his junior, had moved on to Charlotte and a promotion, made everything worse. His funk was aggravated further by the notoriety Miranda received after stumbling onto the solution to her client's poison pen torment, thus exposing Ed's dispensability and increasing his low self-esteem—especially after his squeamish behavior as Miranda faced up to the hapless perpetrator while Ed stayed well back.

Which also meant Ed and Miranda's mutual ribbing was a thing of the past. Lately, there had been no more of Miranda's allusions to Ed's paunchy bod, pasty face, balding pate, and candidacy for early retirement. By the same token, there was no need on Ed's part to tease Miranda about her perennial loser status in the mating game. Hooking up with Harry and receiving more notoriety as a material witness in that so-called Zodiac matter had elevated her stature. Conversely, Ed's fatal flaw—opting to deflect at every turn, let alone face the slightest brush with danger—was, in all quarters, simply a given.

With all this under consideration, plus the way Ed had casually dismissed Skip's charge that someone had absconded with Duffy, Miranda had a lot of ammunition to get Ed on board.

As she drove down two-lane Blue Ridge Road, she pictured him lying in wait in his white-striped black cruiser, about to snag some unsuspecting speeding tourist. Said driver would be completely unaware that this two-lane bypass came with a hidden 35 mph speed limit sign under a shady elm.

Sure enough, there Ed was as always on an early weekday morning, primed and ready to take out all his woes on whatever quarry he could bag.

Miranda pulled over onto the grassy swale a few yards behind the cruiser's rear bumper and got out. With no out-of-town traffic to give him an excuse to pretend to be too busy, she began her calculated approach. She didn't rightly know what exactly made Ed so cynical and jaded. Maybe it was too many false alarms. Maybe he didn't take to the competition and being passed over all the time by younger, pushy cops. Whatever it was, she'd simply have to work around it.

Taking in his protruding beefy arm and the reflection of his aviator sunglasses in his side-view mirror, she eased over to his open window. She stood there, only inches away, expecting no immediate response and receiving none. The silence held for a moment until Miranda came up with "It's not only about a cat this time, Ed."

Ed's left elbow remained jutting out the window as he lifted his sunglasses with his right hand as if it required a great effort. "What is it, Miranda? What do you want?"

"Well now, as it happens, you are the very one who sloughed off the complaint about a pilfered orange tabby."

"What is this? Can't you see I'm busy?"

"Hardly. Plus, the cat happens to belong to my hometown cousin Skip."

"Don't tell me you're in on it too." Ed removed his elbow and sat upright as if it too required maximum effort and pulled his sunglasses back in place. From where she was standing, she couldn't tell whether his posture and tone was a sign he was getting set to let her have it, along with the next speeding motorist who gave him the slightest grief.

"Look," said Miranda, "there's a lot more here than meets the eye. If I were you, I'd pull myself out of this trash wallow you're in, listen up, and turn your life around. And I'd ditch those sunglasses while you're at it. You can shade those shifty eyes, but as some gal at the gym used to say, the body never lies."

Tossing the sunglasses onto a slot above the dash, Ed jerked his head in her direction. "Your smartass mouth is the last thing I need right about now. Just because you made me feel like crap that Halloween night, just because you got your name in the paper and I don't know what all—"

"Drop it, Ed. I bungled into it and know better now than to go into something blind. Besides, if you'd stop giving me a hard time, you could pick up the pieces and get ahead of the game. Stand to get a citation, promotion, or whatever guys who've been passed over yearn for."

Just then, they both spotted a newish white BMW tearing around the bend, racing toward them. Miranda stepped back as Ed flipped his sunglasses back on, turned the ignition key and cranked the Crown Victoria engine to a growling pitch. But before he could put the car in gear, a yellow school bus appeared in the side-view mirror behind them. By the time the bus cleared Ed's front fender, there was no chance for him to turn around and give chase.

Ed killed the motor, hurled the glasses onto the passenger seat, and glared at Miranda. "Okay, woman, this better be good or you will live to regret it."

Miranda stepped forward. The way things were going, she figured she'd hit him with the proposition and give him no time to revert to his old self or take out his frustration over the lumbering school bus on Miranda. "Here it is in a nutshell, Ed. Swiping the cat was only the tip of the iceberg. So was knocking Skip out and sending him to the hospital."

"Knocking him out? Somebody knocked him out?"

"Right. Stick with me, okay? Here is where you come in. After one of this phantom crew assaulted crazy Annie in Swannanoa seeking information as to Skip's whereabouts, Annie filed a complaint with Deputy Roy. The phantom crew member's name is Vin Dupre, and he claims he's got a gig fronting for Bud and Travis this weekend, which is bogus. He was driving an old rusted green Chevy pickup. Circa early 1940s. The kind with artillery-shell-like headlights mounted atop the front fenders."

"How do you know this?"

"Using my sharp little eyes. Anyways, this old Chevy also has skewered Madison County plates and a busted taillight which I also observed firsthand. You will run a BOLO, that's short for 'be on the lookout for'—"

"I know what a damn BOLO is."

"Exactly. You follow so far?"

"Maybe. But what's this supposed to lead to?"

"For me and Skip, a bead on the whereabouts of Duffy the cat who could be starving by now. Lord knows what Vin did with him."

"Who says this Vin character's got this cat?"

"After she was assaulted, Annie poked her head into his passenger side window and screamed she was going to report him, he tossed a spanking new bag of kitty litter in her face and took off into the night heading east."

Ed's face went blank for a second. "Pretty slim, Miranda. I tell you, pretty dang slim."

"That's my lookout, my responsibility. The deal is you contact Deputy Roy in Swannanoa who took Annie's statement and add the assault to Annie along with the cat-nabbing. You factor in a biker in black leathers who happens to be a fixture in Madison County. The same guy who swiped the cat and clobbered Skip and subsequently did a hit-and-run on Pack Square, which left a certain Chris Holden, who knew too much, in traction. Theoretically, the mad biker is also a link to Asheville. And Holden also takes you to Russ Mathews and the Liberty Broadcasting System, right wing conspiracies, and possibly the White House. All of which is about to bust wide open by, at the very latest, tomorrow night by the stroke of twelve."

"Lordy, how in hell am I supposed to follow all this and why would I want to?'

"If even part of it rings true, it takes you far and away from Black Mountain and speeding tickets. It pulls you out of the treadmill of oblivion. It gives you a new lease on life."

Ed slowly got out of the cruiser and began pacing around the swale. At one point he just stood there at the edge of the road. When a bright red Ford GT zipped by him going well over sixty, stereo blasting, busted muffler throbbing and coughing as loud as can be, Ed kept pondering, and Miranda knew she had him going.

When he returned to the cruiser, his furrowed brow indicated he was ready to deal under certain conditions.

The upshot was that he would put out an all-points bulletin for Buncombe County focusing on the Swannanoa Valley and due east to Old Fort. Miranda would run what she spieled about the biker and all by him, clear as can be this time, which he'd record on his digital recorder. Employing this information, he could do some poking around. In turn, he'd check back with Deputy Roy and log Annie's complaint. Miranda would also swear to keep him apprised of any new developments for the next forty-eight hours. In return, he would notify her of any sightings of Vin Dupre's old pickup ASAP.

That done, Miranda slipped him her realty card listing her landline and cell. They didn't shake hands as Ed gave her one of his signature "I don't know about this, woman. I tell you, I dang just don't know. Give me one reason you're so hot to trot on this sorry venture."

"For starters, my cousin looked out for me way back when, and the least I can do is look out for him."

Giving him no chance to counter further, she turned, slid behind the wheel of her SUV, and took off, passing Ed's cruiser and thinking of gunning it. She decided to keep it at 45 mph, giving him no incentive to pull her over and pull out of their deal.

Heading back to her house and Skip, it occurred to her that nothing had significantly changed. Not only was she far behind in the invisible national plot chase, she had no proof that Vin Dupre was a leading culprit, and there was only a remote possibility Duffy the cat had been handed off to him. As Ed had just said, "Pretty slim, Miranda. Pretty dang slim."

Nevertheless, reverting to broker guidelines, you had to have a lot going for you to step in and cross the finish line ahead of the pack. This was Miranda the whistleblower, garnering some leverage.

All she could do at the moment was have a late breakfast with Skip, come up with maneuvers to snatch Duffy and get a bead on Vin's activities. Otherwise known as dragging her heels and waiting till Ed rang back with Vin's whereabouts.

And hoping that quicksilver Vin Dupre too was cooling his heels, waiting for further instructions in the plot to do God knew what in the race toward the closer.

CHAPTER TWENTY-SIX

A few hours earlier, Vin Dupre was tooling around in his old pickup to get the lay of the land and, at the same time, trying to simmer down. Not only was he restless waiting for the van to arrive with the new triggering mechanism and plasticized explosives—far and away better than the nitrates he'd been using—but he'd had to field another call from Russ Mathews. Right off the bat, Mathews started going on about how riled Vin's uncle Lucian was over Vin's failure to nab this Skip character. The second he high-tailed it again, Mathews had been forced to give the high sign for Zeb to take out some other guy who knew too much and who'd tapped this Skip character as an alternate. Which still left Skip on the loose.

Not only did Vin have no idea what either of these two guys had done that led to Zeb's hit-and-run, he had yet to get over being treated like a cat sitter who found himself slamming that slow-witted gal against the garage door before he even had a chance to check the place out—a whole kind of business he never signed up for in the first place.

If that wasn't enough, Mathews asked about Duke and if Vin had enlisted him as the point man. If he hadn't, it was all on Vin's head. At that point, Vin cut him off again, told him to stick it in his ear, and stomped out of the trailer. Which accounted for the way he was gunning the old truck motor as he scouted around for some place to test the new device from a safe distance. The way things were going, it would be a wonder if he didn't blow up a few barns while he was at it.

He switched on the dented FM radio he'd wired into the dash along with an antenna atop the roof of the cab. It was tuned to that folk music station out of Asheville that always helped him calm down some. At this moment, some angel-like gal was singing, "Here's to you, my rambling boy. May all your rambling bring you joy." The rambling part was right on. The joy was all wrong. What it was was more like a charge. Like hurling lightning bolts if and when he felt like it. Akin to the feeling he got when he firebombed that Ocala, Florida, church; then the one in Macon, Georgia; and the one in Florence, South Carolina, two weeks ago that welcomed everyone no matter how sorry looking or weird. But no orders since then, no charge or fun. Just those damn fool errands. He'd kept up being the chill dude in between assignments but, truth to tell, each time Mathews had really gotten to him.

Plus, the gal on the radio's voice was too angel-like, what she was singing too sugary, about "being a pal and a friend always, ramblin' around in the good old days." Vin had no pals, wouldn't even ramble around with kin. That would kill the whole deal of being a chill dude on the outside and a shadow man underneath. Like a bad omen, and before you know it, something flares up. Nobody saw it coming and nobody ever will. And 'cause of him, the world had changed.

But at the moment, everything was hanging.

Edgy as ever, he shut off the radio.

Tearing around here and there, once again he got lost, this

time around a gravity-fed geyser spewing water straight up to the sky in a narrow stream. A couple of out-of-towners— two adults and two little girls, all wearing the same Great Smokies blue T-shirt—stood there in amazement. There was nothing else to look at, just the geyser in the middle of a meadow the size of a ball field. Vin figured it maybe was listed as a tourist attraction down here in Old Fort. He hoped that was it and there was nothing at all like it for miles around and nowhere near the hidden busted trailer and dirt lane that led up to it, yet still close enough where he could try out the new gizmo—a perfect spot to get his blood up and erase this wasted, jittery feeling.

He pressed on.

Pretty soon he came upon a dead end and a dirt track. He parked, got out, and found that the track led to a walking trail marked by a weathered wooden sign with the words "Point Lookout, five miles." The trail was weeded over, but he could still make it out, which told him that hikers and tourists hadn't yet descended and he'd be alone for a while. But the question was, would it take him to a clearing that would be worth the trouble? Better still, would it give him a practice target that would make up for all the grief, dumbness, and being hung-up for days?

With no desire to keep scouting around and getting lost, he hit the trail. At first, there was nothing but more frustration as he kept tripping over bittersweet vines and roots that would take a sharp hoe to remove if anybody had a mind to. Then there were the dandelions, Virginia creepers, and knotweed to tromp through. But he trudged on anyways, moving faster, higher and higher.

As a rule, he never went on hikes. What was the point? What was the payoff? This time, something was propelling him, telling him he would come upon some picture-perfect answer. Maybe it was the edginess and the gusts of wind this early morning. Like the surprises just around the corner that kept him watching action movies and such, with a lone wolf in the lead who finds a hidden route to the drug king-pin's lair back in the canyons. It didn't matter what the hunt was about. All he was interested in was the way the guy handled himself, got in and out of scrapes with no one the wiser. Still a ghost when all was said and done.

He kept moving. He could have sworn he'd sighted a perfect spot while meandering down this way, hunting for the hidden grove and the junk trailer.

Soon enough, the terrain opened up way over to his left. He cut through the stinging nettles and the broom sage tall as wheat, brushing it all out of the way till he could get a closer look. He kept working his way past the brush on a hunch, out of orneriness, just to get through it to some kind of payoff.

Then he saw it. As near as he could make out, the train trestle dipped down out of a tunnel and gradually began to rise again, the single track looping higher and higher until it leveled off. The tunnel was like a gateway for this single-track rail to make it through the Blue Ridge chasm on its way to Ridgecrest and a straightaway westerly to Black Mountain, Swannanoa, and all points west.

He hurried through the thicket to a rise about twenty yards above the lowest loop where he found a gap between the land and the trestle. The top of the trestle was about eight feet higher before the rails tore away from the land. Looking down, the gap fell far below where he could barely make out jutting slabs of granite.

Catching his breath and checking his watch, he recalled Duke tossing new rail ties behind that eatery in Black Mountain. Vin had waited for the freight train to stop at that point around this time, somewhere between one thirty and two. His mind had been fixed on enlisting him like he said he would, no skin off Vin's teeth. He was laid back at that point, foxy behind his chill dude mask with that tavern manager gal sitting close by on the patio, getting a whole earful.

It was when his nice and easy had backfired with Duke that led to this testy mood. All he knew was he had to practice for whatever they had in store for him. Remembering that put all the errand crap behind and jolted him back to chillness.

He spun around, cut back through the brush, down the tramped down track, reached the starting point and scampered down the trail, stumbling over the bittersweet as the downward slope took him to the dead end and his truck.

Vin scouted around till he found a convenience store with a kind of gas he'd never heard of. The scrawny gray-bearded guy behind the pay-first-before-you-pump counter that also featured lottery ticket sales and such was dealing with a dumpy woman in a flowered dress. He kept squinting at her like he was damned if he was going to get some prescription glasses and the cheap ones would have to do. He waited for the woman to make up her mind about which brand of lottery tickets she wanted.

All she would say in a chirpy voice was that the vibes would tell her, but right now she was getting no signs in her head. When she realized someone was standing behind her, she turned toward Vin, stared at him, nodded, turned back and said that gambling numbers would do the trick like seven and twenty-one. Shortly after that, she paid for her roll of tickets, whisked by Vin with a big smile spreading across her face and said, "Thanks for the clue, rambling man."

Vin drifted up to the counter, careful not to seem anxious. Careful not to do or say anything memorable.

"You know anything about that spot in the gorge?" said Vin.

"Come again?"

"Where the trestle meets the tunnel."

"Yup," said Squinty. "Still too early to get a good look."

"At what?"

"Freight train, Norfolk Southern, at that low point outta the tunnel, chugging and strainin', goin' no more than thirty miles an hour. But even at that, still would need a stoppin' distance of half a mile if needs be. But so what? Show only lasts couple of minutes if you happen by at the exact right time and went to all the trouble of hikin' up there. Then it's now you see it, now you don't. You get my meanin'?"

"For sure."

"All in all, I'd lay odds at ten to one of catching it just right."

Squinty was squinting hard now, like seeing double trying to identify someone. Vin decided to end this but not before getting two more answers.

"So is the Norfolk Southern running today?"

"Course it is. Today and most days durin' the week. But too early in the year to get a good look. 'Cause people have to whack all that brush first. You'd best wait at least a week or so till they clear it all out."

Then Squinty finally came out with it. "Tourist, huh? Or hiker? No, I'd say more like—"

"Just make it curious." Vin bought a couple of candy bars he didn't need and a small carton of cream for the cat. Not that he was starting to give a damn about it. Only because his mood was shifting.

Squinty raised the odds to twenty to one as Vin left the store. Vin drove back to the junk trailer, shored up by the thought of the van arriving with the new explosives. State of the art was the way they put it. A dandy gizmo more like, that'd really do the trick like nothing before.

CHAPTER TWENTY-SEVEN

To Vin's mind, the good thing was that the white van with the Confederate/American flag logo on the side pulled in only a few minutes off schedule. It also had New York plates. Must be the exact van cousin Billy used to own and maybe was hard to trace. The bad thing was the guy with the shaved head, gold earring, gray coveralls, wrestler build, and hard Yankee accent. Making it worse, as he stepped out of the driver's side, the scowl on his scraggly face never quit.

"You Vin, right?" the Yankee asked.

Keeping his distance, Vin nodded.

"Figures."

Vin had no idea what that meant and wasn't about to ask. The van was parked deep in the milkweeds, about a hundred yards away from the junk trailer. It was off to the side of the tire marks from Zeb's Harley when Zeb came tearing in the other day.

"I got my doubts about this, I gotta tell ya," the Yankee said, blocking the van's door hatch over the rear bumper as if he was on guard duty. "I mean, the more you think about it, the more lame it gets. I'm talkin' what's been going on."

The Yankee carried on like Russ Mathews, spinning another tale Vin could hardly follow, but obviously testing him just in case, making sure this was all over his head like he knew Mathews pigeonholed him. There was something about a dead end in Hoboken, New Jersey, delivering parts to an abandoned rooming house. Then picking up the latest version of the device, delivering it somewhere else, continuing this way until the triggering mechanism passed muster. The only thing Vin could really pick up on was this Skip character again, caught spying on them across the way. Then following Skip on a Sunday morning, with the orange cat in the back window of that Volvo clunker, crossing over to lower Manhattan where this Skip had no business going.

"Stranger in town. Taking a Sunday drive," Vin cut in. "Letting the cat sun itself."

"Oh yeah? Guys like you from the boonies. What do you know about it?"

Giving Vin a dirty look, the Yankee went on with the same old story, making sure Vin appreciated all the grief this Skip character had put them through, including having to shoot out the window of his dingy flat below street level when he wouldn't play ball.

Vin assumed maybe this Skip blabbed about something but really didn't know what he was doing. Needless to say, Vin didn't give a damn. He began to tune the guy out during the part when the Yankee said, "So this clown heads west and south," his voice getting more and more raspy, "to these boonies, close to the last place you'd ever want him to wind up. I mean, forget about it!"

Vin shuffled over to the oak whose leaves had returned to a full shiny green and offered some shade. But the Yankee followed close on his heels.

"Hey, you getting my drift? This clown is still on the

loose and the way I hear it, you got close but lost him. How screwed up can it get? What's with you, besides coming up with excuses for this clown?"

By now Vin had had more than enough. "I'd like to see the goods."

"Yeah, I'll bet you would."

The standoff lasted a few minutes till the Yankee finally cut it short. He went back to the van, rummaged around, and returned with an old model iPhone and a stick of plasticized explosives, rigged so they looked like sticky short loaves of French bread.

"Okay, Vin, let's call this a test. See if you got anything going for you or you're just as weird and as much a pain in the butt as you're cracked up to be."

Vin hesitated but couldn't help himself. "Where did you get that idea?"

"From what I see. From the way you and your cousin Zeb keep blowing it every which way. Rumor has it you got a screw loose and went off the deep end when you were a kid."

Keeping in check the twinge of anger coursing up his spine, Vin said, "The trigger? How do you set it off?"

"Just like that? You don't want to know the inner mechanism and remote relay they just came up with? You don't want to talk about backpacks, pipe bombs, pressure cookers, and other crap that are so yesterday, it hurts?"

"Just show me the switch."

The Yankee stared at him clutching the old model iPhone, closed in on Vin, and demonstrated slowly as if Vin might be a tad slow-witted to boot.

"Okay, you know how these get turned on and off, right?"

Vin just glared at him.

"Right. So, when it asks for the passcode, you enter 987-4159, which happens to be one of our guy's old numbers down in Boca. You think you can remember it?"

Vin didn't bite this time either.

The Yankee took the silence as a yes and went on. "Anyways, after that, these icons pop up, see—calendar, camera, weather, and so on. You hit the *clock* and then set the timer for three or four minutes—whatever you need to get the hell out of there. The minutes and seconds roll by till the alarm and the blast goes off. I can't tell you how many tries it took timing it with a whole bunch of compact plastics using RPX, C-4—you name it—down in some busted mine shaft on Rikers Island. Rikers Island, New York. Get it? Well? Talk to me."

Vin continued to give him nothing.

"Don't tell me you're hard of hearing too. I'm saying, ain't that somethin'? Ain't it a kick in the head? Ain't you freakin' impressed?"

"Give me some of those plastics."

"You'll get one and that's it. Left you a map of an old gorge about thirty minutes east of here so's you can practice. Way outta the way and just hope you don't blow your foot off or something."

The Yankee took his time rummaging around some boxes in the back of the van till he came up with a shorter bread-like plastic. Looking him up and down again as if still unsure whether he could trust him with anything, he said, "Got to make a call."

Whipping out a smartphone from his coveralls, the

Yankee traipsed off into the woods. As he passed from view, Vin was dead sure they'd sold him short and were making certain he was kept in the dark. He waited till the Yankee was clear out of sight, reached inside the box, and plucked out three larger pieces, and grabbed the map and a flyer from where they were tucked between the box and the corner. On the way to the bin by the shed door, he glanced at the flyer, couldn't make heads or tails out of it, crumpled it up and tossed it aside. He noted the cat litter by his feet, reminding him of that incident with that fat child-gal when he'd tossed the first bag in her face as she screamed at him and threatened to call the police. He was really going to have to watch it, keep from losing it again.

He glanced at the map but was not about to waste precious time scouting for an old gorge way out of the way when he had the perfect gorge waiting for him nearby. He dropped the map into the bin with the plastics just in time to catch the Yankee returning from his secret call. He turned and made his way back over to him as if Vin might be interested in any further instructions.

"I'll be off to Asheville," said the Yankee with a weary moan. "To check with Mathews about the Big Apple end of the deal. When I return, if the world hasn't blown to smithereens, I'll pull in and sack out for a while. Been on the road and ain't had no sleep for over twenty-four hours. So, do me a favor and string a few sentences together so's I can tell Mathews you ain't exactly hopeless."

"Well," said Vin, faking a smile, "ain't that nice of you."

Vin almost enjoyed the fact the Yankee didn't know what to make of that one.

He didn't watch the Yankee get behind the wheel, didn't give him a second thought as he drove off. Sometimes he marveled at the way he could be easygoing and real friendly-like one minute and ice cool the next, so's nobody could pin him down. Like when Duke tossed those rail ties around while he was doing Vin wrong, Vin went from taking it cool and easy to feeling out that spunky gal from the Tavern and being just as sharp.

His play at this point was to be the hired gun from the old Westerns whose ice-blue eyes made him that much more menacing. The shadow no one ever saw coming.

Getting down to business, he calculated the time the freight train came by Black Mountain minus messing with the ties this time, and the distance between reaching the tunnel and the hard going up the trestle and then the miles to Black Mountain. With that ball-park figure in mind, he got out the plastics and placed all four under an old blanket in his trunk along with the old iPhone in a tool kit. He took off, crossed over Mill Creek Road, and took a hard right onto 70, all the while figuring the amount of reinforced rope he'd need.

Twenty minutes later, when he reached Ace Hardware right after the entrance to highway 40, he got the exact number of feet for the coil he needed and asked for directions to the nearest lumber place. Convincing the lumber salesman he needed a yard-square piece of plywood cut and shaped like a kite got him a funny look that stayed fixed on the clerk's face through the whole transaction. But Vin paid it no never mind. Afterward, he tossed the rope and piece of plywood onto the truck bed.

Then it was back on Route 70, dealing with the traffic, the eighteen-wheel rigs that played chicken, daring you to pass, roaring ahead. After that, it was a speedway high up in the mountain pass, plunging down, curving this way and that, cars on all sides hurtling down faster and faster on the way to the Old Fort exit and a little way beyond.

Glad to get off the chase, his old Chevy pickup no match for the new models that passed him right and left like he was in a different time zone, Vin crossed under the overpass and spent a good thirty minutes searching for the spot where the dirt road ends and the bottom of the trail began. The sign that said Mill Creek Road was an old stage route was no help at all.

When he was all but about to give up, the dirt lane petered out and he was home free.

After making certain there was no one around, he got out the coil of rope, iPhone, kite-like piece of plywood, and the plastics. Checking his watch all the while, counting the time he'd lost scouting around for the trail, he got out the twenty-volt drill from the trunk slot, changed bits, drilled two holes and proceeded to affix the four sticky plastics to the wider side of the plywood, looping the rope through the holes and around the plastics several times and knotting it all tight in place. He stuck the iPhone in the inside pocket of his leather-fringed jacket, grabbed the coil of rope and rigged plywood, and began straggling up the trail as fast as he could go, tripping once more over the roots, realizing his fancy boots were a drag when it came to maneuvering fast on foot.

After checking his watch again, he reckoned he had no more than ten minutes to cut through the tamped-down brush and play with the kite, tossing it till he got it high enough so it would snag on the tracks. Another five minutes gone as he reached the ragged clumps of brush, cut through and worked his way to the lookout.

He whipped out the iPhone, wasted another minute till it came on and dialed the passcode. He put it aside and grabbed the plywood-base explosive.

Holding the tail of the makeshift kite, he spun it around and hurled it with all his might over the gap between the land and the rails. It clanged against the trestle but failed to clear the top to the tracks. He hauled it back up and tried again, harder and faster but with the same result. He ran back a few yards, sprinted forward, spinning and hurling like a roping cowboy, just barely missing falling over the edge of the rise. This time it caught somewhere over the trestle past the near side of the tracks.

He plucked up the iPhone and hit the clock icon.

Just then, he could hear the diesel whine approaching the tunnel. He fell on his knees, set the timer for two minutes, and fixed his gaze on the countdown. At forty seconds till the alarm, he figured the train to be twenty seconds away from beginning its climb from the bottom of the trestle, straining and chugging away, hitting the plywood above him and crushing it on its way up till it leveled off.

Any second now if he was lucky, if he'd calculated right, if the damn timer worked. If this freight engine lurching toward his lookout was slower or even more worn out than it looked . . . He held his breath as the train was almost on top of him, then sprang up and ran as the blasts went off.

Sprawled on his stomach, twisting around and peering

through the brush, he saw that the upper trestle had shattered and given way, the momentum of the train engine carrying it partway over the edge. It hung up there suspended like a wounded dragon, smoke in its belly, fire in its eyes, its rasping, squeaking boxcar tail following suit, jammed and suspended. Joining in were the wrenching, popping struts and shearing metal echoing across the chasm, along with the shouts and cries of the brakemen, Duke included probably.

Vin rose up, snatched the remaining length of snapped rope, and walked away.

It was a dang good explosion. As near as he could figure, he'd timed it perfectly. The screams and cries continued— finally a lasting impact instead of just firebomb rubble of unoccupied everyone-welcome churches and folks only talking about it afterwards.

All in all, he was having a good day. And he suddenly was real hungry. Pretty sure he could find a restaurant still open this time of day in Black Mountain downtown around Cherry Street. Heaven knew, he'd earned a little break.

CHAPTER TWENTY-EIGHT

"Fine, there was a derailing somewhere near Old Fort," said Skip. "That's too bad. And what does that have to do with us? What does that have to do with anything?"

"It wasn't just a derailing," said Miranda. "According to preliminary reports, train people were badly shaken up. One of the brakemen who looked out for hazards could have been one of the guys I saw the other day tossing rail ties behind Blue Ridge Biscuit—a railroad man named Duke, related to Vin Dupre, and at odds with one another."

"Now that is really a stretch."

"Maybe not."

They were down in Miranda's den, killing time, still waiting for Ed's call regarding the BOLO on an old green Chevy pickup and a bead on Duffy.

"Anyways," said Skip, restlessly cranking the lever of the vintage Daisy Red Ryder air rifle, feeding it BBs and pouring them out again, "what do you suggest? We drop everything, go to the spot, and help them investigate? Call up the train station authorities and offer them clues as to a Vin-Duke connection? What if it was sabotage by some loony tune who had a grudge against the railroad because he put in an application for employment and was denied?"

"Stop it. That doesn't help."

"You stop it. What have we accomplished the past hour besides playing what-if? All 'cause you happened to turn on a local TV station for no apparent reason?"

"I know, I know," said Miranda, as restless as Skip. She'd been trying to keep things sensible but had been unable to slough off this news bulletin possibly expanding the scope of things.

She took another bite out of her BLT along with other leftovers from the impromptu lunch she'd made for the two of them. She took some more swigs from her frothy bottle of Virgil's root beer when, at last, the phone rang.

She and Skip looked at each other but immediately realized it was Miranda's move, the result of her liaison with Officer Ed, if that's who the caller was. And that was indeed the name on the caller ID.

"Best I can figure," Ed growled over the handset, "from what I got from the patrol car down in Old Fort, it seems a vehicle answering the description was spotted crossing by Andrew's Geyser and then Mill Creek Road. But he lost him when he turned into an unpaved lane and a bulletin came in about a domestic dispute that was turning ugly back at Catawba River Road. You follow?"

"Past Andrew's Geyser, across Mill Creek Road, and up to an unpaved lane."

"I ain't giving you directions, girl. Just tellin' you where he lost him."

"Right, Ed, whatever. Thanks for the tip."

"Speaking of which," Ed cut in, "this was a tit for tat. You were gonna let me in on some big doings."

"Well, so far I only owe you for a lead that trails off somewhere. By the same token, I'll be in touch with the dispatcher."

"When?"

"When I'm closer to whatever is going down before or after sunset tomorrow. What I'm opting for is what Detective Dave Wall calls tangibles and your old partner Tyler calls tangibles and what you label the same. This could be worth your while, Ed, and I kid you not."

There was a lull. Then, picking up on her rushed tone, he said, "You're saying there's more to this than what happened to crazy Annie and your cousin and all. Plus a hit-and-run courtesy of a touring Harley."

She thought she detected a needy tone in Ed's voice. As if he couldn't cover up his anxiety about being over the hill and didn't want to go out having spent so much time shirking with nothing to show for it. No wife, no girlfriend, no promotion, no life.

Dropping the usual flip banter, Miranda said, "Soon as I close in on it for sure." On that note, she hung up and turned back to Skip, who had the air rifle cradled in his arms and a determined look on his face.

"Past Andrew's Geyser, across Mill Creek Road, up to an unpaved lane. Got it, let's go."

Skip headed for the garage door and it was all Miranda could do to grab his arm and stop him. "Hold it. We have to think about this."

"You think about it."

"But we can't just go off half-cocked. Even though I happen to know where Andrews Geyser is."

"Never mind then. I'll go myself, stop at the visitors center and get directions."

"Will you listen to reason for a change?"

"You listen to reason. I'll go find Duffy."

"Will you wait a second?"

"No. Item: So far I've cut out, hightailed it down here, and failed to keep track of Duffy. Item: Stalking a baddie, I got clobbered, froze in the dark while poor, slow-witted Annie covered for me and got assaulted. Item: I cut out again while Chris Holden got pummeled by the selfsame biker who clobbered me in the first place and snatched Duffy. I mean, good grief. We've waited, got the call, and this time, by God, this time . . ."

"Okay. While hanging back."

"What do you mean?"

Perhaps it was sensible Miranda humoring him. Then again, perhaps it was tomboy Miranda itching for action. At any rate, she blurted out, "The costume party up at the mansion on the hill. We were wearing army fatigues, remember? I was about twelve, you were about—"

"Eighteen. So?"

"The orchestra was playing 'Moonlight on the Wabash.' We were just checking things out from a safe distance and didn't know what to expect."

"Gotcha," Skip said, clutching the air rifle, scurrying onto the driveway and climbing into Miranda's SUV. "You're on. I'm riding shotgun."

"Hold it, why are you taking that old BB gun?"

"Hey, you never know. It's useful for creating a diversion.

Hitting dangling outdoor chimes and such just in case while your comrade drifts off to investigate."

"Taking stock. Hopefully adding a telling piece to the puzzle."

"Hopefully, at the very least, snatching Duffy."

Miranda got behind the wheel and let any further discussion go. She knew it was the train wreck that was the kicker. Things happening whether they pertained or not while she was standing still.

She hit the ignition and began to head east to the off ramp onto I-40, eventually crossing the crest at the continental divide and taking the swerving cascade downward to the Old Fort exit and something irrepressibly beckoning.

CHAPTER TWENTY-NINE

Miranda pulled over by the gravity-fed geyser, which had apparently become defective since the last time she was here.

"What are you doing?" asked Skip. For the past few minutes he'd been venting his frustration over the detours, fire trucks, and the like linked to the aftermath of the train derailment and the effect it might possibly have on Duffy's situation. At the same time, he'd been worried about what shape he would find the cat in, talking himself into the proposition that the brand-new litter bag this guy Vin had tossed in Annie's face was a sign Duffy was okay and in his custody.

"I repeat," said Skip, "now what are you doing? Why are you stopping?"

"I'm thinking," said Miranda, "do you mind? Instead of a geyser, it's trickled down to a waterspout. Meaning that not only would there be no tourist trade hanging about, the locals wouldn't be hanging about either. Especially on a weekday in the middle of the afternoon what with all this excitement in the background."

"Is this what it's going to be like? Can you picture a pair of Brit commandos doing this? 'I say, shall we discuss the pros and cons of this prospective raid a bit further? So many distractions. I'm having a deuce of a time trying to concentrate.'"

"Knock it off, will you, Skip?"

"I want to know why we can't get cracking?"

On one hand, she knew Skip was right. They'd come this far. As card players would say, you play it as it lay.

The only bone of contention involved the Daisy air rifle. Since there was no way she could handle Duffy no matter what state he was in, she'd have to play lookout while Skip scouted around whatever they found. If Vin was out and about, they'd have to call the rescue ploy off and go back to the drawing board. Or, if anything was amiss, she would have to fire well over to the side at anything metallic. The pinging sound, as Skip had noted, would create a diversion so they could hightail it out of there back to the car.

Which brought up another consideration. They had no idea how far it was down the dirt lane to where Vin was holed up. They had no idea how isolated it was or what in the world they'd encounter, let alone where Duffy might be caged up or if he was even there.

But, given Skip's prodding, she took off on the chance they'd come across something that at least put them inside the playing field.

It was less than half a mile to Mill Creek and the access across Mill Creek Road tapered off a few yards beyond. Except for a weathered, one-story frame farmhouse, there was nothing ahead but the designated dirt lane, more narrow than she'd envisioned, flanked by tall spindly pine trees.

She turned off into a bed of pine-needles and coasted until the car was partially hidden under a canopy of towering maples. The car would be out of sight from anyone traveling in either direction.

"Okay, gotcha," said Skip. "Commando rules."

Somehow Skip expected her to recall the maneuvers used on their approach of the mansion on the hill during days gone by, determining the logistics in their attempt to crash the party. Luckily, she did. "Same hand signals."

"You bet."

"If the coast is clear, you take a minute to look for Duffy. If we're up against it, we chalk it off and make for the car."

Miranda expected a forlorn look on that narrow face of his as he considered the latter, but all he did was break into an expectant grin.

And so, they took off without saying another word, as though the only thing that had changed was the nature of the raid.

In the lead, using the air rifle as a thresher, Miranda had two advantages. The first, as a seasoned hiker, swimmer, and a person who frequented the local fitness club, she had it all over Skip, whose only apparent exertion came by way of acting routines cavorting around a stage. Her second advantage was knowing which vegetation to avoid. And so, as she bypassed the patches of thistles and skirted around the thorny low-lying goldenrod, she glanced back now and then and caught glimpses of him gingerly picking thistles from his trousers and dress shirt. Why he chose to wear that same outfit was beyond her.

The thistles and goldenrod finally gave way to wildflowers, tall coneflowers, and waist-high grasses like waving fields of wheat. But there was still no sign of an old, green pickup.

She did note single tire tracks that left deep ruts in its wake on the dirt lane to her right. When Skip caught up and she pointed it out, all he could say was, "Got to be from the same mad biker's big fat Harley. Hope it and those double treads were headed away from here."

Moving on, they came to open fields on both sides of the lane blanketed with dandelions. And off in the distance, as near as either of them could make out, a grove of sycamores. Nestled inside the grove was the outline of a rusty old trailer, a van well off to the side by a huge oak, and a shed in the foreground back over to the left. But no old Chevy truck.

"I'm for the shed," said Skip.

"It's not that easy, Skip. We don't know who's in the trailer or the van for that matter or if either or both are occupied. We don't know who's going to come barreling in here at any second—biker or truck or both. We don't even know if this is a total wild goose chase."

"Commando rules, remember?" Skip dropped down into the beds of dandelions and grassy weeds and began to scamper forward. Following suit, as if she was twelve and ticked off at the same time, she found herself cradling the air rifle as they covered ground like extras in an old WWII movie.

Continuing in this way, Miranda gradually took over again and motioned for Skip to lie low. And there they waited. And waited some more.

Soon enough, a brawny figure in gray coveralls and matching T-shirt barged out of the trailer draining the dregs of a carton of orange juice. He hurled the carton into the weeds, yawned and flexed as if showing off his gym-toned biceps, peered down the dirt lane, and yelled, "What the hell, Vin?" He shambled around, slipped inside the back of the van, cursed, and slammed the van doors shut, temporarily sealing himself off. Once again, all was still save for the sound of buzzing insects all around them.

Miranda looked over to her left and saw that Skip had retreated a few yards and seemed frozen to the spot. She went over and knelt beside him in the grassy weeds. "What's the matter?" When he didn't answer, she said, "Tell you what. I make it T-minus five. If there's still no movement, I'll scout around nearby. You cover. Five bucks gets you ten, if Duffy's here, he's penned up in the shed, hidden, out of everybody's way."

"Right. I guess that figures."

"Okay, you set? Aim for the flanged pieces of metal way over the wires where they must have siphoned off electricity for the trailer."

"You think?"

"It figures if this is where Vin's been holing up."

She handed him the air rifle, but he still hadn't responded. "Come on, Skip. Snap out of it. What happened to all that talk about not being able to live with yourself? What happened to the great mission to rescue your beloved tabby?"

Skip took the air rifle. "Fine. Let me know."

Miranda sprang forward, bending low, telling herself that the street character seemed to be waiting on Vin's return and may be sacking out in the meantime. She scampered over in the direction of the shed to her left and stopped short as she came across a crumpled flyer. She unfolded it, glanced at the colorful header, crumpled it back up, dropped it, and kept going until she noticed traces of kitty litter in a direct line with a bin at the side of the shed door.

Reaching the shed, it took nothing to unlatch it and peer inside. At first it seemed empty except for some empty paint cans and rakes. Stepping inside, she tripped over a bowl. In the shadows of a far corner, a cat raised its hackles and hissed. As she stepped back, the cat ran around in circles, meowing like crazy. Keeping it from racing outside into the woods, she spun around, latched the door shut, and retreated. Keeping low again, she kept going until she reached the grassy weeds where Skip was crouching, still aiming the air rifle way over to the right where the electric wires dissolved into the tree line.

They waited until they were fairly sure the street character hadn't heard the ruckus inside the shed and all was still again.

Nudging Skip, Miranda said, "Your move, buster. I don't know what to make of all this. All I know is the cat is in that shed climbing the walls, and you've got two minutes to get off your butt and do the deed."

As Skip remained in the same fixed position, Miranda said, "I'm talking right this minute. Before Vin comes tearing back and the street guy comes busting out of that van to greet him." She snatched the air rifle out of his hands and used it to shove him out in the open.

For a second, Skip seemed caught in limbo. A glance at the van, the tire-rutted dirt lane, and back over to the shed snapped him out of it. With his gangly legs covering as much ground as possible, he cut through the weedy field, careened to his left, burst into the shed and, seconds later, emerged clutching the twitching cat around the back of his neck. Miranda expected him to stop and join her, but he sprinted past her, through the field of dandelions and low-lying shrub. Twisting around, she could make him out until he disappeared in the thistles and tall coneflowers. He was doubtless working his way back to her SUV where he could comfort Duffy in the shade of the ample back seat.

The low, grumbling sound of an old truck engine filled the air, and she had no choice but to follow in Skip's wake, keeping low in starts and stops just as she'd approached this hideaway. A few moments later, she lay in the grassy weeds as the old truck passed by, not daring to raise her head to make sure of the color and make. The slam of a car door and a bellowing "What the goddamn hell, Vin?" in the distance was all the proof she needed.

She took her time working her way back. Skip in the back seat, coddling and soothing the purring tabby, was a given.

The surprise came when she asked, "Okay, tell me. What happened to you back there?"

"Didn't you see the Confederate/American flag logo? Didn't you hear the guy's New York accent? That's the same van I saw, the one that picked stuff up and dropped stuff off at the ramshackle boarding house. The same one that followed me with Duffy sunning himself in the back window as we checked out Lower Manhattan around the World Trade Center. To check out St. Paul's Chapel, 'the little chapel that stood' and survived 9/11. It's like, after all this, it's all come around again."

For the briefest moment, Miranda had an inkling of the

bigger picture. In all the commotion, she realized that even the nasty New Yorker couldn't keep up with the exact way things were shaking out.

CHAPTER THIRTY

A short while earlier, Vin drained another cold bottle of Corona on the deck of the Veranda Eatery downtown on Cherry Street. The tingling sensation from the massive explosion stayed with him this whole time, which was all he'd hoped for. Why he'd thrown in with his uncle on this deal, whatever it was, was a question he still had no answer for. For the time being, let the Yankees up there mess about with however it all figured in. Much better to stay—what was it some older gal called him? *Mercurial*, that's what it was.

In fact, that was what attracted women to him. He looked young but maybe he wasn't. He seemed easygoing but then he'd clam up. He may or may not take it out on anyone who poached on his preserves. Then again, you'd never know, and he'd might as not drop the gal just like that. Like the words to that old song, "That's what you get for lovin' me."

He kept reminding himself he was absolutely the chill dude. The rebel looking to cause havoc when the occasion called for it and then sitting back, cooling his heels in the shade.

The sound of the screams filtered through his mind. So did the sight of the crunching, splintering metal, all of which had done him a world of good. What he needed was the promise of more. Some way to top it and keep it up, which he could see now was up for grabs.

He recalled an old Flying Wallendas poster in a roadhouse honky-tonk up in Madison County. The caption was "Life is on the high wire. All the rest is waiting." It became his motto as a kid. It was still his motto. The thing of it was, how could he or anyone keep on flying? Above it all? Make the greatest impact and slough it off till the next opportunity, bigger and better?

Then it finally came to him. They were using him, but when you came right down to it, he was using them. Best of all, he was the only one who could make things happen. Sure, Duke could ramrod if he had a mind to, but that was about all. Besides, among the wreckage, Vin had blown him clear out of the picture. So far they'd jerked him around and riled him to the point where this blast was on their heads and to his credit. Truth be told, he was in the catbird seat. Mercurial. Now you see him, now you don't. Just like always, only a million times better.

He could feel the smile spreading across his face. Now that he had nailed the long and short of it down for well and good, all that was left was to scope out and come to terms with this fuzzy scheme. From then on, the rest would follow suit.

Glancing over at the only other occupied table, he could tell the blond in the flowered sun dress was still nursing her ice tea, peeking up when she thought he wasn't looking. Reminding him that he could always turn on the country boy charm. Like he did with that perky gal while Duke was giving him a hard time. Testing her. Teasing her. Telling her all about the glory days of the Dupres. Seeing if he could get a rise out of her. Then being cool about opening for Bud and Travis this Friday when she called him out on it. Maybe he actually would open for Bud and Travis after this shindig was over tomorrow night. That is, after what he just pulled off, get it by his uncle. Call up those two boys and work his way in.

Why not? The way he was seeing things now, he could pull anything off.

This time when the sun dress gal caught his eye, she spoke. "You from around here?"

"No, ma'am."

"Just passing through, huh? Just like me."

"You could say that." He liked the look of her, not too old, not too young. Low syrupy voice, no accent. Maybe from the Midwest. His uncle said this operation would relay to the Midwest to boot. He'd have to keep that in mind.

He thought about Duke again and the surly Yankee who was probably back by now. He thought again about something he never considered, what they call repercussions. Something he'd have to answer for. Or erase, one way or another. Since it had gotten bigger, involved other people, other unknowns including that damn Yankee, there was no way of telling.

Except that he was above it all.

"So," the sun dress gal said, cutting through the silence, "how long do you figure? You sticking around, I mean."

Not giving anything away, he said, "I might have a gig at the Tavern this Friday. If you're still around."

"Folk music?"

"Kind of."

"Acoustic? Old favorites?"

"Not exactly."

"Original tunes?"

Vin nodded.

"Well then. Have I heard you on commercial-free or the Asheville station?"

"Could be."

He rose, left a tip, and gave her one of his forefinger salutes.

"What's your name?" she asked, hanging on to her syrupy voice.

"Just make it Vin."

As he left, he wondered whether it was wise to drop his name like that. What if someday it caught up to him?

Not a chance. Not the way things were going.

As he descended the wooden steps to the street level, he knew he had his work cut out for him. He was entering unknown territory. But, then again, there was nothing he liked better.

Though it was getting easier to locate the dirt lane, he'd never had someone waiting on him before who might try to hold him accountable; never had to skirt around fire trucks and sundry which he was the cause of. Feeling good about himself was tinged with more new thoughts. Like if it turned out that the Yankee had not only come back from his rounds but wasn't sacked out like he said. No matter how wasted the guy was from hightailing it down the whole eastern seaboard, he was bound to have gotten wind of the blast close by and all the commotion. So now what? Who had the Yankee been talking with? As if he didn't know.

It took a lot of skirting around and doubling back before he was able to ease into the dirt track. And, sure enough, there was the Yankee, waiting up on him. Sitting on the tail gate of the open van like a parent fit to be tied. Vin pulled in, jostling over the rutted track, veered to the left, and got out. The Yankee yelled, "What the goddamn hell, Vin?" In response, Vin tossed him the gizmo, turned away, and went inside the junk trailer. He got himself a cold one out of the squat little fridge, sauntered back over, pulled down his own tail gate, leaned back and waited him out.

Winning the game so far, Vin peered over his shoulder and took a deep pull from the frosty Corona as the Yankee called out again, "Guess who's been expecting you?"

"Figures," said Vin. "Where's he at?"

"Downtown Asheville, Haywood-Park Hotel, executive suite."

"Uh-huh. I'll look into it. And don't give me no more maps. I'll manage."

The Yankee eyed him for a time and then said, "Pretty cool, ain't you, for someone about to be thrown under the bus?"

"Oh?"

"Add it up, bozo, starting with you and your biker cousin blowing your assignment to nail down that radio clown."

Vin gave him a sideways glance but that was all.

The stillness that followed just hung there. For no reason, Vin got up, sauntered down to the shed, noted the crumpled flyer by the spilled cat litter, picked it up this time, and tossed it in the bin. He took another swig, pulled open the shed door and peered inside. Thrown at first, then nodding to himself, he latched the shed door and went back to his truck.

He had no idea what happened to the cat, but at the moment, it was one more waste of time off his list.

As he repositioned himself against his tailgate, on purpose taking his time draining the rest of his beer, the Yankee marched straight over, snatched the bottle out of his hand and tossed it into the woods.

"What is this? You think it's some kinda game? Blow up train tracks just for the hell of it? On your horse, pal. You better come up with something and hope all systems are still a go. You better pray you haven't tossed a wrench into the works and screwed up the trajectory. 'Cause if you have, I'm gonna personally take it out of your hide."

Vin moseyed around to the driver's side of the cab. He knew he had his work cut out for him to make his case and carve his niche at the top of his uncle's ramrod list.

The afternoon was wearing down by the time Vin was set to handle anything thrown at him. He'd only seen his uncle a couple of times when he dropped in unannounced at the old homestead. The first was soon after he blew up the moonshine hidden under the haystacks. Everyone thought it was such a mystery, but his uncle kept giving him a cold eye, his thin lips curled up in the slightest smile. And that's when Vin knew Uncle Lucian was a man of few words who appreciated how Vin kept everything close to the vest. There were a few other times as well, especially when Vin was around nineteen and set his first barn on fire. It was then, as his uncle peered under those dark glasses while the family was busy helping in the kitchen, Lucian said, "Someday I might call on you."

All this while, Vin had kept this last part firmly in mind.

As he veered off onto the downtown Asheville exit, there was something else to keep in mind too, but it was so vague Vin didn't know what to make of it. He recalled a few other times when he spotted his uncle alone at the dining room table, mulling over something while he played with some hand puzzle. Maybe it calmed him down or helped him to think. Once it was a set of cubes held together with a round pin he kept twisting this way and that, trying to make the colors line up. Another time it was three metal rings forming an atom or some such thing with a blue marble in the center. The trick was to take it apart and put it back together exactly the way he'd found it, with the blue marble in the center. When he had it down cold, his pencil-thin lips curled up in that strange smile of his and he put the whole thing back in his jacket pocket.

Vin let all this go as he found locating the hotel and a place to park required his undivided attention. Some half mile away and quickening his pace was not his style, but damned if he was going to add being tardy to the list of issues. He'd simply start right in once he got past Russ Mathews, who was bound to interrogate him first. Stood to reason given the fact that his uncle, as far as he knew, never cottoned to what they call preliminaries and Mathews was obviously the point man.

Skipping over any formalities went double for the way

Vin was dressed in his leather-fringed vest and all, compared with the suits he found decked out in jackets and ties lounging around the lobby, reading their *Wall Street Journals* on armless couches scattered around the shiny waxed floors.

He walked right up to the reception desk and told the skinny gal with the short, lacquered black hair that Mr. Clay was expecting him.

She flashed a disbelieving smile and said, "Mister Lucian Clay?"

"We're kin. No need to buzz and bother him."

When she still seemed like she wasn't buying it, he noticed the numbers flashing by the elevator, figured S stood for a high-priced suite, ignored Ms. Lacquered, and took the elevator to the top.

Sure enough, sitting on a padded bench in the foyer of a suite that took up the whole floor, heavyset Russ Mathews, walrus moustache, thinning gray hair, and all, worked on what must have been his umpteenth black cheroot. He appeared to be more than ready to quiz Vin before Vin took another step.

"Hold it right there, Dupre. This time you don't cut me short. This time you answer to me first and face up to this whole fiasco. Starting with this fly-in-the-ointment Skip picking up on the codes and blabbing it all over the airwaves, down to his run, to every freaking loose end, covering the entire screw-up to what you just pulled."

Though Vin still had no idea of what the Yankee called the trajectory, let alone anything about this dang Skip character, all he gave Mathews was, "What do you mean, the codes? And what do you mean, his run?"

"Never mind. Never mind all you don't know and never will know. Let's just say as a backwoods character, and Skip a fish out of water here, you only had to track him down. But you totally botched it. Have mercy, how screwed up can it get?"

Vin pulled back a few feet till Mathews simmered down a bit. Then he said, "Seems to me, it really don't make no never mind. Have you heard hide nor hair from him? Even when you had him stashed in the limo, seems he crawled away, still wanting no part of it."

"Now you look here."

"No, you look and quit jerking me around. Whatever happened, happened on your watch. My guess is you were put onto us Dupres to sweep it under the rug 'cause we were handy, 'cause we weren't on any Fed watch list. Countin' on Duke to ramrod, not knowing diddly that just like this Skip fella, he wanted no part of it. And working on me, not knowing squat that I wouldn't take to being treated like a damn errand boy. Not knowing squat about anything except for mouthing off behind a microphone."

Rising, his face reddening, mottled fists clenching and unclenching, Mathews hissed, "What makes you think you can talk to me like this?"

"'Cause if it's really about to go down, seems you'd best hightail it and get back in harness stead of fussing over some fool no-account and a trial run."

Chewing away on his unlit cheroot, Mathews seemed to be reaching for another comeback but came up empty. It might have been Vin's tone, or Mathews was far out of his depth and he knew it. Memorizing the Liberty Broadcasting System script (which Duke called "hand-me-down propaganda") was another reason Duke wanted no part of this. Which was why Vin had Mathews dead to rights. Mathews was only a mouthpiece.

Emitting a deep frustrated sigh, Mathews said, "Let's just say you're in for it and brought it all on yourself." Chewing some more on his cheroot got him nowhere. After another deep, raspy sigh, Mathews barked, "Stay put while I confer with the man."

As Mathews exited through the double doors leading into the suite itself, Vin gave himself high marks for getting through the first exam and began working on the second hurdle.

Ten minutes went by. Even through the tinted glass windows and Asheville skyline, Vin could see the late afternoon was clouding up. Which, in a way, was all to the good.

Mathews finally reappeared through the double doors, sat down on the bench, head bowed, and nodded.

Upon entering the huge suite through a brightly lit alcove, Vin spotted his uncle under a large glass chandelier. He was in all his glory behind an oblong dining room table. Same thin, chiseled features, dark glasses, dark suit and tie. No puzzles, but this time a shiny deck of cards which he cut twice, shuffled and dealt like a casino dealer. He proceeded to arrange the cards in four piles, one card face up, six face down.

Vin couldn't swear to it, but he got the feeling that he had until the end of this game, if not before, to come through.

And the way the cards were flipping around, he had no more than five minutes.

"We'll bypass how you took your time getting here," said his uncle in that same matter-of-fact icy delivery. "Plus, your stab at excusing the broadcaster sub from Indiana, the one who appears to have instigated this turmoil."

Another card flipped faceup on top of others that were facedown.

"Well," said Vin, "in any case, no harm done. No matter how many rounds of tag Mathews has been playing. Nobody but you knowing the whole plan, that is."

For a second his uncle stopped dealing, thought it over but gave Vin no sign he'd scored any points. In fact, he began slapping down the next set of cards and glared at Vin before he spoke. "And where do you get off, swiping more sticks of plastics than you were allotted? Raising all kinds of hell. Not miles away but close by. Where they're still sorting through the mess."

"That's right," Vin said, seating himself in a fancy wooden captain's chair, leaning back like an opponent holding a superior hand. "Including how in the world it happened, yards away from solid land and up on the trestle tracks. Not to mention timed so the engine would stop before the whole kit and caboodle sailed off. Not to mention it was my first try with a newfangled gizmo. Which I figure was my first and only test."

Receiving no reply, Vin carried on anyway. "How about how I firebombed those churches from Florida, Georgia, and South Carolina? Lying in the shadows, not giving off a trace. Never mind the dumb orders from Mathews, but this munitions man whose idea of practice was so lame only some Yankee peckerwood could dream it up."

His uncle paused in his card flipping. "And what is the pattern we're trying to keep under wraps till the optimum moment?"

Reaching back, recalling the word the Yankee used, Vin said, "The trajectory."

"Meaning?"

"Must be what comes before, leading to the one coming up." He wanted to toss in one by the World Trade Center. *Meaning without the one coming up, the whole thing's probably a shot in the dark.* Instead he said, "Meaning without me making it happen, there ain't gonna be no payoff."

"What isn't going to happen? What is the kicker?"

"Damned if I know," said Vin, springing up from his chair. "Which doesn't change diddly. I'm still a mystery. Nobody's come even close and you know it. Matter of fact, you could say you and me are two of a kind. Staying in the background, 'cept I take all the risks."

More than frustrated now, Vin continued, "You said I'd be up for the big time someday. Well I damn well figure that day has come. Which is the only reason you dropped everything and flew all the way down here. 'Cause everything is riding on it."

No answer as his uncle started placing aces above the cards in separate suits, drawing from a reserve deck, looking for lineups in diamonds, hearts, clubs and spades. Finally his uncle said, "Going off half-cocked won't do. Won't do at all."

"Well, if by now they ain't got a clue, they ain't gonna

have one. I'd say what I done has got everybody on edge and makes it that much better. Makes this whole operation that much better off. Keeping a threat in the air which, Duke says, is what Mathews is all about."

His uncle rose out of his dining room chair and left the room. Just as quickly he returned with a box labeled from a Broadway costume shop.

"What's this?" asked Vin, expecting Lucian to hand him the box. He didn't.

"If you really didn't slip up, if there're no leads pointing to that old beat-up Chevy of yours, come back first thing tomorrow and I'll let you know."

"Let me in on the big score, you mean."

"Let you continue."

Vin waited for something more encouraging in vain and left. Noticing that Mathews was still waiting out in the foyer working on another cheroot, Vin asked, "Cutting it kind of close, ain't he?"

"Figures whatever was bound to go wrong would rear its ugly head by the last minute."

"And who did he have in mind to carry out this last-minute deal if I blew it?"

Regardless of any no-smoking regulations, Mathews puffed away out of sheer frustration till he was sure the cheroot was good and lit before saying, "Nobody."

Taking that in, Vin took the elevator down to the lobby, gave the gal with the lacquered hairdo one of his forefinger salutes and made his way outside into the glare of the streetlights. The feeling he'd done good holding his own lasted all the way down the brightly lit city streets till he reached his old pickup. Then a nagging feeling he'd kept under wraps slipped to the surface.

What if Skip, that northern radio fella, had tracked down the shed where his cat was stashed? An orange stray deep in the boonies only he gave a damn about. But how could he manage—how could that happen? Some things in this world just didn't figure.

CHAPTER THIRTY-ONE

T hat evening, Miranda watched Skip play with Duffy down in the den, toying with slivers of tin foil attached to a piece of wire. It was good that the cat had stopped being skittish, came out from beneath the cot, and finally seemed more or less at home. On the other hand, given a window of some twenty-four hours when something awful was due to happen, there was no way Miranda could simply call it a night. Couldn't make do with surviving a stint at playing Commandos Strike at Dawn.

Even Skip had started in again, yelling at himself for freezing, wondering what would have happened if Miranda hadn't pushed him out there in the open. The van and the sight of that big guy who stepped out of the trailer had really rattled him. Coupled with the prospect of Vin Dupre—who'd shoved poor Annie against the garage door while he cowered in the shadows—about to return, the idea of both guys catching him in a vise had really done the trick. When he'd rushed to the shed, nabbed Duffy, and started hightailing it through the prickers and the brush, he felt like he could've kept going forever. Miranda telling him he did good under the circumstances caused him to momentarily drop the subject. But not quite.

"The aim," Skip said, "is not a pat on the back. If there has to be a tagline, when the smoke clears, one lady says to another, 'Who was that masked man? I didn't get a chance to thank him.' That's the objective. To come through and exit unsung."

"That happens in old movies. In old comic books. Now will you please drop it?"

"Maybe. If there was some way I could do better next time."

But they didn't have a productive next step on tap.

Skip came up with the notion of informing Officer Ed of the hideout they'd uncovered. After all, it was his tip that sent them down there. But Miranda quashed that idea. It was well beyond Ed's bailiwick—you don't go barging in without a warrant or probable cause (something her ex had duly impressed upon her). More to the point, they had no business trespassing and ransacking someone's shed.

And so, yet again, they were at an impasse. Only Duffy, at long last, was perfectly fine.

Miranda got to her feet, went upstairs to her office, and for the umpteenth time got in touch with Harry.

"No," said Harry, after asking how she kept coming up with this stuff. "The tips you've given me—whatever your source—don't provide me with any kind of pattern. Little nudges here and there but nothing imminent that's going to kick in by this time tomorrow. Nothing of national import. Moreover, you still haven't told me how the cat suddenly showed up. Said cat supposedly the be-all and end-all of this whole farrago."

"As it happens, one Ed Wheeler of the local constabulary sent out a BOLO, got a lead and . . ."

"And? What is a BOLO? And since when is Officer Ed Wheeler hot to trot about anything, let alone stray tabbies?"

"Never mind, Harry. All I ask is that you go over your notes coupled with my indicators and see what you come up with."

"As I keep telling you, nothing rings any bells."

"Look, I gave you a deadline. Deadlines are your stock in trade."

"Deadlines are based on a story that's going somewhere, replete with a lead, development, and the promise of a satisfying conclusion. Not dead-end bits and drabs. Not scatter shots in the dark. And while we're on the subject, may I remind you of Watergate and how much shoe leather Woodward and Bernstein wore out, how many months it took until Deep Throat told them to follow the money. Then some screenwriter had to come along, sift through mounds of material, and write *All the President's Men* to make it comprehensible. And you want me to come up with a through line in a matter of hours?"

"A hot lead, early on, by tomorrow. Which will still leave two whole days to . . ." She caught herself then and there. She had no intention of telling Harry she was directly involved, a prime player, or any such thing. She switched gears and said, "But okay, okay. Getting ahead of myself, only want Skip to have a little piece of mind. We'll just have to sleep on it. But I'd still like to factor-in Lucian Clay's background and a set of explosions coming this way from Florida, Georgia, and South Carolina."

"Oh, is that all?"

"And, while you're at it, did you happen to get wind of the train wreck outside of Old Fort?"

"No, I haven't."

"Come to think of it, let's not forget there's the stalking horse, diversionary measures, and the thrill of chaos as operative factors."

"Enough, Miranda. Give it a rest, will you?"

"Sorry. Yes, sir, I will indeed."

She hung up and reached for some means of doing just that. She'd heard that the purring of a cat was calming and therapeutic. Duffy had been purring like crazy. But his great adventure was over, all nine lives intact, and he could afford to purr.

Usually at this time of night she could count on the freight train rumbling by the old depot at the bottom of Cherry Street. But someone had even taken that away from her by blowing up the trestle.

Maybe if she and Skip hadn't come across that van with the New York plates and the Confederate/American logo, maybe if that creep with the tough New York accent hadn't emerged from the trailer, she could buy Harry's theory of dead-end inklings. But the proliferating pieces only served to corroborate Skip's plight in terms of what was going down.

And so, what do you do when you feel something has to be done, is none of your business, and comes down to you anyways?

All she was left with was the same hopeless cause that wouldn't leave her alone.

CHAPTER THIRTY-TWO

O nce again, Miranda was up bright and early before breakfast. She scoured the daily Asheville paper, listened to the local news on radio and TV, and could only garner the fact that the authorities had no leads in the rail explosion episode down in Old Fort but would welcome any eyewitness accounts of suspicious activity in and around the vicinity.

After they'd had their coffee and muffins and could do nothing beyond giving each other blank stares, Skip took off in search of pet supplies for Duffy. In turn, Miranda announced she was looking into a longshot that was so remote it probably wasn't worth mentioning. But they did have a window of two more days.

Saying that did nothing to lessen the strain of being at her wits end. The only other time she'd been at her wits end was the point when she was willing to try anything to fix her hopeless relationship with her ex. She had mentioned her predicament to her mechanic, Benjamin Watts. She told him she'd looked at the couples' compatibility problem from every angle and wondered what she was missing. Where had she missed the boat? Where had it all gone wrong?

Little had she known that burly Benjamin was also a part-time Unitarian minister for a tiny congregation off the beaten path in Swannanoa. All she knew about the sect was that it was a place where you went to question your answers. Pretty soon, Benjamin started talking about synchronicity, or a set of pointers that the universe sent out that you weren't picking up on. He mentioned things like broken glass, broken mirrors, and things like that which hinted at picking up the pieces, recommended discarding them in the dumpster and moving on. Going along with this notion, Miranda had started complaining about such things as worn fan belts (which was why she was at his garage in the first place). Then pushing it a bit, she had mentioned that her Bradford Pear tree was unable to withstand the last windstorm and had cracked open, the sealant on her driveway hadn't taken hold, and none of the hairdos she'd tried were getting her anywhere. So, she told Kim, her hairdresser, to lop it off and keep it short, which was her style anyway and fit her carefree personality.

"You see?" Benjamin had said, seemingly out of the blue. "It doesn't hold, none of it. What have you got going here except for something physical? Think about it. Synchronicity is the key. When all else fails, synchronicity comes along and rings a bell."

"You mean you're getting signs?"

"Exactly. In your case, the signs are telling you that you can't patch something up that ain't never going to hold. These worn belts of yours can be replaced, but I can't order a spanking new Dave Wall for you that'll foot the bill. He's always going to have no sense of humor. Always going to be hung up in his police work even if nothing is coming down the pike. He'll keep looking for trouble because that's why he got into law enforcement in the first place. It energizes him."

Recalling all this while driving over to Benjamin's garage on Blue Ridge Road, desperately needing a mental jump start, she tapped into something but for the life of her couldn't figure what. If straining her brain and doing her damnedest to be logical was getting her nowhere, why not give synchronicity another try? If it reframed things once, why couldn't it do it again?

As she might have guessed, Benjamin's first response was to defend his work. With his head under the hood of an old MG he said, "Don't tell me, Miranda. Your belts are near new, your SUV checked out fine. What is it now?"

"Synchronicity. Look, I don't have time to explain, I've beat my head against the wall, and I'm open to anything right about now. Tarot cards, crystals, feminist incantations—you name it."

"Are you making fun?" said Benjamin, coming out from under the hood.

"No, I swear. My on-again, off-again partner Harry is strictly logical which, admittedly, has rubbed off on me. But hard as I try, he's not buying my maximum efforts at being reasonable." She rattled off her dead-end clues as fast as she could and threw in right-wing propaganda and nationalism to boot.

"Well no wonder," said Benjamin. "You call that logic and reason?"

"I know, I know. But it could add up if I could break the code."

"But it doesn't work that way. You see this old MG I'm grappling with? It looks like it has a dual carburetor but is really fit for a motorcycle. All the parts under this hood including the motor, clutch, shift mechanism, and I don't know what all are recycled. They don't belong. This here is a '72 British racing green, which on the outside is all well and good. Except they stopped making them in 1980. The carburetor is leaking, the float doesn't hold, there are no part numbers, and I'm going to have to order dual parts from a California outfit that fabricates such things and hope for the best. You see, nothing dang well belongs. Any purist will tell you, you take care of it and keep anything foreign the hell out of the way."

"Is that what you tell your parishioners?" The second she blurted it out, she pulled back. "Sorry."

Benjamin cut it short the second he looked at his watch. "Got to get cleaned up and put on my calm and collected face for a board meeting at the church. The only reason you found me here was because this MG is like to drive me round the bend."

"And synchronicity?"

"Let's give synchronicity a rest for a while, okay? Let's turn it over to the metaphor folks, foreign parts to the importers, and do our best to keep everything where it belongs."

"All right. Thanks anyway. Didn't mean to interfere. Just call it a shot in the dark."

She left the garage with the uncanny feeling Benjamin had put her on to something. But she wasn't at all sure what, and the clock was ticking away. The best she could do at this point was send Harry a voice mail and ask him to nail down

Lucian Clay's political clout. And what in the world he had in mind on this cloudy day that would turn him on. She was driven by the vague clue of a bunch of foreign parts and things that didn't fit, with time running out in less than two days.

No matter how much he'd protested, Harry had taken a renewed interest in what might be going on apropos of the current political scene. Though he and Miranda had vowed to respect one another's personal space, he couldn't help wondering where she was getting these pointers. Perhaps it did have a lot to do with spending time with her cousin Skip, who'd come across all kinds of things during his short stint on a major network in Manhattan.

Her comments about a recent set of explosions heading this way and some blasted railway trestle outside Old Fort couldn't be dismissed out of hand. Neither did an attempt to shoehorn these occurrences into "a stalking horse and the thrill of chaos." Like Watergate, you couldn't dismiss anything that was percolating.

And so, while randomly making another stab at it, he discovered that Russ Mathews was back live at the old stand. Not only that, he seemed to be intimating that sometime after the sun set this evening, "there is a good chance things were going to take a turn for the better, as long as certain Southern moderates in the Senate finally begin to see the light. We'll be well on our way to taking back our country."

Harry had long since given up trying to fathom the ins and outs of the Do Nothing Congress. The current Senate majority leader was constantly refusing to bring a bill onto the floor even if it passed the House. The Speaker of the House was forever refusing to bring a bill onto the floor even though it had gone through some committee or other because some faction was certain to vote it down.

Even though Mathews had apparently returned last night after some involvement in Skip's plight according to snippets gleaned from Miranda, Mathews's current message was mixed in with the same old drivel about proposed bans on lawless immigrant hordes streaming into America. How it was high time to bring refugee admissions to a screeching halt and root out enemy cells lurking in sanctuary cities and that zero tolerance was the only way to confront the antics of weirdos becoming more and more brazen.

Harry had taken all this claptrap with a grain of salt. Like a throwback to the Civil War and the carrying on of warring tribes. It wasn't a matter of a difference of opinion—viewpoints weren't based on evidence anymore. Pundits like Mathews were using the term "alternative facts." Claiming conspiracies emanating from something called "the deep state," whatever that was. It was on social media. Drivel as bad as the stuff plastered over the tabloids at the drug stores and supermarkets.

Yet how many were buying it? How many closed their eyes to conclusive evidence in favor of following extreme right-wing claims?

Granted that Harry still knew next to nothing about Lucian Clay, it did make sense that someone behind the scenes may have his hand firmly on the till, capitalizing on all this percolating fear and anger.

As a shortcut to figuring Clay's clout, he tried using Wikipedia. But he only gleaned that Clay had served as a political consultant for far-right candidates in state-wide and national campaigns in the Deep South and Midwest. There was some vague reference to his being on the board of the Liberty Broadcasting System. There were references to his being a top strategist in a burgeoning current administration out to protect the homeland at all costs, an advocate of populist nationalism, and a person nostalgic for the 1950s and the days when women were content to take care of the home. A belief was attributed to Clay that history was cyclical and a new age was dawning. There was also speculation that Clay was born and raised in the Madison County northwest section of Carolina's Blue Ridge.

There was nothing to suggest that Clay had been a backwoods militia commander. But there was nothing to dispel the notion that Clay may have the current president's ear.

Moving on to the *Washington Post*, there was a leading news item about an upcoming bill and attempts by staunch conservatives to convince certain moderate Senators to quit riding the fence. Plus, an op-ed piece in the *New York Times* about Harper, the selfsame current commander in chief elected by the skin of his teeth, who had a pressing need to surmount his wishy-washy good-guy image and sign on to some tough measures to keep the country safe. To finally and firmly take charge.

The ultra-conservative author of the op-ed piece ended by posing this pithy question: What would it take to shake things up and get America back on track?

Try as Harry might, the weight of these implications could not be casually cast aside.

The circumstances were made all the more pressing by another item Harry came across in the news wire. It seems that President Harper had not only been in constant touch with his chief strategist, but Lucian Clay hadn't been seen lately at the White House. There was some rumor he'd been called out of town but would certainly return in time for the crucial vote on homeland security tomorrow evening.

CHAPTER THIRTY-THREE

Vin's plans to meet with his uncle at first light were cut short by the incessant rapping at the junk trailer's door. While straggling out to the front stoop in his pajamas, he came upon the Yankee's scrabbly, unshaven face and the costume box his uncle had displayed the night before, coupled with a thin laptop and a box of plastic explosives. All three items were plunked on the ground by the Yankee's work shoes.

Without giving it a second's pause, the Yankee started right in. "Your uncle caught an express flight to DC. from Charlotte. Got it?"

"No," said Vin, stifling a yawn.

"Like a shark, has to keep moving. Unlike you and yours, his moves are calculated, nothing klutzy and lame."

Before Vin could take in this latest putdown, the Yankee went on. "Plan A had Duke slated as lookout, keeping tabs on you. And if anybody needed a short leash, you're the one. Including the topper of wrecking the train trestle so there was no way Duke could put in for his usual day off."

Vin could have told him Duke wanted no part of this anyways, but Vin was more interested in the two boxes.

Predictably, the Yankee kept at him. "Which means, given your cockeyed, lone wolf, twisted farm boy routine, I've been saddled with making sure this time I've struck brain.

Because there ain't nobody on standby and everything is riding on this. Why your uncle's putting a plug nickel's trust in you is beyond me unless he's positive you don't want to be left holding the bag. Someday, somebody is going to have to explain how it came down to you and that backwoods loose cannon, Zeb."

It didn't matter the exact reason why the Yankee had it in for him, and there was no call to go into it and give him any more call to let off steam. All Vin said was "Hold it. Give me a minute."

Vin went back inside, warmed up some coffee, and got into his usual outfit, including his fringed vest and hand-tooled boots. All the while, the Yankee was outside telling him to get a move on, and where was it written that country boys had to be slow on the uptake?

The next thing Vin knew, the Yankee barged in and stood over Vin as he was finishing his cup of coffee.

"Like I said, bubba, giving you any space and leaving you to it is asking for it. Of course, this could be an act, but whichever way you slice it, it's all on your head and the clock is ticking." The Yankee reached inside his coveralls and yanked out another flyer. "I seen where you crumpled up the one I gave you. Well, this time you're gonna treat it with respect."

Pointing to the colorful, bold headline, he added, "This time consider it a gospel warning. You read me, hillbilly?"

Vin didn't at all like feeling hemmed in in these close quarters. He rinsed his cup in the sink, peered out the smudged window, and felt claustrophobic. "I do better out in the open." He stepped past the two boxes into the cool, early morning air.

"No dice," said the Yankee, right on his heels. "You're not shaking me and you're going to have to damn well listen up." Grabbing Vin and pivoting him around until they were face to face, the Yankee began reading Vin his marching orders.

"First off, you will check out the area designated on the laptop, then case it firsthand till you know it real good. You will make sure your screw-loose biker kin knows it just as good. You will come up with an escape route using him and his Harley."

Breaking out another one of those snide looks, the Yankee said, "If any of these instructions are too much for you, or if I'm going too fast, raise your hand."

"I got you."

"Phase two." He kicked the costume box. "You will practice wearing the outfit until you got it down cold. You will come up with something new to conceal the explosives, something nobody would suspect, not some dumb backpack or anything just as lame and suspicious. Since you've already got the hang of the trigger mechanism, you will return to the designated area and work out the logistics. Designated area and logistics, you copy? Just nod your head."

Vin didn't respond. The Yankee went on anyway.

"Phase three. You will put the plan in action to fit with the opening activities indicated on the flyer, which should peak around seven and payoff exactly with the action in DC. Plus, if you pull this off, we'll get wind of it back in the Big Apple too, exactly on time."

"How?"

"Never mind."

"You're saying an instant big payoff."

"What do you want, a blow-by-blow, chain reaction, change the course of history? You think I'm gonna trust you with anything if I wasn't forced to lay out the springboard? Give me a break, will ya?"

The more the guy went on, the more Vin was reminded of those old movies on TV he used to watch as a kid. Especially a couple where some Nazi war hero generals were plotting to get rid of Hitler. The plan was to leave a briefcase under the table of a big meeting Hitler was attending. One officer was to flip a buckle on the briefcase, excuse himself, and everyone attending would get blown to bits. The plotting officers would have saved the world. But each time Vin watched one of these, he shook his head. You never walk away and figure it's all going to work out. Sure enough, while the guy who left the briefcase was off somewhere to answer a phone call, some joker at the meeting moved the briefcase further away from Hitler to give himself more room and the whole thing was caput. Never while Vin was handling things. There would be a big impact because he would make sure of it.

He'd do it, watch it go all to smithereens, and then disappear. Not like at the railroad trestle when it could've been really something, with the whole train going over the edge, everybody including Duke screaming their heads off—instant buzz, way bigger than watching the moonshine splattering under the haystacks. Way, way bigger than the empty everybody-welcome churches. The kind of thing he'd always been waiting for.

"Hey," the Yankee said, "are you flaking out on me? I'll be damned if I'm going to repeat myself. I got to hit the road. Now, where was I? Oh, yeah. Check out the little modifications to the phone. Guess we should count ourselves lucky you tossed me the practice one instead of losing it or leaving it behind."

"Go on, will you?"

"Yeah, right. Strictly for coordinating the action, there's an LED flash that'll be seen easy from a block away for your biker pal. I repeat. Check out the preliminary on the laptop. Work it out with your boy Zeb so's you've ditched the outfit in the most conspicuous spot that's sure to be noticed and get your butt outta there at least a minute before the timer goes off. As soon as all hell breaks loose, call the DC number listed so it jibes with the optics, so it jibes with the breaking news every which way. As soon as you get off the Harley at the hotel, go to the front desk. You'll get instructions how to locate the safety deposit box with the dues you're owed for all four jobs. Plus the two Zeb pulled. But you blow it, you screw up, forget about calling any number. Forget everything. I don't want to know you, your uncle never heard of you, you're left twisting in the wind."

"But if I pull it off without a hitch?"

"How about this guy? He's got three empty firebombed churches to his credit, lost track of a hightailing clown, barely managed to cage a cat, and just now went off and blew up a train trestle that almost cost us the whole shooting match. And he's already thinking past this big one. Well don't. You screw up, we got us a short circuit, and the whole operation is shot. This country is shot and—" He broke off, then finished with "Never mind, we're through here. Wise up. Try for once to get a goddamn grip!"

The Yankee folded the flyer, shoved it in Vin's vest pocket, and reminded him that the instructions for wearing the costume piece were in the box. He didn't bother to say another word and headed over to the van, fired up the motor, and took off down the rutted track with not so much as a honk of the horn.

Vin couldn't help wanting to holler, "Don't never sell me short, Yankee!" But that wouldn't fit the style of a bona fide chill dude. Still and all, he damn well had to take stock.

Casting his gaze to the cloud-capped Blue Ridge, he realized Duke had been right. By going along for the ride and some extra coin, Vin had put himself in this potentially exposed position for the first time. Even though Duke had told him the Dupres were being used—including Billy forking over his van—because they were handy, Vin persisted despite the fact he and Duke had no use for each other. Had second thoughts and still persisted, despite having to put up with the likes of Mathews and this hard-ass Yankee. Kept in the loop, despite having to put up with Uncle Lucian treating him like he was still a little kid looking for a pat on the head.

But Vin wasn't actually in the loop. And all that was gonna change. First thing, after this hullabaloo was done and dusted, he would seek his uncle out up in DC and put things straight. Which meant he would have to get in front of whatever was going down. And then set himself up and be treated like the real ramrod.

Muttering "Damn straight," he unfolded the flyer and gave it a good glance this time. He noticed the rainbow heading and different skin tones and facial features of those pictured. It reminded him of making peace with the Cherokees as long as they stayed where they belonged—due west of here in their own territory. Which was why he hadn't cottoned to that breed he ran into at the Tavern the other day. But the mashup on this poster of all kinds of foreign and weird types was beyond anything someone who hailed from first settlers could cast a blind eye to. It still gave him no clear idea of his uncle's overall scheme, little Yankee church and all up north. But as the chill dude with a knack with explosives, he sure was itching to do his part.

Vin picked up the laptop, reached into the box of plastic explosives, grabbed the new trigger mechanism, and took them both inside the trailer. The latest rigged cellphone was bigger. The second he turned it on, the LED greenish light attached to the back of the phone lit up and cut through everything, making him feel like a scout in an old war movie signaling his platoon dug in over the hill to advance. It could easily do to signal Zeb from a block or two away through the glare of the Ashville street lights and headlights on a busy street.

He shut the gizmo off, turned on the laptop, and opened the first of two icons on the desktop—a video reel. A viewing window opened, bright and clear, that cut through the dimness of the trailer. From what he could make out, according to the date/time stamp, someone had taken a video of the scene in a park around twilight a week ago from a steep angle looking down. As the camera panned here and there, Vin saw that there was a large, flat play area where a few kids were fooling around with hula-hoops, Frisbees, and skateboards. They also had a variety of skin tones. The camera then focused on a bank of three levels made up of short walls of bricks topped by concrete fanning out, each level leading closer to the busy street beyond. A wrought iron staircase ascended through the middle of the three levels. A few foreign-looking adults sat on the first two levels, a scattering of them on folding beach chairs. The top level was cut off by large, leafy trees through which you could spot the busy traffic going by and the outline of a line of shops across the way.

Though the sights and sounds weren't much to go on, he got the point. He was supposed to imagine the first annual festival advertised on the flyer. More than that, he was to picture a three-tier outdoor theater filled to the brim with those foreign types looking down on whatever was going on on the floor level.

The other icon opened up a browser, the starting page showing a map with a route that would take him from the trailer to the park and a short getaway route to 1 Battery Park and the hotel. All of this what the Yankee called "a preliminary, Vin doing his homework."

Next, Vin looked inside the costume box. The typed instructions called for his wearing this "kaffiyeh, symbol of Arab revolt." The gimmick slowly began to come to him. His uncle once notified him that the Dupre clan didn't hold with foreign invasion. No unwanted Englishmen way back then—given the Boston Tea Party and such (dress up and blame it on the Indians)—and no undocumented immigrants ever. Nothing that threatened their traditional way of life. Which must be what Uncle Lucian had in mind that day he said someday Vin would be called upon. But Vin sure as hell never thought it meant being disguised as a foreigner to get rid of foreigners.

By noon, Vin found himself battling with the speedier traffic cutting in and out. A lot of things were pressing in on him, including the fact that he'd stuck to the mountains, hills, and backroads. Playing his country songs at little roadhouses, taverns and honky-tonks after dark. Totally avoiding the crowds that had spilled out at all hours and taken over the cities he wanted no part of.

After he maneuvered here and there and finally found a place to leave his pickup, he had to walk a good piece to get to this park. Once there, what he'd glimpsed on the flyer and on the video began to hit home. A one-arm Mexican was sitting on the second of the three-level brick tiers practicing a few licks on his silver cornet. A bunch of Hispanic kids were playing tag below on a flat cement circle that Vin figured would be the dance space. Kids who should've been in school along with other brown-skin folks who should've been at work or had nothing better to do were lollygagging around. Even worse, a couple of women snuggling up to each other seemed to be practicing their moves, as were an Asian-looking man and maybe a woman from Iran or some other Mideastern place. People that, if things were at all normal, didn't belong in the park on a nice, sunny, spring day around these parts.

The amount of foreigners was guaranteed to multiply in the next six hours. A humongous blast would scatter the whole crew and put a big bloody dent in it all. Helluva more of a buzz than firebombs, women and whiskey. Make him the cause of what the Yankee called changing history.

As easygoing as can be, he checked out the tiers, glanced at one of the lollygaggers, and made a mental note of the size and shape of the folding chair. Moving on, he made his way up the wrought iron steps in the center, slipped through the trees at the top and spotted a couple of tall, iron-mesh wastebaskets to the side, perfect for tossing away the outfit. None of that leaving the briefcase like the old plot against Hitler and hoping it would pay off down the road in five or ten minutes. Here the blast would take only a matter of seconds as he stepped off the curb.

A single step, that is, onto the street as the heavy traffic passed by honking their horns. Another glance over to the right and it wouldn't take much to signal Zeb as he double-parked his Harley for a minute by one of the plate glass shop windows.

It was as if the whole hullabaloo was meant to be. Zeb had no trouble with the traffic. He'd ridden with other bikers all over to rallies and such. He knew his way around so good it was nothing for him to put that other radio broadcaster out of commission. The dents were only minor collateral damage no matter how much Zeb went around the bend over it. All Vin had to do was mark the location of the park where he'd be stationed, and it could be set up with a quick call.

Nodding to himself, Vin spotted a little restaurant across the street where he could get a bite to eat. At least some ham and eggs to tide him over before taking care of the other few matters before the big show. After all, it was all cut out for him, a job that would take only a few minutes of his time.

Despite Mathews, the damn Yankee, and his super-cautious uncle, it really was just a walk in the park with nothing or no one standing in the way.

CHAPTER THIRTY-FOUR

A t around this same time, Harry had another idea. So far, he'd been dickering with the alternating charges and counter charges between the far right and the liberal progressives. That and Mathews newfound urgency while employing the same old hyped-up expressions like the breach in the castle walls, the tide is changing, etc. If you did happen to add Skip's and Miranda's contributions, there was also a stalking horse and references to WWII maneuvers and tactics.

There was also the deadline Miranda had been going on about.

So, what was actually slated to take place? This question led him back to today's Do Nothing Congress as legislation got stalled or never progressed out of committees, leading to more finger pointing. All the static he'd since given up on. All the hot air that was never brought to the floor for a vote.

So what legislation had been kicked around that was actually pending? What crucial vote regarding homeland security?

Tracing bills that had been modified over the past few months, he came across a notion of raising grants to Central America as a means of beefing up their own security and curtailing the flood of refugees seeking asylum, clogging up the borders with women and children. There were different approaches to handling the children of illegal immigrants who were now of college age facing deportation. There were travel bans from Middle Eastern countries. There were measures to block Mexican cartels from drug trafficking across Texas, Arizona, Southern California, and trickling through Canadian borders.

But which one had actually made it all the way and had any chance of passing and getting the president's signature?

Realizing the clock was really ticking away, he got back on the Internet news cycle seeking anything imminent. As luck would have it, he came across one item that might be promising, made a note, and returned to the legislature agenda for congress. And there, in practically no time, he hit upon it.

He dialed Miranda on her landline, found that she was in, and ran his findings by her. He underscored a right-wing sponsored bill to establish a comprehensive task force to root out subversive elements, including illegal aliens and anyone harboring them, plus homegrown terrorists in so-called sanctuary cities—all justified under the umbrella of national security.

"Okay, Harry," said Miranda, seemingly unable to take this all in. "Here we go again. What's the upshot?"

"That's it. The so-called impending deadline."

"But what about Lucian Clay?"

Harry groaned. "What more do you want? A chronical of his history and evolving philosophy? His belief that what goes around comes around in cycles? Déjà vu. Right now, he's back in Washington. He hasn't given me access to his agenda."

"Say that again."

"I don't believe this."

"Come on, will you, Harry? Do me a big favor and spell it out for us simple folks. Mention the cycles and how they figure in with what's going on right this minute."

The last thing Harry needed right now was to try to link his tracking with breaking news, but he reluctantly came out with, "If you had to link Lucian Clay's theory of history and cycles repeating themselves . . ."

"Go on."

"According to the hawks in the Senate who are more than impatient with their moderate colleagues still dragging their feet . . ."

"Yes, yes?"

"The sons of illegal immigrants are becoming radicalized. About to sow more chaos now that we've been allegedly naïve enough to continue with our open door policy. Thus, this impending vote on homeland security. Quite a leap, wouldn't you say? And, speaking of spelling things out, I still don't get what you're up to. You act as if you yourself had some stake in all this."

But there was no mutual disclosure forthcoming. She only said, "Thanks, Harry. I'll get back to you if this, at long last, pans out" and hung up on him.

For her part, Miranda rushed down the stairs, went into the den, erased everything on the dry-erase board, and stood back.

She was alone for the moment because Skip had gotten

so anxious with every passing hour, he'd made arrangements with a pet boarding service in East Asheville to take care of Duffy until this whole thing blew over. In fact, the more antsy he got, the more he entertained the notion that the nasty guy in the van may have set about to trace the cat's whereabouts the moment he discovered Duffy was missing. And/or Vin Dupre was the prime culprit, which was more likely, apparently just as nasty in his macho hand-stitched cowboy boots assaulting Annie—a guy who might also stop at nothing.

In any event, she welcomed Skip's absence because there was no way she could fend off Skip's concern over Duffy's safety and come to any conclusion as to the mysterious, dire plot at hand with time speedily slipping away.

She made a fresh list incorporating other things Harry had tossed into the mix. She underlined indications that Lucian Clay was a firm believer in historical cycles, but she wasn't at all sure where that would take her. She added notions of radical immigrants. By the time she was done, she was so beside herself, she didn't know where to take the jumble of pointers. It was like those connect-the-dot puzzles when she was a kid that would soon reveal the big picture. Only in this case, there was a smattering of dots, along with dots in a row, and a slew of missing dots. And nothing actually clicked into place.

As this quandary began to get to her, she took a break. She went into the garage, got out the new bag of seed earmarked for songbirds, ripped the bag open, and went out back. She filled the new bird feeder with the anti-squirrel shut-off mechanism, spilling some on the ground in the process, and waited in the shade of a dogwood tree.

It was the old saw about finding an outlet that gave your fevered brain a break, and then returning to the problem at hand with fresh eyes and a fresh approach.

She gave it another few minutes, but no songbirds arrived or even a pesky squirrel eager to try out the new squirrel-deterrent model.

Back in the house, deciding whether or not to make herself a bracing cup of Kenya AA coffee, something finally came to her. It all had to do with the sporadic cat rescue and centered on the crumpled flyer she'd glanced at just as she was following the trail of cat litter to the shed in the boonies. An image which was just prompted by a little spillage of bird seed.

She got on the phone, got hold of the Asheville Chamber of Commerce, and asked if the First Rainbow Diversity Festival advertised on the flyer was still on for this evening. A lady with a syrupy Southern drawl said it was, but the organizers only got the permit after they'd finally agreed to the caveat.

"Meaning?" Miranda asked.

"No protests. It was all understood, mind, but still and all, now it's hunky-dory official."

"Protest over what?"

With a voice getting even more dreamy, the lady said, "The big vote I expect. If I'm not mistaken, that is."

"In congress? In the senate?"

"That's it, darlin. Seems our ethnic folks and such don't take kindly to Asheville being called a sanctuary city harboring hordes of illegal immigrants. Don't take kindly to being called anything special at all. Just live and let live as always."

"So there'll be . . ."

"Crowds, music, and dancing, I reckon. Lots of cameras and reporters to boot. But no speeches, no ma'am. From the look of things, you'd best arrive early if you've a notion to attend."

As Miranda was taking this all in, the lady said, "Well now, don't mean to rush you none. Whatever you decide, you be sure to have a good day, you hear?" Her goodbye and the click of the receiver was as soft as can be.

It was back to the dry-erase board, more notations and something Harry mentioned about senators still riding the fence. When Miranda got back in touch with Harry, she immediately asked about the holdouts.

"Good grief, Miranda. What do you think it's going to take for any one of them to get off their backsides? Special session or not, the passage of the revised bill hinges on the foot-dragging four, making it the longest shot among long shots. In other words, Miss Davis, don't hold your breath."

"Uh-huh." Jumping right back in, Miranda asked, "Tell me, which states are the senators from?"

"One who hails from Ocala, if memory serves, and the other three from Georgia, South Carolina, and North Carolina."

"Right. Now then, so what if this was all coming to a head in our own bailiwick?"

"In your dreams, Miranda."

Miranda gave him another "Thanks" anyway and rang off.

She hurried back to the dry-erase board and noted the firebombed empty churches in Georgia and South Carolina as well as the one in northern Florida that might very well do the trick, let alone another that possibly sprang up from here skipping over to New York and that chapel—the very iconic "little chapel that stood" she recalled as she jogged her memory further. The symbolic church by the 9/11 World Trade Center that once a year on the anniversary date was always cited as a beloved emblem of American resolve. The church Skip unwittingly was eyeing with Duffy in the back window while the nefarious van tailed him.

With her mind clicking away, she also recalled her Unitarian mechanic Benjamin Watts's tussle with an old MG and parts shoehorned in. Foreign parts that didn't belong. A thought which led her straight to tonight's diversity festival smack dab in western Carolina, plus a relay up and over to Manhattan where Skip had possibly been followed by that selfsame, surly driver. The one who'd yelled in that backwoods clearing "What the hell, Vin?" Or at least one of his ilk in cahoots with this whole scheme.

Maybe she was spinning her wheels, really losing it this time—but then again, maybe not. If only she could come up with some graphic pattern, a complete set of dots that clearly nailed what in the world was going on.

While she studied and altered her list, Skip wandered in muttering, "Safe and sound, under state-of-the-art lock and key." When Miranda failed to respond, Skip added, "Thanks for asking. But there is no way anyone is going to get to Duffy before D-Day has come and gone and the smoke has entirely cleared."

After the next pregnant pause, Skip too began to peruse the dry-erase board, noting the changes, asking for the source, joining in so the two were like math students attempting to solve an impossible equation.

Suddenly, before she could stop him, Skip took the red marker out of her hand, circled the word *cycles* and *what goes around comes around* and began erasing and making another crude drawing of the United States. He stood back when it was complete.

"And what do you think you're doing?" asked Miranda.

"Wait a minute, I think it's coming to me."

He attacked the sketch of the crude map and made dotted circles around it. "That's it. Don't you see? Don't you get it?"

"Are you kidding?"

Undaunted, Skip carried on. "I've been so busy dodging the bullet and playing hide-and-seek it never dawned on me. When I listened to Shep Anderson as a kid, he used to reminisce about World War II stories when he too was a kid and this fearmonger Walter Winchell was broadcasting from the very exact New York radio station. Back in Indiana, slipping under the covers with his crystal set, it got so bad that Shep began wondering if there might be enemy spies everywhere, maybe even hiding in the corn crib. So, here is Mathews doing a riff on Winchell and me doing a riff on Mathews, not realizing it really was coming around again."

Making dotted lines crisscrossing the country joining the circles, Skip went on, speaking even faster. "Winchell, you see, kept hollering about the Axis powers threatening to invade from all sides. Mathews does the second coming of World War II, and I'm picking up fans from old insomniacs who remembered. But the threatening calls coming in came from guys who, unlike me, knew it was code. Fully believed history was cyclical and coming right back at us. The circle was unbroken, the aliens were out there, it was déjà vu all over again."

"Fine," said Miranda. "But could we slow it down for a minute before I go into brain lock?"

"Not when it's up to us lightfoot lads and rose-lipped maidens. Who else is in a position to decipher imminent clues like D-Day and a stalking horse?"

"Even if we could decipher it, what do we do then?"

"All I know is Winchell yelling over the air waves to round up the foreigners and—"

"Mathews saying we've got to reconstruct America. Make it safe and sound with our own kind."

"Bingo."

Skip got absolutely nowhere at the dry-erase board. Returning to Miranda's side, he said, "Okay. First rule of life. When all else fails, you improvise. Boil it down. Who, what, why now, and so what? I say we opt for the gimmick: the stalking horse and who's going to carry it out."

"A scapegoat, you mean. Something in disguise to get folks all riled up. In this case, four senators, duped at last. Champing at the bit to join their colleagues and clamp down on dire threats to national security."

"Senators?"

Ignoring him, Miranda declared, "The stalking horse has to be a disguise the perpetrator can hide behind to keep from spooking the rest of the herd."

"What herd?"

"The foreigners. The diverse celebrants, of course. So what can be done between now and the next five hours to stop whatever dreadful thing is in store? Who has what in mind, and how is he or they going to go about it to ensure the bill gets passed?"

Completely stumped, Skip hollered, "Okay, I'll bite. What bill? What in the world are you talking about?"

"Later. Right now we need a stopgap to foil who, when, what, and how. And who but our very own Officer Ed is wavering? If I can talk the talk, be convincing, I can hand him the ball. He can then work it through law enforcement, and we can stand back in reserve."

Still stumped, Skip just stood there motionless.

"If I can play it right, we can still close the deal. Put aside all the sputtering and pretend I've been steadily connecting the dots and now have it down cold. Have earned my stripes and can talk to Ed about reconnaissance and the Liberty Broadcasting System."

"Who, from all indications and in case you haven't noticed, are relentless and highly professional. Professional reconnaissance requires you to fly over, take soundings, take out any resistance. You then set up installations, your stalking horse or whatnot. You set things up so that all systems are go for—"

"D-Day. You get the cigar, the brass ring, and the old Skip I used to know award. Now if once, just once, the perpetrators would just hold still for a minute."

"Before they do what, pray tell?"

"Oh, didn't I say?"

"No."

"Ever hear of the Diversity Festival in dear old Asheville slated for this very evening?

"Of course not."

"That's because, my dear, it's the very first gala of its kind."

CHAPTER THIRTY-FIVE

V in walked up and down congested Patton Avenue in downtown Asheville in order to make absolutely sure. Then walked behind Prichard Park and came across a long building marked Art Station, found a slot between the back corner and a dumpster wide enough to squeeze in his pickup. Since there were no hours posted at the front of the building, nothing to indicate it was operational on this early Wednesday afternoon, he figured he could stash his truck here with no one the wiser. Afterward, after he'd done his worst as folks scattered hollering and screaming a few minutes after seven, and after finishing up his business at the hotel, he could have Zeb drop him back off, squeeze into his truck and take off for Old Fort and the trailer. Again, as ever, with nobody being the wiser.

But he still wasn't sure of the logistics right before the explosion.

Walking around to the front of the Art Station, he saw that there was a good twenty yards between the sidewalk and the park, which made this side of the park the entryway. Few would want to enter from the curb by the traffic on Patton way on the other side and slip through the trees by the metal trash cans, walk down the top tier and the wrought iron railing, looking to see if there was any space left to sit or put their folding chairs.

So he reconfigured the whole setup from this entrance way. Crowds of all stripes wandering in at around six thirty, cameras likely already in place atop the huge flat boulders on both sides. Cornet players, drummers, and whatnot set up on the first tier and below on the edge of what Vin labeled the concrete dance floor.

Which meant, as it was filling up, dancers and such would be approaching and taking their place on this flat, oblong surface, followed by the musicians as older folks squeezed by them and up with their camping chairs to the second and third tiers on both sides of the aisle. Which meant that he needed to get his camping chair positioned smack dab in the middle, leaving only one tier higher to navigate as he exited, passed through the trees, signaled Zeb down at the end of the block, hit the clock, shed the outfit into one of the trash cans as traffic zipped by. Then hop on the Harley before anyone knew what was happening, meshing with the humongous blast taking out dozens as the TV camera guys on their boulder perch took it all in, posting it back to their stations and whatnot, in time for one of those "We interrupt this broadcast to bring you . . ." And then the relay to some spot in New York the Yankee mentioned was some kind of kicker.

Taking this all in, he stood still at the entrance, paying no mind to the cornet player and two giggling little girls passing him by. The overweight brass man was grinning away, wishing Vin something in Spanish or with some accent Vin couldn't place, Vin still being too busy with the pictures in his mind to reply.

He could see himself for once taking in the results of his work, watching it up close on the hotel TV bar screen, then collecting the keys from the front desk to the safety deposit box, getting his due and driving back. Followed by ambling into the Tavern in Black Mountain a day later, talking Bud and Travis into booking him and slating him first. Or, failing that, turning on the easy country boy charm till that feisty gal manager let him front anyways for the Friday night duo, featuring his best down-home songs. If and when anyone mentioned the humongous blast at Prichard Park and all the casualties, he'd say that all the while he'd been polishing his act down in a clearing in the woods by his old camper and, truth to tell, hadn't heard a thing.

After that, during the lull, he'd ditch his old truck, buy his airline tickets, and kiss the junk trailer goodbye. Track down his uncle in DC or wherever and take his rightful place as chief honcho in charge of stirring things up.

As the daydream tapered off, he eased away from the park and headed back to his pickup, reminding himself he still had three more things to take care of.

Vin certainly didn't figure on Zeb giving him a hard time the second he reached him on his cell.

"Don't mess with me, Vin, pulling my chain again. I tell you, I have had it."

"I am not messing with you. Just simmer down, no worries."

"Now where have I heard that before? First, it's the rebel

yell, pride of the Dupres, Duke in charge, no worries. Then it's not exactly a rebel operation, Duke's backed out, some mouthy Yankee name of Mathews is calling the shots."

"I know."

"You know? Did Mathews play you like a fool? Have you swipe a damn cat and then take out some beanpole fella twice? Will that do 'er? Oh no, oh oh oh no. When Mister Beanpole scoots out of a limo and away in all that traffic, I get the topper—a nod from Uncle Lucian to Mathews to take out yet another Yankee gunnin' the throttle full tilt. And my Harley ain't been the same since. And now you want me to—"

"Let it ride. Piece of cake from now on. I'm telling you, Zeb."

"Oh yeah, fat chance. What kinda rinky-dink outfit is this anyways? You know what they say. You want to make the Almighty laugh, tell him your plans. What in hell is this all about? I swear, I am taking off for the lost highway where nobody can pull my chain ever again."

"Ain't exactly pulling your chain. They got their reasons."

"About the right hand not knowing what the left is doing and all that horse pucky. In case one gets caught and forced to rat out the others. Talk to me dammit, Vin. Let me in on it or plain forget it!"

But Vin had no intention of letting Zeb in on it. No telling what he could do, who he would tell, at the rate he was going. Instead he promised to fill him in on what the great impact would be the second it all went down and Vin relayed his simple job following the green signal during the timed getaway. Right afterwards, getting hold of his severance pay in the bargain from the safety deposit box in the hotel. But even that made Zeb start in again.

"All the same, one more fool fandango and just guess what'll happen."

Vin didn't have to guess. He knew full well. Everyone in Madison County knew what happened when the Black Knight got really riled. He'd go berserk. Run roughshod over anything or anyone in his way.

"I hear you," said Vin.

"Then on your head be it."

For emphasis, Zeb banged down his cellphone so hard, Vin wondered if he busted it.

Tooling back down I-40 east as he kept to the right-hand lane so the semis and fancy new cars could pass him by, being the slowest vehicle on the road began to get to him. It put him in mind of how the territory and the stakes had expanded. Like having to drive the highways instead of the backroads to firebomb those churches. The congregations a jumble of folks it had always been easy to steer clear of. Strangers from parts unknown. Foreigners speaking fast and funny, showing him clear as can be things were getting way out of hand. And now Asheville, where it had spilled out weirder and more mixed up than ever he could've imagined.

On the other hand, it was the very reason he'd been handed this opportunity. On nobody's wanted list, person of interest, or someone the Feds should keep a close eye on. He didn't exist but was about to be smack dab in the center of things. Causing what they called collateral damage. Making every foreigner pouring into this country think twice. And making the ones already here dying to go back to where they came from. Providing Vin ten times more fun was the chance to use the very latest equipment.

"Oh, oh," he sang to the tune of the old Neil Young song, "the damage done."

Hell with Zeb anyways. He could have his damn lost highway and welcome to it.

He took his time eyeing the folding camping chairs at the Wilderness Shop just east of Black Mountain. The perky little redhead kept offering her assistance, but he kept brushing her off. He did it offhandedly and friendly like, not to leave any bad impression but not wanting to get into any specifics that might come back on him afterwards. He reminded himself to leave her while flashing his hey-you-never-know smile and his forefinger brushing his brow goodbye. Keeping the promise and the mystery going that gals liked so much. It always struck him how dumb it was to come on strong and tip your hand. That killed the mystery and what really turned women on. What that lady had called *mystique* along with *mercurial*.

Scuffing here and there, he settled on the sturdy chair with the steel frame and blue canvas back, seat, and deep-hanging side pockets. Each pouch was about two feet wide and twenty inches deep—perfect for three full-sized plastics on either side. He reached down and tugged on the Velcro tabs that made fastening the pockets a cinch. At first glance, nothing would give away what was hidden there. It could be tanning lotion, soft drinks, a collapsible umbrella, a Thermos—no telling what or how much.

Folding the chair up and following the redhead to the checkout counter, he got set for the small talk that was bound to follow.

"That your old pickup out there?" asked the redhead. "Still runs, does it?"

"Yup."

"Still holds climbing up the mountain passes?"

"You bet."

"All these years?"

"Yes ma'am."

"Haven't seen one that old. Golly. What must it have been through all this time?"

Vin thought for a moment and came back to the words of one of his old songs. "Hard travelin', hard ramblin', hard gamblin', Lord."

She paused, gave him one of those come-on looks and said, "Hey, you know something? That could make a good country hit."

"Hmm? Maybe I should give it some thought."

Another look as she bade him good luck. He gave her a forefinger flip and a "see you around," tossed the folded chair into the flatbed behind the cab, secured the tailgate, and was soon heading for the hidden clearing.

Back in the trailer, sitting on the sprung couch, he opened the costume box and stared long and hard at the oversized checkered black-and-white shawl. Then he read the note that only told him it was called a kaffiyeh and was a symbol of Arab revolt circa 1939 as WWII was revving up and was a po-tent symbol still today. Which, at first glance, meant nothing to him. The jumble of types he saw at the park wore nothing like this, and neither did those in the photos on the flyer. So, in a way, the shawl fit right into the mixed-up diversity thing, but in other ways it didn't. At any rate, he just keyed on how to wear the dang thing.

It took him a whole bunch of tries. First you were supposed to fold it in half to form a big triangle. Then you held the folded side to your forehead with the left side short and the right side long.

But it kept getting frustrating as he tried to tuck the longer end under his chin, pull the shorter side across his face like a mask exposing only his eyes, secure both ends behind his head with a knot, the rest of the material flowing behind his shoulders.

He riffled through the box and came up with an old movie poster of *Lawrence of Arabia*. The actor had blue eyes like Vin himself and was also trying to pass himself off as an Arab stirring things up. But all they had back then around the start of World War II were rifles and sticks of dynamite and fuses you lit with a match. The movie itself, which he once tried to watch on TV, was too long. And besides, this Lawrence was always carrying on and showing off. Vin had to keep a low profile and skedaddle out of there before anyone noticed. Or, the thought just occurring to him, were those who survived supposed to have noticed him, so as to point the finger at homegrown terrorists in disguise or some such thing?

That was the trouble with dealing with Uncle Lucian. He played his cards so close to the vest that, as the Yankee said, if you screw up, he don't want to know you.

Anyways, by the time he got back to the hotel TVs, he'd be able to get a handle on what this whole scheme was about or at least have himself a number of theories.

More stabs at it and in time, he got pretty good at tying the thing right. He put the shawl away for a while, got out a full pint of Jack Daniels from the stash he'd bought from a package store up in Madison County, and strolled outside. But just when he was starting to feel pretty good about things, he came across some cat litter he'd spilled, like Hansel and Gretel bread crumbs leading their way home. Except these crumbs led to the shack where the tabby had been kept shut-in tight.

A cat he was supposed to keep cooped up. A cat who didn't let itself out.

As the liquor started to do the trick, it also prompted him to retrace his steps and wonder when he might've slipped up. Maybe, like the plot to blow up Hitler, something wasn't figured on. Funny how some no-account details can stick in your craw.

A couple more good swigs and his worries began to ease. The cat was just a wild, hissing stray and wasn't fit to be looked after. Mathews had no call to saddle him with its keeping. It had nothing to do with plans to change the course of history like the Yankee let on. Nothing to do with turning the tide back to where things belonged.

CHAPTER THIRTY-SIX

A short while before, holding forth down in the den, Miranda had been working on Skip to come up with a little white lie. But Skip kept insisting everything be above board, as if the whole operation pitted the forces of good against the Axis powers of evil.

"But that's not what happened, Miranda. I grabbed Duffy and ran."

"I know that's not exactly what happened. But Ed will want to know how come you just lucked out. Harry still wants to know how you got your cat back, while making sure I've been hanging back, playing it safe."

Skip hesitated. "Okay, you're telling me that even though Officer Ed supplied you with the clue about the old pickup, we had no business being there. It was trespassing around the time and near the location of the railroad trestle bombing, and it will open up a whole can of worms with time running out. And we need Ed because . . ."

"We have no clout. And who else are we going to recruit in the next few hours? Who better than a local cop who needs to make up for all the times he's turned a blind eye? Who else'll see this as a last chance to redeem himself before he's put out to pasture?"

"You're saying he's hungry."

"I'm saying he's starving."

Skip stalled a little more, running the pros and cons to himself and finally said, "All right. But after the smoke clears, you'll at least explain this crucial Senate vote you say is hanging in the balance."

"Fine."

"And how in the world it all links up with the flyer you came across by the shed where Duffy was locked up, and this big diversity to-do that's going down tonight, and a string of bombings that—"

"For now, call it a right-wing conspiracy to shake up a handful of conservative senators so they'll get off the fence and pass some bill to root out and boot out foreign terrorists."

"Lurking in our midst, you mean? Like Walter Winchell during World War II, scaring everybody about a fifth column of enemy agents plotting to strike against the heart of our democracy?"

"Yes, yes, words like that."

Nodding, Skip peered up at the ceiling like a kid at a spelling bee making sure he had all the syllables correct. He turned back and said, "Okay, how does this grab you? Following Ed's lead, you asked around. After all, Old Fort is a little town and everybody knows everybody, right?"

"Right," said Miranda. "In no time, a chatty guy at a grocery store put me on to a cat lady who heard that something fishy was going on down the very dirt lane where the old pickup was spotted. There was a strange van with New York plates, plus motorcycle tire tracks and . . ."

"A crummy trailer siphoning off electricity from a main power line. Not to mention a poor kitty locked in a shed."

"So, in the name of the Humane Society, the cat lady

snatched Duffy and put out an all-points bulletin via the grapevine. Almost immediately, the grocer called me, and voila."

"Plus," said Skip, "plied you with news about the van that had been dogging me, and the biker who'd snatched Duffy from me in the first place. Plus, the pickup and the frustrated guy in the hand-stitched cowboy boots I spotted earlier while cowering in the shadows. Satisfied?"

"That'll do it."

Skip glanced at Miranda and said, "So, now can we toast the regiment and get this show on the road?"

"No rose-lipped maidens and lightfoot lads till I enlist the man in blue and someone, somewhere sounds the all clear."

Skip nodded once more and pulled back, lingering, gazing off into space.

Miranda was no psychologist, but she could tell from the strained look on his face that it had finally caught up to him. His war to retain his childlike illusions while skirting hard, slippery reality had all come down to this very showdown.

Taking that into account, Miranda patted Skip on the shoulder. Then, promptly sent Harry one of her cut-to-the-chase propositions.

If there's a local link, this bailiwick coupled with greater national implications, will you cover it? One of two words will do it. Yes or no?

Less than five minutes later, she got her reply.

If you'll sit tight and keep out of it, it's a yes.

In that moment, Miranda couldn't help recalling her mom's patented admonition: "No more nonsense. Hold still and behave yourself, young lady. Remember you've got a birthday coming up if you want to receive any presents."

It was that spring when she'd just turned twelve and Skip dropped in out of the blue with a bottle of pricey crème de menthe topped by that very same regimental toast.

Miranda was all but convinced she was primed for any contingency no matter how many second thoughts Ed came up with. Not only did she have a number of years behind her in nailing down clients getting cold feet before making a decent offer, she'd made a coherent case of that loopy poison pen fiasco and impressed all and sundry as a material witness. A feat which even got Skip's attention up in the Big Apple and had a lot to do with this outlandish predicament.

True, she'd done a lot of floundering this time. But, she kept telling herself, she was set and loaded.

At last, the two of them found themselves alone on the creaky porch at Dynamite Coffee on old US 70. Ed had long since finished his shift at the station and was sporting a John Deere cap to cover his bald pate, his pasty face still shaven but his denim work clothes were completely out of character. Even though his outfit should have enabled him not to stand on ceremony, Miranda still had her work cut out for her.

Fielding his next bout of deflections, Miranda pushed even faster and harder this time. "What do you think I've been doing the past five days? I've got Harry on it. Filled in the blanks from Skip's ordeal. Got pointers from Arlo at the Tavern, bluesman Chase, and even glommed some leads from Trish the cleaning lady."

"From who?"

"Never mind. The powers that be have completed their

reconnaissance, taken out any resistance, doubtless have their stalking horse in place, and are set to strike."

"Cut the doubletalk, girl. What do you mean, taken out any resistance?"

"How about yourself, if you think about it? Skip comes to you and, in typical fashion, you don't do squat. So much for the Black Mountain police force. So much for clearing the decks as far as any opposition is concerned."

As if taking his cue from the weather, which was running hot and cold—now sunny, now cloudy and breezy—Officer Ed threw another monkey wrench in the works.

Sliding his mug of coffee to one side, Ed came up with "Not so fast, not so fast. Aside from this shady plot you've been cooking up here, what's in it for you? Don't tell me you're all fired up out of some kinda civic duty all of a sudden. I mean, let's get real here. You're a broker. What kind of commission you gonna get from your cousin from wangling the return of his kitty thanks to some cat lady horse pucky you're throwing at me? What's your payoff?"

Miranda might have known he'd pull this one. But the broker reference was apt. After all, it was common knowledge what she would put up with for the sake of keeping her brokerage going.

"I didn't ask for this. I even tried to slough it off, plying myself with thoughts of a birthday hike, taking a break in the Smokies, leaving it all behind. But this threat is hanging over me like a time bomb."

Before he could come up with another deflection, she said, "In a nutshell, Ed, any way you look at it, it's come down to this. Cousin Skip desperately needs this dangerous game to end. You need to square things with your chief and prove you can handle something besides speed traps while hiding in the bushes. And quit shying away from trouble every chance you get. Forget about me, will you? Call it a win-win and let's cut the tap dance."

Crinkling his beady eyes, Ed said, "Forget about you, hell. What in the world has come over you?"

"Life. Frustration. Does it every time. Good grief, Ed, what is it going to take? I told you this is high profile. Collateral damage and a possible relay to lower Manhattan. At this late date, you are the only thing between catastrophe. Plus, Harry is waiting in the wings to write it up."

Ed shot back, "While you're after some high-profile coverage and publicity to feather your cap."

"Wrong. Damn it, Ed, will you quit stalling?"

Throwing up his beefy hands in mock surrender, Ed said, "Okay, okay. Anyways, there are things I gotta know. Can't just take off for Asheville out of uniform. So simmer down and give it to me plain."

Realizing she finally had him going, she moved in. "In the first place, you will get all the credit. As for Skip, he will also serve as a spotter. And even if by some miracle he took any kind of stand, he'd have to slip away. Couldn't take any credit. Code of the regiment."

Noting Ed's raised eyebrow and funny look, Miranda added, "Besides, the last thing he needs is to be mentioned because he and his cat cannot take any more hounding. At best, he'll blow the whistle and split."

Ed thought that one over but still kept it up. "And the write-up? How do I know your boy Harry is gonna come through if it's anyways near as high profile as you say with TV cameras and such? Get in the papers and news and turn my reputation clear around? If I do step in, that is? And it ain't a whole bunch of smoke and mirrors?"

"Because Harry is hooked. Because he's been champing at the bit. Why? Underneath it all, he'd like nothing better as long as guys like you are taking all the risk. Because Harry just agreed to cover any local link, which means you—Officer Ed Wheeler."

Ed's face went blank as he absentmindedly stirred his mug of coffee. In the meantime, traffic whizzed by down on the main route to US 40. The cloud cover broke, barely allowing the drifting sunlight to stream through the mountain passes before closing off again.

Ed squinted and dropped his spoon on the wooden table. "And if nothing happens? I get caught up in all the Asheville traffic, all this first-time festival hoopla for nothing. Waste a perfectly good evening when I coulda been at the ball game in Swannanoa. Easy to get to it too."

Springing up, Miranda let him have it. "Get off it. You don't want to be at the ball game. You'd never be able to get over it if innocent people and children get killed. And what could be more heroic than being one of those out-of-uniform guys you read about who happened to be there, steps in, and saves the day? You could live on that for years. Especially if the TV cameras and smartphone devices catch it all. For God's sake, Ed, what do you have to lose?"

More spoon rattling, more making sure he'd covered all the bases. "And suicide bombers? What about them?"

Miranda hovered right over him. "How many suicide

bombers hail from Madison County? How many folks in that neck of the woods could even tell you what one was? For once in your life, put something on the line!"

"But if it's not one of those rednecks who've dogged your cousin. If it's a woman sent from Charlotte carrying something or with a bunch of grenades strapped to her belly."

"Black hijab, fixated eyeballs, set to pounce? She'd be spotted right off."

Ed got up and walked over to the wooden railing. "Look, this is a parcel of loose ends, just grant me that. Then again, last time I sloughed it off, you wound up on top. Along with Detective Dave Wall and my wet-behind-the-ears partner Tyler."

"Bingo. And so?"

"And so, this is the way it's gonna shake out. You cover the front and I don't care if the head scarfs are pink or pistachio. If she's bulging in spots or carries a large handbag, you stop her and give me a shout. Your cousin'll cover the opposite end—I'm talking the traffic on Patton Avenue. The slightest chance that biker is on a hit-and-run like I hear tell terrorists do in Europe, he'll give me a shout and I'll head the biker off. In the meantime, I'll hunt high and low for any luggage left around and the like, and my little walkie-talkie'll be primed to notify the bomb squad, which I'll check out before heading over there. We're talking prevention, right? That's it. No active shooter or any such thing?"

"You got it."

"All right then. So no guns, no service revolver or Glock strapped to my ankle. No gun play at all, which is bound to backfire in close quarters."

"And if you do have to apprehend someone?"

"I'll cuff her before she has a chance to get away. Are we clear?"

"Crystal."

Ed went back to the table, downed the rest of his coffee despite the fact that it had to be cold by now, and said, "But it still could be a whole lot of hogwash. Playin' the fool, blinkin' and duckin' for cover."

"Which is your stock in trade."

Ed barely held on to his temper before coming back with "Gal, how any man puts up with you is beyond me."

Another beat passed before Ed checked his watch and sprang forward. "Lordy, look at the time. No percentage hanging around if we're really dead serious about this."

CHAPTER THIRTY-SEVEN

With only a little over an hour to spare, Vin practiced wearing the oversized head scarf that ran down his back, carrying the folding camping chair, and setting it up. He'd gotten used to the scarf by now, but the steel chair loaded on both sides under the flaps with the plastic explosives was still awkward. It was designed to be heavy duty, plunked down for a spell in rough terrain, and not at all flimsy like a folding beach chair you carted looking for a likely spot to light and then afterwards, plucked it up and scooted back to your parked car. This loaded camping chair was much more cumbersome.

And so he practiced, starting from a few yards in front of the shed up to the stoop in front of the junk trailer, unfolding this extra wide thing like it was nothing, and easing into it like he'd done a half dozen times.

Next problem was sitting still, careful not to give himself away. For the first time ever, he was going to be in some open arena and more or less conspicuous. As he sat there peering straight ahead, the trick was to count on all the commotion, what with people dancing down below on the cement circle, women with women and men with men, the drums and whatnot beating, the cornets or whatever horns foreign folks blow on blaring.

His thoughts shifted to the possibility that even with all

the racket, somebody might jostle him or say something looking for a response. If they spoke in Spanish or Iranian or some such language he could shrug. But if they spoke in English, what then?

Same thing, he decided. He practiced giving a little shrug and continuing to look straight ahead, which made the most sense. Even if it was a gal in a head scarf next to him, she was bound to be in a bright color to go with this rainbow shindig. And he'd heard tell folks all over the Middle East were forever fighting with each other, speaking different ways and having rival religions. So a shrug would do for the short time he planned to be sitting there.

Then he practiced standing up as if he had to be excused for a minute. Looking at his watch, slipping his hand in the inside pocket of the shawl they'd sewed in for the phone gizmo, touching the screen so the eerie green light snapped on, keeping it secure and hidden above his jeans, and walking off. He didn't have to practice what to do after that. Then it was a simple matter of tapping the clock, unraveling the scarf, and tossing it in one of the metal bins under the trees by the curb so that the cloth draped over and couldn't be missed after the smoke cleared. Next, flashing the light, signaling Zeb down the street to take off, cut in front of the traffic so's he could hop on the back of the big Harley and be off and out of there.

But even so, it meant missing out on the fireworks. Not seeing and feeling the result, taking in the greatest high, bigger than all the whiskey he'd ever drunk and the wildest nights with the wildest gals put together. He was the cause but wouldn't be there to soak it all up. Just watch some of it on the hotel TVs as he'd figured, which was good as far as it goes but not nearly the same.

To this day, folks still talked about the ruckus when the moonshine exploded, everybody running helter-skelter as he gazed in wonder and had so much fun. But that was the price you pay for causing the greatest pandemonium ever. If he knew his uncle Lucian, there was no way he would have gone to all this trouble, including flying down here and monitoring it and all, if this wasn't slated to be one for the history books.

After all, Vin was what they called the perpetrator, in disguise, sitting smack dab amongst the victims. Still and all, he'd disappear like a deadly phantom in the wind.

CHAPTER THIRTY-EIGHT

As revelers filtered into the small stadium-like park, it was evident there was no rhyme or reason to their movement. Things seemed to take place of their own accord.

Checking it all out from the entrance, Miranda caught a glimpse of Ed in his street clothes atop the flat rocks and boulders to her immediate right, flashing his identity card, hobnobbing with the TV cameramen as they set up their equipment. Apparently, they were giving him the benefit of the doubt that from this higher vantage point he was better able to carry out a stakeout. Knowing Ed, at the same time he likely was making sure the cameramen were primed to home in on him if ever he did swing into action.

Her attention shifted to the pale lavender twilight and the outfits the gals were wearing as they made their way inside. In contrast to her own signature bib overalls and white peasant blouse, the fashions began to overwhelm the space. She caught sight of tube dresses in every vibrant color, print dresses, kaftans ruffled and tie-dyed, feather dresses, strapless sun dresses, Hawaiian blouses and skirts embossed with bamboo and tropical flowers. As if that wasn't enough, out came gathered outfits as if just yanked off the racks of a drapery shop. She also spotted a flaming orange elastic dress, a floral cardigan blouse with a kimono top, and a short gown made up of bright patches latched with a knitted rope to keep it all from coming apart. Pretty soon there were too many variations to count in the whirling kaleidoscope.

Just as the dance space became flooded, as if on cue, instrumentalists started to slip in from the top tier through the opening between the trees, drifting down the wrought iron banister aisle. To her left appeared a marimba in three sections, replete with players striking the wooden bars with soft mallets as the ladies in their flowing dresses began to sway. Dark- and light-skinned barefoot men joined in wearing pleated wedding shirts, batik long-sleeved cotton tops, and print shirts of every shade and hue. Before she knew it, other musicians slipped down from the top tier, and the beat picked up and receded along with the movements of the dancers.

By this point, Miranda didn't know where to focus as more and more elements vied for her attention.

The gaggle of instruments began to play off each other. The marimba chimed in and established a lilting tropical mood with some of the swaying dancers singing along: "Don't you worry 'bout a ting. Every little ting gonna be all right." Soon enough, shakers, rattles, and wood blocks took over along with finger cymbals, castanets, timbales struck on the metal sides of a drum, and the ring of a cow bell, all replacing the marimba in the lead.

Miranda felt jerked around by the sights and sounds, here, there and everywhere. Musicians added something wild, making the dancers undulate and wave their hands in ecstasy, then suddenly call out, making sharp trilling sounds with their tongues. Impatiently, the hand-slapping beat of bongos knifed through; a brace of deep timbered conga drums picked up the beat, driving it forward. A mixed batch of little kids raced by, each moving in his or her special way.

At this point, Miranda was so jangled she felt she had to at least touch base with Skip. He was supposedly up top, through the trees on the sidewalk by busy Patton Avenue. This urge was strengthened by images of the threat of a crazed biker out there somewhere. There were parents and grandparents sprinkled on the upper tiers leading beyond the trees to where Skip was stationed. A biker could ramrod past him, streaking up over the curb, through the trees and down onto the upper tiers, ploughing into anyone in the way.

Ed still peered down above her right shoulder on the rocks, but that didn't help any. And, for the first time, there was the crystal-clear sound of a cornet cutting through it all. An instrument, for all she knew, that possibly didn't belong.

She confronted a gyrating black woman sporting a feathered African headdress and asked, "A cornet? Horns? Is that okay?"

"You serious?" the woman yelled back. "Manu Dibango and his sax from Cameroon. Ladysmith Black Mambazo and the South African sound. Hugh Masekela and his horn. Where you been, girl? Besides, this ain't no show. We just getting started, feeling each other out. No telling who gonna turn up!"

"Right," said Miranda, letting the woman jump back into the fray and twist her torso like mad as the tempo picked up again. Then and there, Miranda realized not only who was about to drop in was up for grabs, but also who might slip out.

More and more, she wanted to touch base with Skip. A smiling, heavyset cinnamon-skinned man pushed past her carrying what she took to be that very same cornet, followed by two female couples arm in arm sporting cargo pants and coral spangled jackets.

Miranda turned and kept track of the exiting cornetist. She scurried atop the rocks, past the newsmen from NBC and CNN affiliates, then tripped over a narrow instrument case. She told herself that it might very well belong to the cornetist or it might not, an observation she shared with Ed. But as Ed hopped down, rushed forward, reached the case, and was about to peer inside, the cornet player, accompanied by a woman in a silk kimono, accosted him. Ed shrugged, apparently made some lame excuse, and returned to his post atop the rocks.

With their brace of bongos between their knees, a trio slapped away in alternating rhythms; the cornetist let loose his frustration wailing away in counterpoint, the overall effect like an angry duel between factions echoing the ill feelings Ed had just caused.

In turn, Miranda knew she couldn't keep up this anxious flitting to-and-fro. The full complement of TV cameras in search of breaking news was yet another intensifier. The starlit sky and the remembered announcement of voting on the threat to homeland security bill slated to take place on the senate floor—all of it underscored by an even more insistent, driving drum beat that had taken over.

The more she scanned the scene, the more she sensed the impending timeline. She glanced at her watch. She forced herself to take stock. To see how this plot was ostensibly going down, clear up to D-Day.

It led her to thoughts of the right-wing TV network setting up the progression of fire bombings, incorporating the blown railroad trestle perhaps; a plan to set off a bomb right here—the cameras capturing the chaos, helicopters called in filming shots of crowds fleeing and screaming, programs interrupted, broadcasters attempting to make sense of the footage, news reaching the Senate floor right before the vote. Another blast going off in the vicinity of Manhattan's St. Paul's Chapel, the moderate senators who'd been dragging their feet now casting their swing votes to root out illegal aliens and their cells in every nook and cranny of this country.

In that same moment, something caught her eye. Peering harder, she caught sight of an oversized black-and-white checkered shawl covering everything but a guy's eyes. He was seated on a camp armchair by the aisle on the second tier. Two women in black headscarves carrying much smaller camp chairs eased past him and sat by his side.

She wondered why he didn't acknowledge them. Why he continued to stare straight ahead. She thought about different sects—Sunni and Shiite if memory served. Which was what this gathering was all about: the colors of the rainbow coupled with black and white, an opportunity for all and sundry to learn to get along.

But the percussive beat, the impending timeline and all its implications were really getting to her now as she surged forward and weaved through the dancers and the ring of players blocking her way to the wrought iron staircase. She had to touch base with Skip and compare notes. Perhaps there was something she had totally missed and hadn't even crossed her mind.

She rushed up the stairs just as wooden flutes and a penny whistle added to the fray from somewhere at the far edge of the top tier, like a flock of angry birds that burst free of the trees, trilling and piping.

She cut through the trees onto the sidewalk, glanced here and there till she spotted Skip hurrying toward her, his jaw set, his gangly body tense as can be.

Raising his voice over the noise of the traffic, Skip said, "What are you doing here? It's got to break any minute now. Look at the time. You're supposed to be a lookout as we cover both flanks in a pincer maneuver."

"This isn't an old combat movie, Skip. Ed's down there covering but can't call it in because he's got nothing to go by and neither do I."

"Which still makes it a two-pronged attack. What if the biker zips by and hurls something over the trees and another guy pops up from nowhere where you could've spotted him, and he does God knows what?"

Before she knew what was happening, Skip ushered her back through the trees, telling her to look harder for a signal or something planted and pre-set, his tone as frantic as the flutes and pounding heavy drums.

Just then, while they were jostling through the throng on the upper tier, the shawled figure rose below them blocking their way. Skip called down, gesturing wildly, trying to communicate, asking him to step aside, and suddenly yelled, "The cowboy boots!" Reflexively, Skip lunged forward, grabbed the top of the scarf and jerked the figure so violently he fell, the back of his head smacking against the edge of the brick tier and iron railing as a piercing greenish light flashed from his clutched hand.

As people began screaming right and left, Miranda fixed on the frozen blue eyes and look of utter disbelief on the twisted features of Vin Dupre.

Putting Vin in a choke hold and holding on with all his might as Ed made his way toward them with his dangling handcuffs, Skip shouted, "Miranda, Miranda, the Harley, the motorcycle! Watch out for him, do something!"

Keying on the eerie blinding light clutched in Vin's hand, Miranda pried his fingers loose, grabbed the light, and took off.

With the blur of images Skip had planted in her mind of a maniacal biker, Miranda spun around, brushed through the trees down to the sidewalk and began prowling the main drag until she heard the deep-throated growl of a touring bike not far off.

In seconds, she spotted the visor, down as advertised, and dark leathers as a big Harley sped toward her with the traffic on the other side by the storefronts, weaving in and out. Moving in his direction, it occurred to her that the eerie green light might deter him—like some nighttime infra-beam exposing him in the semi-darkness and calling him off. Or, failing that, would at least throw him off stride. She dashed ahead, flashing the beam back and forth like a berserk traffic light and crossed over despite all the honking until she was in the middle of the street.

But the flickering glare only made him pick up speed,

passing cars on the other side, as if hell-bent to squeeze between lanes, gun the motor, and run her over. But there wasn't room for a big-throated touring bike to ram its way toward her up the meridian between the two-way traffic. Blasting its horn, a huge Mac truck clipped the handlebars from behind, hurtling the bike into the path of an oncoming limo from the opposite direction. The limo brushed by Miranda's side, its screeching brakes meshing with the piercing din of mangled, scraping metal.

She heard voices calling for an ambulance. She could have stuck around and checked. But there was no way she could have explained what she was doing in the middle of the road flashing this strange green light as a speeding biker sped hell-bent toward her, intent on taking her out.

Working her way through the bumper-to-bumper traffic jam, she decided the better tack was to rely on eyewitness accounts that a berserk biker was hurtling forward while some pedestrian was stranded on the meridian trying to cross over to one of the shops and then must have thought better of it.

She no sooner started back when Skip came running toward her, said he heard the crash just as Ed was dragooning Vin away. Then he suddenly froze.

Pointing at the eerie glowing device, he said, "Holy cow, Miranda, the gizmo! What if it's primed . . . on countdown . . . ticking away?"

He snatched it out of her hand and headed back to the festival. As she traipsed after him, she could hear him calling over his shoulder, his voice mingling with the noise of the traffic accident behind them, saying that maybe he could pass it to somebody in the bomb squad in time.

So there Skip was, carrying a possible triggering mechanism like someone racing to toss a grenade in a lake or out of harm's way that might go off before he got there. In a daze, she went along, too late to stop him, cutting through the trees past the wire mesh trash basket.

Reaching the top tier, she found everything in disarray. Some of the dancers and musicians had lingered, led by the marimba players and percussionists as if doing a reprise, while a few TV newscasters and cameramen had left their perch on the rocks in pursuit of anyone who might give them a clue what had caused the short-lived commotion. Everyone else seemed to be hanging around outside the front entrance.

The dispersal of the news crew left the rocky area free as Miranda waited for Skip to return. She was so shaken at this point all she could think of was a what-if. What if the gizmo was actually primed, ticking away? What if while she was out there on the meridian, the blast had gone off, killing and maiming all those people and kids at the festival?

When Skip finally returned and revealed that members of the bomb squad had this last piece of the puzzle in hand, she tried to put a positive spin on it all as they hung back, trying to remain incognito. She told him about the biker and began whispering that he had saved the day. But Skip would have none of it, claiming that the Feds and the bomb experts Ed had contacted would issue some final verdict that hopefully would leave him out of it.

Continuing to wait it out just to make sure, Skip thought Chris Holden would want to be notified that the biker had cracked up and could do no more harm. Miranda offered to relay the message after everything had calmed down and somebody had indeed issued an all clear.

The next thing she knew, Skip was gone. He'd evidently slipped away when she wasn't looking, doubtless at the same time the news team began to trickle back in, spreading the word that the bomb team had already surreptitiously spirited a cache of plastic explosives away.

Which is when Ed drifted back in.

When she confronted him, it took some prying until, out of earshot, he admitted that he was taking no chances on being in the vicinity of an explosion. As a result, the bomb squad had been in position an hour before, scouring every inch in and around this place. Which meant that the only option was somebody departing early and leaving something behind. As it happens and the way things stood, the only thing left turned out to be the bulging side pockets of the steel camp chair right after Ed called the squad back in. At the same time, he'd had already alerted the Feds so that they were on the scene within minutes and took the handcuffed fake Arab guy off Ed's hands.

Ed also admitted if none of this had panned out, the worse that could happen was being accused of crying wolf. But as long as he was in one piece, that was an easy price to pay.

Ed tried to shrug this ploy of covering his back off, faked a smile, even gave a nod to Skip for flushing the culprit out. But after getting nothing from Miranda, who still felt shaken, he gave her a quick pat on the back, shrugged again, and walked off.

In the meantime, as though picking up from where they'd left off, the trio of marimba players carried on, soon joined by the percussionists, the cornetist and the flutists following suit. In practically no time, the dancers reentered, swaying once more, and the festivities were in full swing, including the kids who seemed fully determined to join in, oblivious of anything that may have happened.

Moments later, a cute little Latina, no more than five or six, scampered up to the second tier, flounced around in her frilly red-and-white embroidered dress and plunked herself down in the oversized blue camp chair like a princess surveying her domain. She remained there waving and clapping her hands in time with the beat.

When her parents told her someone may want their seat back, she stood up and made a little fuss. "But we go together," she said, twirling around the chair and pointing her finger. "See? We're red, white, and blue."

CHAPTER THIRTY-NINE

In the aftermath, Harry was still beside himself trying to come up with a through line. Of course, it was his own fault, jumping the gun like this, telling his editor who, prompted by the competition and the twenty-four-hour news cycle, notified the parent company that the story behind the story involved national security and cried out to be syndicated. A narrative initiated by firebombed churches in northern Florida progressing all the way up to the White House. (That business about the White House was a hype on his editor's part. Harry only suggested that it might all hinge on the votes of four key senators. Plus, the influence of the newly elected president's chief strategist on the commander in chief who was under a lot of pressure to show some gumption and take a stand.)

As for the firebombing springboard, in terms of any corroboration, it didn't exactly hold water. Conceivably, Miranda shared some of the blame for getting him going and jumping the gun like this. She'd tapped into some secret longing on his part to join the ranks of reporters hot on the trail of a big scoop. She may not have spelled it out, but all along she knew which buttons to push. Especially when, in between assignments, he began plugging into that selfsame twenty-four-hour news cycle after he'd fallen so far behind.

Moreover, as he'd told Miranda to keep her from champing

at the bit, stories take time to unfold and a lot of digging and skirting around dead ends. Truth to tell, all along he knew better than to expect to come up with a full-blown exposé in a matter of a few days just by playing armchair detective.

And so, with a deadline looming, he was going to have to cut his losses and modify a possible right-wing plot to sow paranoia throughout the land.

Miranda's newfound indifference only contributed to his dismay. When he told her on Thursday that the senate bill failed to pass, she simply took it in stride. When he informed her right before the big Friday do at the Tavern that a certain Vin Dupre was in custody after a botched bombing ploy in Asheville, she took that in stride as well. And when he further told her that Dupre claimed he was simply a country singer-songwriter who was slated to open at the Tavern that night, she merely said, "Nobody performs unless I book them."

Which led Harry straight back to his unsubstantiated national security piece. Though Dupre's fingerprints were discovered on the plastic explosives inside the Velcro-bound pockets of a folding camp chair, as yet the Feds apparently could find no link between Dupre and the highly sophisticated triggering device. Moreover, other fingerprints were found on the explosives and still more on the triggering device by the time it found its way to the lab. Dupre was on a person-of-interest list harkening back to suspicious barn burnings in this neck of the woods, but that's as much as the Feds were willing to disclose. Supposedly, Dupre kept sticking to his story of blue-eyed innocence while arraigned as a subject in an aborted hate crime.

As it happens, on that same Wednesday evening in

question, the Feds' field office in Manhattan came across an empty van in the vicinity of St. Paul's church that contained traces of bomb making materials. The van was traced back to a cousin of Dupre's back in Madison County, but that's a far as the news item went. Needless to say, Harry sensed there was a lot more to this story that was totally beyond the purview of a wary armchair feature reporter.

Even when he looked furtively into a Lucian Clay connection, the only inkling was a memorandum from the White House chief of staff that Clay's services were no longer required.

There was an item in the Asheville paper about a victim of a motorcycle hit-and-run in Pack Square who wished to bring charges but was so heavily sedated, his ramblings were incoherent. The only reason Harry even noticed the clipping was the fact that in her poking around, Miranda alluded to a biker on the rampage who may have also had something to do with her cousin's predicament. In a more recent incident, an unidentified would-be biker assailant was also mentioned whose condition was touch-and-go. But Harry didn't see what bearing these two incidents had on his pressing assignment.

Which reluctantly brought him back to Plan B: making do with a profile on the exploits of local police officer Ed Wheeler. But that too was proving to be problematic. Contacting the station for background information before zeroing in with a face-to-face interview revealed that Officer Ed was the least likely candidate for off-duty heroics. In fact, it seemed as though he'd devoted his life to avoiding any such distinction. Traveling to Asheville immediately after his shift to intercept white supremist machinations at a first-ever celebration of diversity was well beyond his MO. It was more likely that he'd not only slough off any such activity but to make the case that any such action was foolhardy. Among his standard excuses while on duty were "It's probably just a false alarm." By and large, his only forte was traffic violations and apprehending speeders.

Nevertheless, while trying to come up with apt questions for his upcoming interview after being apprised of criteria for commendations, merit, and promotion, Harry couldn't help thinking it would have been so much more promising if he could have started with Skip. So much more rewarding if Skip's plight had amounted to anything.

But, aside from what he'd gleaned from Miranda, Harry's only actual contact had been over the phone for a few minutes. And how in the world could anyone base a high-profile story on a spooked Hoosier and his stray cat who, yet again, had flown the coop?

Then it occurred to him that Miranda only offered him a local angle "with greater implications." The way things went, that was all it amounted to.

Unbeknownst to Harry, by Friday afternoon circumstances had taken another turn. By now Vin was having the worst time trying to cool it and hang on to his chill dude act.

Needless to say, he'd never been cornered before, let alone locked up in a holding cell. It had gotten to the point where, hemmed in by these close quarters, he'd started pacing as if he could somehow walk himself out of this jam. And come up with an answer to how in the world some clown had scrambled behind him, waving his arms and screaming just as he was about to take off. The next thing he knew, the damn shawl was pressing against his Adam's apple, jerking him backwards so hard he'd like to have blacked out; the same guy holding him down, getting him in a choke hold, screaming at someone. Vin found himself staring up at that feisty little gal from the Tavern tearing away at the lit gizmo in his hand. How could that be? How could these things happen?

But for the umpteenth time, he couldn't walk past it and couldn't wake up out of this bad dream. All he could do was try to hang in there before that Fed came back flipping through his notepad, needling him with the latest thing that had cropped up.

Sure enough, next thing he knew, there was that dark blue suit again—steely eyes, square face, pencil-thin lips, shaved head. Flat tone like he was reading items off some ticker tape, letting Vin in on the latest strikes against him. Vin had been so lost in thought this time, he hadn't even heard the cell door crank open.

Vin spun around and slumped down on the hard cot as if it was all going to be fine and they'd soon let him go. He even stretched out in the most lackadaisical pose he could muster.

But as he might have known, it was a no go. Flipping a couple of pages of his notepad, the suit said, "Still trying to track down the snapshot of the guy who body-slammed you. Fuzzy image considering the pandemonium, but we're making progress."

Vin hung on to his cool pose.

"Next," said the suit, "mentally challenged homeless woman down in Black Mountain identified you and your old beat-up pickup. Cross reference with the BOLO, busted taillight, and her filed complaint. Starting to add up if you figure in the guy at the convenience store who also identified you asking about the freight train schedule down in Old Fort."

Vin continued to hang in there. The suit seemed to have run out of items for now. But then he flipped to another page. "Not only adding up, but getting more and more incriminating, spilling out all over the place."

Despite himself, Vin said, "What's that supposed to mean?"

"Means we're going to have to alter your profile in the database. If you take into account the links to your firebombing those churches of late, plus all the rest of it, like accosting that homeless woman."

When Vin sat up straight, the suit said, "Not only that, but tossing a bag of kitty litter in her face."

The suit started to go, flipped through his notes and then turned back. "I mean, why would a longtime homegrown terrorist give himself away like this? And why would you ever want a cat?"

CHAPTER FORTY

The sunlight continued to sparkle that following Saturday morning, the sky a clear Carolina blue, the hovering Seven Sisters mountain range just as verdant as the week before. But nothing could touch the funk Miranda found herself in. Even when forced to field a wake-up call from Ed, she couldn't muster enough gumption to cut him short.

"Hey, don't you see, don't you get it?" said Ed, pressing even harder. "Saying I got an anonymous tip just don't wash. The chief ain't buying it and your boy Harry'll be here any minute now set to plaster my lame tale all over hell and gone."

"Just a second, Ed."

Miranda shuffled over to the kitchen sink, poured the hot water from the steaming kettle into a mug laced with instant coffee and brown sugar. She took a few sips and, just as lethargically, came back with a few ploys to get Ed off the line.

"Start with Annie's bruises, the culprit driving an old green pickup, a crummy trailer siphoning off electricity in a clearing down in Old Fort."

"And then what? Toss in the cat lady snooping around? How does that figure and why? What we got here is a bunch of rabbit holes."

A few more sips of coffee until Miranda said, "Connect the dots. Make up a story. That's what you're good at, Ed."

"What dots?"

"Okay, then toss in the railroad trestle blast."

"You think? Maybe . . . I don't know. But that still don't cover the anonymous tip and what in the world got into me."

"Just confess you were that desperate. And didn't want to admit . . ."

"I was relying on a nosy cat lady. Good lord, Miranda."

"Whatever."

"Hey, don't hang up on me now. So let's see . . . Maybe I track the old pickup to where they're holding this rainbow shindig. And I figure on some Klu Klux Klan angle. How did I spot this Dupre fella I'd never laid eyes on?"

"Annie's description."

"Uh-huh. Right. Go on."

"The cowboy boots."

"Come again?"

"Jeans and cowboy boots don't go with Arab garb."

"Dang, woman, that is good. I owe you one. I'll make it up to you, I swear."

"Forget it. I gotta go."

With that, she hung up. Truth to tell, she didn't have to go anywhere. It was her birthday, but she had no plans. This was the day she and Harry were to leave bright and early for the Smokies and get away from it all. Harry had obviously forgotten all about it. But that wasn't the crux of this empty feeling.

She knew there would be the usual well wishes on social media. And the book on spring gardening from her mom with the gift card suggesting it was high time she settled down. But that didn't cut it either.

Mostly, there was Skip. Gone without so much as a goodbye. Leaving only an envelope embossed with a cat's paw-print and a generous check for services rendered, a check Miranda had no intention of ever depositing. For all she knew, he was scouting around for another hideaway, far from any chance of notoriety and the crafty far-right forces seeking him out.

Or perhaps he really had followed his fantasy code of the regiment and slipped away into the night. You're not supposed to stick around to receive any credit. After all, what would Jack Armstrong do? Or even Jack's sidekick Billy if, for once, he laid something on the line?

She sat down at the kitchen table with her cup of coffee. Thoughts of Skip and derring-do led her to the fruits of their labor. The waffling moderate Republican senators could be seen on MSNBC TV offering more or less the same comments. There was no imminent call for drastic measures. When their name came up during the roll call, in tandem they ensured that the measure to clamp down on unverified alien threats went down to defeat.

At the same time, Russ Mathews could be seen on Fox News calling for the condemnation of those turncoats who, by foregoing their patriotic duty, placed the country in jeopardy at the hands of foreign elements "polluting our once pristine villages, towns, and cities." This message, according to the commentator, was repeated throughout the Liberty Broadcast system.

But all that really mattered was the fact that the lives of innocent men, women, and children had been spared.

Her thoughts drifted to her attempts to raise Chris

Holden's spirits at the hospital. Though she was a perfect stranger, she'd told him the mad biker was out of commission. At best, all Holden could offer was a thumbs-up before drifting off again. She wanted to tell him the whole business with Lucian Clay and Skip's Shep Anderson impersonation and flight was resolved but realized it was useless. So was harboring any ill will toward Holden and his part in Skip's plight. She even tried repeating that favorite Black Mountain expression "It's all good" to no avail.

All of it as hopeless as the night before during Bud and Travis's sold-out country favorites when everyone tried their best to pick up her spirits. Which was surprising because she was the MC and always gave a hearty sendoff to the advent of spring. She attempted to fake it but, at best, was going through the motions.

And so she was just plain stuck with this gnawing ache. It wouldn't go away. It had no name and there was nothing that could be done.

Never one to feel sorry for herself, not after a lifetime of admonitions to "Grow up" and "Face it, that's life, missy," she forced herself to pick up the pieces. Got ready to make the rounds at the tailgate market, glom some fresh baked goods from Trudy the pie lady, and go through the rest of the routine.

Which meant another round of "How was your week?" from Trudy and a halfhearted "Same old, same old" on Miranda's part.

Which led to second thoughts about Harry and telling herself that was par for the course. Like most guys she'd known, he'd come around later with a bouquet of flowers.

And like Ed, he'd say, "I'll make it up to you first chance, I swear."

More or less set by around a quarter to nine, just when she was about to leave, the doorbell rang. Taking her time, she opened the front door as a freckled-face delivery boy scurried away, turned back and said, "Good deal. Caught you in the nick of time."

There by her feet was a silver bag. Before she had a chance to look inside, her landline starting ringing again. Bag in hand, hoping against hope it wasn't Ed still in dire straits, she retreated to the kitchen and picked up the handset.

The first thing that greeted her were opening chords on a ukulele, followed by Skip's warbling rendition of happy birthday. Without missing a beat, he segued to "As I dream about the moonlight on the Wabash. As I dream about my Indiana home."

Then it was "Look into the gift bag yet?"

"Not yet," said Miranda, reaching down and plunking out a fancy pint bottle and matching tumbler.

"Ready?"

"Just a sec." She unscrewed the cap and poured a few fingers of the shamrock-green crème de menthe. "Okay."

"Here's looking at you, kid."

With tears welling up in her eyes, she raised her glass and said, "To rose-lipped maidens and lightfoot lads."

As the tears ran down her cheeks like they had so long ago, she gently began to sob. And it was all good.

ABOUT THE AUTHOR

Shelly Frome is a member of Mystery Writers of America, a professor of dramatic arts emeritus at the University of Connecticut, a former professional actor, and a writer of crime novels and books on theater and film. He is also the film columnist for Southern Writers Magazine and writes monthly profiles for Gannett Media. His fiction includes *Sun Dance for Andy Horn, Lilac Moon, Twilight of the Drifter, Tinseltown Riff,* and *Moon Games.* Among his works of nonfiction are *The Actors Studio* and texts on the art and craft of screenwriting and writing for the stage. He lives in Black Mountain, North Carolina.

OTHER BOOKS BY
SHELLY FROME

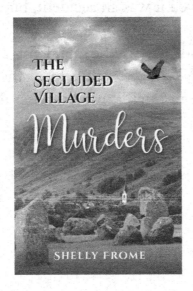

Written in the style of a classic British Mystery with a contemporary young American woman as the amateur sleuth. Entertaining. Keeps you guessing until the end.

From a small secluded village in Connecticut to the English Countryside, readers are taken on a roller coaster of events and quirky characters as amateur sleuth Emily Ryder tries to solve a murder that everyone thinks was an accident.

For tour guide Emily Ryder, the turning point came on that fateful early morning when her beloved mentor met an untimely death. It's labeled as an accident and Trooper Dave Roberts is more interested in Emily than in any suspicions around Chris Cooper's death. For Emily, if Chris hadn't been the Village Planner and the only man standing in the way of the development of an apartment and entertainment complex in their quaint village of Lydfield, Connecticut, she might have believed it was an accident, but too many pieces didn't fit.

As Emily heads across the pond for a scheduled tour of Lydfield's sister village, Lydfield-in-the-Moor . . . she discovers that the murderer may be closer than she thought.